W9-DES-341

LEGACY of COURAGE

A Holocaust Survival Story
In Greece

By

FREDERIC J. KAKIS

This book is a fictional account of a true story. Places, event and situations are based on the recollections of the author as a young boy. Consequently no absolute historical accuracy is either claimed or intended.

© 2003 by Frederic Kakis All rights reserved.

No part of this book may be reproduced, stored in a retrieval system, or transmitted by any means, electronic, mechanical, photocopying, recording, or otherwise, without written permission from the author.

ISBN: 1-4107-1357-1 (e-book)
ISBN: 1-4107-1358-X (Paperback)
ISBN: 1-4107-1359-8 (Dust Jacket)

Library of Congress Control Number: 2003090389

This book is printed on acid free paper.

Printed in the United States of America
Bloomington, IN

1st Books - rev. 04/24/03

Table of Contents

PREFACE

I postponed this writing for many years because I did not want to relive the period of starvation and fear, the constant hiding and running and the bizarre way I grew up.

I was trying to distance myself from the unpleasant memories of life during the Nazi occupation. At the urging of friends and family I have finally decided to tell the story, because the memories are fading and I think its important for my children and grandchildren to know their roots and appreciate the value of fighting injustice and tyranny.

This book is inspired by the trials and tribulations of my family during the German occupation of Greece. It is a story of a Jewish family attempting to evade capture and deportation to the death camps and its struggle for survival.

There are many books written about the Holocaust. Most of these involve survivors of concentration camps and depict the horrors they have witnessed, the tortures of innocent people and the death of millions in the gas chambers. However, there are very few stories describing survival based on defiance and the will to resist and fight the Nazis.

This is such a story. The events described stem from my recollection of things that happened a long time ago, when I was just a young boy. Consequently no absolute historical accuracy is either claimed or intended.

The heroine of the story is my mother whose intelligence and sheer guts were, more than any other factor, responsible for our survival.

There are numerous incidents depicted where mother's ability to stay cool and not cave-in in the face of eminent danger have saved our necks. Another factor was her broad education and knowledge of several languages that included German. Her stubborn refusal to conform and submit to the German directives despite the advice and urging by relatives on both sides was proven to be the right course of action.

All those that were criticizing her for risking our lives by defying the Germans were killed. They helped the Germans put a rope around their neck and were deported like lambs to the slaughter. All of these relatives who were urging my mother to comply with the German orders died in the concentration camps of Germany and Poland.

In these days where one hears frightening accounts of a Nazi resurgence and a rise in anti- Semitism it is imperative that the world does not forget the horrors of the past. Finally I want my family to know that no matter how bad they think their life is at times it can actually get a lot worse. Thus be prepared to face adversity, if it comes, with courage and dignity and an uncompromising belief that good eventually triumphs over evil.

List of Illustrations

Photo 1. The town of Drama

Photo 2. Our House In Drama

Photo 3. Father With Medals (Ca. 1920)

Photo 4. Mother and Father (Ca. 1940)

Photo 5. The Town of Salonica

Photo 6. The Family (Ca. 1940)
From left to right: Zack, Albert, Mother, Myself, and Carmen.

Photo 7. The Island of Skiathos

Photo 8. Zack and Resistance Fighters
Zack is the fourth from the left looking towards the right.

CHAPTER 1

The Calm before the Storm

The sky was gray and gloomy in the predawn hours. Dark clouds lined the horizon. The deserted dimly lit cobblestone streets were wet with the morning dew, reflecting a strange and eerie light.

Parked in front of our family home in St. Barbara's street were two Phaetons ready to transport us to the railroad station. The horses were nervously kicking their hoofs onto the pavement making ugly noises that seemed to pierce the tranquility of the sleeping town. Clouds of steam came out of the horses' mouths as their hot breaths came into contact with the chilled morning air.

Mr. Vournas, the cashier of the movie house, which was one of my father's business enterprises, climbed the double staircase that lead to our quarters and timidly knocked at the door. When my father opened, he said in his characteristically high-pitched voice: "Mr. Emil, I've got the railroad tickets and I have two carriages waiting downstairs as you instructed me."

Mr. Vournas had been in my father's employ for as long as I could remember. Because of his high pitched voice, his tiny stature and the fact that the box office at the movies was built in the shape of a birdcage, Mr. Vournas was nicknamed the "nightingale". In addition to his duties as a cashier, he performed a variety of other chores, which ranged from hiring workers to supervising repairmen.

Among other things Mr. Vournas ran errands and did the shopping for my mother on all the occasions when a dinner

1

party was planned. My father, who was a very sociable and outgoing person, was frequently known to invite dozens of people to our home for dinner, often with little or no advanced warning to my mother's great dismay and exasperation. The guests were frequently performers who appeared on the stage in my father's theater.

Because of this, I was exposed in my early childhood to a variety of talented people, from concert pianists to opera singers, and I have developed a life long appreciation of the theater and the performing arts. The opportunity to hear some of these artists at their best within the confines of my own home was a rare treat that I cherish forever.

As part of his being an all around "gofer" for my father, Mr. Vournas also had the responsibility of making the appropriate reservations, buying the tickets, arranging the transportation and overseeing the entire process, whenever my father or the entire family was planning a trip.

Standing in the dimly lit hallway of our home with my brothers and sister and staring at the long row of neatly lined up pieces of luggage I had the distinct feeling that this was somehow not going to be just another of our excursions.

I heard my parents arguing. My father insisted on taking a neatly folded large canvas tent, one of his souvenirs from the British Army of World War One, that was destined to play an important role in our family's fight for survival. My mother thought it was totally unnecessary to drag it along and it was one of the few times that she was wrong.

This departure had an unmistakable air of sadness, yet my young mind could not process the information and come up with a reasonable explanation of why it felt that way. The early morning departure, the excessive amount of luggage and the long and somber faces of my parents were all signals that something was wrong. Also the white sheets that were covering all of our furniture made the interior of our home look weird and strange and reminded me of coffins or dead people wrapped in their shrouds. We had never in the past bothered to take the time to cover everything in the house before going on vacation.

All of these omens filled me with uneasiness and a mixture of fear and sadness. As it turned out, there were good reasons for my feelings.

For weeks there were persistent rumors that the invasion of Greece by the German Army was imminent. Also it was reported that Bulgaria, an Axis power and a long-term enemy of Greece, was concentrating a large amount of troops and artillery along the Greek border.

The Greek government, trying to avert panic and a massive exodus from the towns along the projected path of the would-be invaders, was asking the people to be calm and stay put.

My father, a highly decorated veteran of World War One, had very vivid memories of the death and destruction that occurs in the path of invading armies and decided, for safety reasons, to move the family to Salonica the home of his parents. The intention was to return to our home in Drama after things had quieted down and it was safe to do so. This never happened. In fact our home was completely looted by the invading Bulgarian hordes and partially destroyed.

When we descended the two spiral staircases to the street I had a strange but unmistakable feeling or premonition that something very bad was about to happen.

I turned around and looked at this beautiful and happy home of my early youth, the home where myself and my siblings were born, not realizing at the time that all of our personal effects would be lost and we would never occupy this home again.

Our Family Home in Drama

I could never imagine, how quickly our lives were about to change. We boarded the carriages that were waiting and began our journey to the railroad station. The town was just beginning to stir in the early morning hours. Lights started to appear in the windows of the buildings along the way and some workmen began to appear in the dark streets rushing to their morning shifts. The noise of the horses' hoofs on the cobblestone streets was piercing the night silence. Click clock, click clock, click clock. I remember hearing the jingle of the bells around the horses' necks and the occasional hissing sound of the coachman's whip.

Traveling as a family in the past always meant going on a holiday which was a joyous occasion filled with excitement and anticipation. The ride to the train station on a horse drawn Phaeton, the busy platform filled with travelers of all shapes and colors and the line-up of the trains on the tracks with copious black smoke spewing from their chimneys were all sources of pleasure and wonderment for my young and impressionable eyes.

I remember the peasants with their wives dressed in the local colorful costumes dragging an assortment of children by their hand and carrying the water filled "Stamnas", clay pots shaped as carafes, to quench their thirst, during their train ride. Many of them carried along livestock such as chickens and roosters with their legs tied together and their heads dangling in the air.

There were also the priests with their long white beards and black robes and their hair tied in a knot at the back of their head that carried a tubular, chimney like, hat with a flat top. Occasionally, a peasant woman will kiss their hand and receive the customary blessing: "May the lord be with you".

Among this crowd were also all types of vendors selling food for the travelers that did not carry their own provisions: Chestnuts and corn on the cob roasted on charcoal, "couluria" a giant bagel-like bread covered with sesame seeds and of course the traditional Greek "suvlaki", a small charbroiled skewer of spiced morsels of lamb.

Also present on the same platform were the businessmen in their Sunday suites accompanied by their robust heavily made up and somewhat overdressed wives, who somehow seemed to be out of place striking a strange note in the cacophony of sounds that emanated from the melee of people who were waiting to board the train.

But in this bleak, dreary morning when we reached the railroad yard we encountered a different scene than the usual one. Despite the early hour the platform was full of people pushing and shoving to get on the train. There was also a heavy presence of soldiers and uniformed policemen trying to control the crowd.

With the help of a porter hired by my father, the coachman, and the faithful Mr. Vournas, we managed to load our entire luggage on the train and get aboard. I was both touched and surprised to see Mr. Vournas say goodbye to us with tears in his eyes. He embraced my father and assured him that he will look after the movie house until my father returns.

"Don't you worry Mr. Emil" he said, "I will personally take care of things and watch the business until you get back as if it were my own".

My father thanked him and boarded the train. No one had suspected that on that fateful dark winter morning of 1941 Mr. Vournas had performed these duties for our family for the last time. He was captured, tortured and murdered by the Bulgarian Army of occupation shortly after.

Mother & Father (Ca 1940)

CHAPTER 2

The Nightmare Begins

On April 6,1941, only two short months after our narrow escape from Drama, the German forces crossed the Bulgarian border and invaded Greece. The entire northern front, which included Yugoslavia, collapsed like a house of cards under the mighty punch from the awesome German war machine. The Greek army, ill equipped and already weakened by the fighting in Albania, was no match for the German panzer, artillery and mechanized units. Despite this, the Greeks refused to surrender and tried to resist. As a result thousands of young Greek soldiers were killed or wounded in their heroic but futile attempt to defend their country.

The all-powerful Wehrmacht that had plowed through the entire European Continent in a matter of weeks was virtually unstoppable. The valiant Greek effort to resist was instigated by the British who wanted time to get on their war ships and escape the slaughter. As a result the flower of Greek youth died in vain fighting an enemy that they could not possibly defeat. Within a matter of days the German army had completed the occupation of Greece and the nightmare began.

Shortly after the German invasion the Bulgarian troops on the North and the Italian troops on the South joined their German Allies. The Germans, while maintaining a presence and control over the entire Greece, placed the eastern Macedonia and western Thrace territories under "titular" Bulgarian administration. The southern part of the mainland of Greece as well as the Ionian Islands and the Cyclades were placed under Italian administration.

Frederic Kakis

This allowed the Germans to maintain a grip over the country without tying up a lot of their troops that were badly needed for fighting on the Russian Front. For the Bulgarians this was the opportunity they were dreaming about for years to have access to the Mediterranean and for the Italians a chance to save face for their humiliating defeat by the tiny country of Greece.

On October 28, 1940 Mussolini asked for the unconditional surrender of Greece. The Greek Prime Minister Metaxas, although himself a fascist, gave the historic one word reply to this ultimatum: "OXI" which means "NO". Italian troops then attacked Greece through Albania that was already under Italian occupation.

Despite their superior numbers and the infinitely better equipment the Italians lacked the fighting spirit and were quickly repulsed by the Greek army. To the great embarrassment of Mussolini the Greek army had chased the Italians through half of Albania. Mussolini was changing his commanding generals practically every week and pouring in his most elite units but to no avail. This was the first defeat of the Axis powers. The news infuriated Hitler who then ordered his army to invade Greece and teach the Greeks a lesson. The rest, as they say, is history.

Because of ignorance coupled with a healthy dose of stupidity for most young people, including my siblings and myself, war was viewed as some kind of adventure, something that would break the monotony of our drab and uneventful lives. We were looking for excitement but what we got was hunger, misery and death.

Drama was overrun by Bulgarian troops and several thousand Greek men, women, and children, in the immediate vicinity, were slaughtered for no apparent reason. This was the earliest example of ethnic cleansing in this century. Homes were looted and destroyed and young girls were raped.

The brutality of the invaders was beyond description. The Bulgarian authorities immediately began to drive out the Greek inhabitants. Over 100,000 Greek refugees fled westward from the Bulgarian zone.

Our home was one of the firsts to be hit. Everything in it was carted away and shipped to Bulgaria. Among the early victims were Mr. Vournas and Mr. Boubniev.

Mr., Boubniev was a Russian colonel in the Czar's army, who, like many of his fellow white Russians, fled because of the Communist revolution and found himself in Greece without any profession or marketable skills. Fortunately he was an accomplished pianist and my father hired him to provide musical background to the silent films and to give us music lessons.

Mr. Vournas got shot when he refused to provide the Bulgarians with the keys to the Movie Theater and Mr. Boubniev was arrested and thrown in jail accused of being a Russian spy. After being repeatedly beaten and tortured he made good on his promise and committed suicide by swallowing the contents of the cyanide vial he always had hidden on his person.

Before the German occupation forces began to pour into Salonica we experienced our first bombardment. German dive-bombers pounded the city leveling buildings and creating a scene of death and destruction that provided a quick cure for any romantic notions about war that we might have had.

I remember watching the sky completely dumbfounded, hearing the piercing sound of the air raid sirens, the whistling noise of the falling bombs and the thundering explosions, unable to move and really having no place to go since no one had bothered to build shelters. In a short time, just as abruptly as it was started, the bombing stopped and the tedious and sad job of cleaning up the mess started.

My grandfather's house in Salonica was located in an aristocratic neighborhood known for its impressive looking mansions and elaborate gardens. It was really not one but three buildings or structures on the same lot. The largest structure was an L shaped two-story house with the short part of the L facing Queen Olga's Boulevard, one of the major thoroughfares of Salonica.

The front was enclosed with a four-foot wall supporting a highly ornate wrought iron fence flanked on each side by a huge, heavy wrought iron door. The massive vertical members of this fence had sharp points at the top, which made them look like the spears used by the African tribes. In addition, in the front, there were four huge, over fifty feet tall, cypress trees proudly pointing towards the sky. The trees were very old and served as a point of identification for the house.

Both floors of this huge house at one time served as the quarters for my grand father's household, which consisted of himself, his wife, six children (4 boys and 2 girls) and a multitude of servants. The house had an endless array of rooms that included a baking room. This enormous baking room housed a commercial size oven of the type used by the local bakeries.

My grandfather, who was a wealthy tobacco merchant, did a lot of entertaining and his dinner parties were legendary. Obviously my father had inherited that trait. There must be something to this business of genetics after all.

On the left side of the lot, also facing Queen Olga's Boulevard was a one-story structure with a spiral staircase behind it that led to a terrace on top. This structure was actually a store, a commercial pharmacy in a rather strange location amidst a high-class residential area.

At the rear of the lot was a taller three-story house. This became our home away from home.

Both houses had ornate ceilings with elaborate white plaster moldings and rosettes in turn-of-the-century Italian style. Each room had its own small balcony, which gave it a bright and spacious look. There was electricity but no central heating. Wood or coal burning stoves heated the rooms. Cooking, bathing, and the washing of clothes also involved burning wood or wood charcoal since there was no other way to heat water.

Between the houses and the front entrance there was a beautiful garden filled with flowers and trees. The garden was irrigated by water derived from an artesian well and pumped by hand by means of a red, cast-iron pump.

On the side of this garden there was a large shed used to store shovels, rakes, wheelbarrows and other agricultural tools. This tool shed was to play a role in one of the many adventures of our life under the German Occupation.

The aerial bombardment was just the prelude to the main event, the actual occupation. There were persistent rumors that the Germans had broken through our lines and were advancing towards Salonica. The entire City was in an uproar. The biggest turmoil was in the harbor area where dozens of ships were scurrying to avoid capture and sail before it was too late.

Thousands of people, mostly young, were pushing and shoving to get aboard the sailing ships to escape from the German occupation. Among them was my oldest brother Zack accompanied and assisted by my father. A melee of people, vehicles and equipment lined up the entire waterfront creating a panic situation and trampling one another.

The Government had ordered all reserves of fuel destroyed so that they would not fall into German hands. As a result several fires had erupted in the pier area and rivers of crude oil were flowing through the streets. The Police were making a desperate but vain effort to control the crowd but it was quickly apparent that this was not an ordinary situation.

Eventually my brother was able to board one of the ships by grasping one of the ship's mooring lines and sliding upwards on all four like a giant rat until he reached the deck of the ship. My father satisfied, that my brother was safely on board, fought his way through the crowd and started to walk home. When my father finally made it home his shoes and pants, up to his knees, were immersed in crude oil, his face and hands were black with soot and his hair was full of black and white fly ash.

Most ships escaped. The rest were purposely sunk to block the entrance to the harbor. All the news reports made it clear that the fall of Salonica was imminent. The hearts of the people were filled with fear and uncertainty, wondering what life would be like under German occupation. We didn't have to wait long: On April 9, 1941, Salonica fell into German hands.

The news that the Germans were entering the City caused thousands of people to line both sides of the streets to catch a glimpse of the invaders. Filled with morbid curiosity and fear we also stood at the gate in front of our house and watched the arrival of the "super race" as they paraded through Queen Olga's Boulevard.

The city of Salonica

First there were rows of motorcycle riders wearing helmets and goggles, black leather boots and green-gray capes. Hanging from their necks there were large, horseshoe shaped, plaques with the words "FELD GENDARMERIE", (which meant "MILTARY POLICE"), that glowed in the dark. Smeizer submachine guns hung across their shoulders.

Our first impression was one of fear mixed with awe. These riders looked like alien creatures from another planet and did not resemble any soldiers any of us had encountered in the past. Following the motorcycles was a very long array of armored vehicles, personnel carriers and Tiger tanks. Behind them the infantrymen came marching-in and a new sound was introduced into the city's repertoire, the sound of hobnailed boots pounding against the cobblestone pavement.

Every now and then a vehicle with powerful loud speakers would go by proclaiming that the Germans were our friends and that they came to liberate us from the British imperialists. They also said that the Greek people had nothing to fear as long as they obeyed the rules.

We sat there for hours dumbfounded and with our eyes glued to what seemed to be an endless parade of German military might until one of us noticed that one of the vehicles that went by that had special identifying marks, went by again. Then we understood the old German propaganda trick. They were marching their troops through the main avenues of the city and when they reached the end they diverted them back through the smaller streets to the origin and send them through again. This way it appeared to the casual observer that an enormous armada had invaded the city.

As soon as the Germans set their foot on Greek soil two things happened almost immediately: All the banks were seized making all deposits worthless and all news media came under German control and censorship.

Frederic Kakis

Thus, all at once, by a flick of a switch called fate, my father lost his entire fortune except for any real estate that he owned. His sizable deposits in the Greek National Bank, which included special savings for the education of each one of us, became worthless. Consequently our family went from riches to extreme poverty in a matter of hours. The only thing of value that remained was my mother's jewelry.

My father always bought expensive jewelry for my mother. He believed that buying jewelry was a form of catastrophic insurance. He used to tell us: "whenever you have extra money buy jewelry for your wife. It is good insurance against unforeseen emergencies because you are not likely to sell it unless you are starving and if that should happen you will have something valuable to trade." None of us knew at the time how prophetic those words would turn out to be.

The Germans started tightening the screws gradually. One of their first orders was that all firearms, regardless of age or condition, and all short wave radios must be surrendered to the authorities. Anyone caught in possession of either a radio or a gun past the deadline was to be shot.

We had a 38-caliber revolver, a Browning automatic pistol, two antique dueling pistols and, of course, a Phillips short wave radio. The radio was the result of my father's being the exclusive agent for Phillips in Greece.

After a brief discussion of the pros and cons it was unanimously decided to ignore the German command. We hid the weapons in the roof of the laundry room under the ceramic roof tiles and the radio in an armoire behind the hanging clothes. Each night we would take out the radio, hook it up to the antenna, and listen to the BBC while someone always stood watch to warn the rest for any possible surprise visit.

I can still hear the beginning sounds of Beethoven's fifth symphony that marked the start of the transmission. Dum, dum, dum, dum. Dum,dum,dum,dum, "This is London Calling, the

14

European service of the BBC". The news that followed was our only link to the outside world and the only source of truthful information about the conduct of the war. The Greek radio stations and newspapers were entirely in the hands of the German propaganda machine and they only broadcasted the fake "victories" of the glorious German forces.

At the end of each broadcast a hand written summary of the day's news events was made for circulation to our friends and neighbors. The radio was then immediately returned to its hiding place. We had enough sense not to press our luck by listening to it more than was absolutely necessary to gain some knowledge of the world events.

One dark and rainy evening, shortly after the BBC broadcast, there was a loud knock on our front door. When my mother opened the door an SS officer in black uniform wearing an armband with a swastika faced her. Accompanying him were four German soldiers armed with automatic submachine guns and a Greek traitor who was brought as an interpreter. My mother without losing her composure or appearing scared, addressed herself directly to the Officer and said to him, in perfectly pronounced German, "We don't need the services of this gentleman because I speak fluent German".

The officer then turned to the Greek and dismissed him by simply saying,"Rouse" which means, "Get out".

With that my mother asked them all to come in and we could see a visible change in the attitude and manner of the German when he heard his own mother tongue spoken by an attractive, well mannered lady. My mother then proceeded to ask, "What can I do for you?"

He replied, "We have reliable information that you people have a short wave radio."

My mother laughed and said, "Did you say a radio? I am a poor refugee widow with four young children. Where will I get the money to buy a radio?"

To that he replied, "Nevertheless, this is what we were told. You don't mind if we search the house?"

This was a rhetorical question and my mother knew that regardless of whether she minded or not they were going to conduct a search. So she immediately said, "Of course we don't mind. We are always happy to cooperate with the authorities" and upon finishing her sentence she opened the door of the room where the radio was hidden and said,

"Why don't you start here"?

The officer turned to his soldiers and issued an order.

"Search the rest of the house. I will search this room myself".

He undoubtedly thought that since she opened that room first the radio would most likely not be there. He then proceeded to make a perfunctory search of the room, looking under the bed and opening some of the drawers in our dresser. He also opened the door of the armoire, looked at the shelf inside but did not part the clothes.

In the meantime he and my mother continued to have a pleasant conversation in German. My mother was asking him questions about his family and the place where he was born and raised and telling him that she was a philatelist, a collector and student of postage stamps, and that she had correspondence with other ladies from his part of the world for the purpose of exchanging stamps. He said,

"You speak very good German, where did you learn it?"

My mother told him that she had attended the German Academy, which was a lie.

Shortly after the four soldiers returned and reported that they did not find any radio. The German officer then clicked his heels saluted and said,

"A million pardons, gracious lady for disturbing your home. Obviously we were misinformed."

My mother replied, "Please think nothing of it, I've enjoyed talking to you. It is not very often that I get a chance to practice my German."

The two of them then side by side were slowly heading towards the front door when he noticed an antenna wire coming down from the ceiling. He quickly made an about face and shouted,

"Aha! If you don't have a radio why do you need an antenna?"

We all realized at that critical moment that our lives hinged on my mother's reply. We stood motionless, paralyzed with fear holding our breath and waiting to hear what she was going to say. My mother then smiled and said,

"Now I know why you have information that there is a radio here. The previous tenant had a radio but he left a long time ago and I've never bothered to climb up there to remove the antenna wires since they don't really bother me."

He took another look at her, saw how calm she was and said, "That makes sense" and with those words he opened the front door and left.

We took a deep breath glad to be alive and watched mother collapse into the nearest armchair.

My mother's remarkable performance and amazing self-control was to a large measure due to her upbringing and education. She was born in the town of Kavala on the Aegean Sea. Her father was a wealthy tobacco merchant, thus she grew up in an affluent environment surrounded by servants. Consequently she developed poise and was able to take charge and issue orders.

At the time my mother was growing up Kabala was still under the control of the Turks. The Turks did not have public schools, thus she was educated in a private school operated by French Nuns. While enrolled in that school she had to learn a foreign language, so she studied German. This minor detail would soon prove to be a vital factor in the complicated web of events surrounding our family's struggle for survival.

My mother's musical training as an opera singer taught her several other languages. As a result she was able to tune in on the short wave radio and listen to the broadcasts emanating from several European Capitals.

She was thus extremely well informed on the state of the world in these uncertain times just prior and immediately after World War II. Additional information was obtained from her correspondence with several people in Europe with whom she exchanged stamps. This knowledge turned out to be crucial in terms of our decision to defy the Germans.

My mother was a handsome woman with a long aristocratic face, black eyes and black hair. She was very well organized, logical and a no-nonsense person. She thought more like a man than a woman. I have never known her to indulge in the frivolous behavior so typical of women of that era.

She was a very able person and performed with extreme dexterity all the domestic tasks from knitting to baking. She was a great hostess and her dinner parties were legendary. She was very imaginative and artistic.

This talent particularly flourished during the "Apocries", the Greek equivalent of Halloween. She always came up with the neatest ideas for costumes for all of us. She personally designed and executed the construction of the outfits. My brothers, my sister, and I, dressed up as Pirates or Maharajas, and became the talk of the town each year that holiday rolled by.

As part of the ritual we always had to pose for a professional photographer to immortalize the occasion. These were some of the exciting and happy times of my otherwise weird childhood.

My mother was not a very demonstrative person. I am sure that she loved all her children dearly but I do not recall her ever being overly affectionate or her babying or cuddling any of us. If we told her that we did not like the food that was prepared she simply said, "Don't eat it", but she would not offer a substitute. Her reasoning was that if we were hungry enough we would eat and if not, so be it. As a result of that we grew up with very few, if any, hang-ups about food and learned to eat everything.

Her attitude about other matters was similar to that regarding food. She was a strict disciplinarian and believed in making sure that we understood the difference between right and wrong. She was rather inflexible and stubborn and would not compromise when she thought that her position in a certain matter was right. Every one in our family, fortunately or unfortunately, inherited this characteristic. Above all my mother was a very courageous and decisive person who did not easily cave in at time of adversity.

Surely the sum total of her life experiences was the sole reason she was able to outwit that German officer who came looking for our radio.

CHAPTER 3

Father Killed in Battle

My father was an average height, heavyset man with a clear complexion, penetrating blue-green eyes and a full set of wavy hair that was prematurely gray. He was a very neat person, meticulous about his appearance and his personal effects. He was a man of many talents, extremely handy and able to fix anything. As a young man he went to Italy to learn all about electricity that was just becoming available on a commercial basis. He then returned to Salonica and opened an electrical supply store with one of his younger brothers. He was the first person to install electric doorbells in town and electric lights to the "White Castle", Salonica's most famous landmark.

When the store burned down in the early 1900's from a fire that destroyed nearly half the city, he bought a portable projector and started touring the nearby villages showing movies to the peasants. This brought him to the town of Drama, where he decided to open his first Motion Picture Theatre.

The Town of Drama

Drama is a small town in the northern part of Greece about half way between the Aegean Sea and the Bulgarian Border and within a day's drive from Turkey. Drama and its surrounding villages are located in a valley between Mount Falacros and Mount Pangeon. The primary occupation is farming and the primary crop is tobacco.

The problem was that Drama did not have electricity at the time. Such minor obstacles did not deter my father in the least. He rigged his own power generator and produced enough electric power to not only operate the movie but also to provide light for part of the town.

Father was what we call today an "entrepreneur". In addition to the Movie Theatre he was involved in several other business enterprises. Among other things he was the exclusive agent for Phillips Radio in Greece. As a result of this we always had the latest model Phillips Short Wave Radio in our home.

I remember my father as having a generous nature, an honest and decent man that intensely disliked lying and liars. He had a hot temper and a short fuse. Despite this I have never known my father to raise a hand to my siblings or me. He had an alert and creative mind.

Although his formal education was minimal his encyclopedic knowledge was remarkable. He spoke several languages, which included German. The big family joke was that he learned how to speak English after he signed up with the British Army as an interpreter!

Father with medals.

My father made a quick recovery from the devastating news of his complete financial ruin and put his fertile mind and able hands to work for survival. He started to buy parts of machinery from many junk sources and rigged-up a small mill for grinding grains into flour. He then built his own power generator and started a business in a tiny store that was in a remote area of the city.

The payment for doing the grinding for clients was in flour not money. The flour could not only be used to bake bread but also had a high trading value for other essentials. This operation had to be conducted in secrecy because if the Germans got wind of it they would confiscate everything and arrest my father for operating without a license.

This meant that the grinding had to be done at night and as silently as possible. One had to be continuously on the lookout for German patrols. Every time one such patrol would approach the grinding was stopped and the lights were turned off. We then waited in absolute silence until they passed by and then resumed the operation.

The next challenge was getting home at that hour without being spotted. The Germans had imposed a curfew and only those with special permits from the Gestapo were allowed to be in the streets after hours. Armored cars, equipped with a spotlight and a machine gun, were used for the patrols.

Whenever they spotted anyone moving they put the spotlight on and ordered him or her to stop and show their permit. If they made the slightest movement they were mowed down by machine gun fire. Since the mechanized patrols used primarily the main streets and avenues we had chosen a much longer but safer route for circulating after curfew that involved back streets and alleys.

One night when my father was returning from the mill the back way he turned a corner and suddenly came face to face with two German military policemen. It was too late to flee. They shouted Halt! And my father froze in his tracks.

"Papier Bitte" said one of them.

My father reached in his pocket and pulled out an old bank savings passbook. They pulled their flashlight and examined the photo but of course they could not read the Greek writing "Where is your circulation permit?" They asked.

My father replied,

"I am a Doctor and I was summoned in the middle of the night to deliver a baby. I did not have time to get a permit nor did I know that I would have to go out."

In the mean time the entire conversation is conducted in German. The soldier said,

"You speak good German, where did you learn it?"

My father decided to go for broke and answered,

"I have studied Medicine in Vienna."

Fortunately two totally unrelated events enabled him to pull this bluff and made his lies convincing. First, his older brother, my Uncle Gabriel, who was a dentist had actually studied in Vienna and married a Viennese nightclub singer. As a result he knew the name of the Medical School and the address where my uncle was staying while he was studying in Vienna.

Secondly my mother and father had actually visited Vienna before the war on a vacation when they were celebrating their tenth wedding anniversary and thus had some familiarity with the city and its sites.

The soldiers seemed satisfied that he was who he said he was and for a moment it looked that they were going to release him when suddenly one of them said,

"Her Doctor, one of our comrades is very sick. Do you mind coming with us and taking a look at him?"'

My father was terrified but he knew he was stuck so he smiled and said,

"I'll be glad to do what I can but as you can see I don't have any of my medical instruments with me. Not even a thermometer".

The soldiers replied,

"We have a thermometer and an emergency kit in the barracks. Please help us."

My father was trapped. He had no choice but to go along, getting deeper and deeper into trouble.

When they arrived at their destination he was ushered into a room. Laying on a wooden bunk bed was a soldier still wearing his uniform except for the boots, moaning and perspiring heavily. They produced a thermometer and my father checked his temperature. It was 105. My father asked them,

"How long has he been ill? "

They said," a couple of days."

"Did he have chills? My father asked?"

They said "yes."

My father then said authoritatively and with a tone that reflected confidence and certainty,

"Your friend is suffering form Malaria. We must give him a cold bath to reduce his temperature and Aspirin to keep it down. We also must start him on Atabrine. Give him two tablets four times a day. I'll stop by tomorrow morning to check up on him. Now please give me a pass so I can go home safely and get some sleep."

They thank him profusely, gave him the pass and sent him on his way. My father had seen enough cases of malaria among the Greek population to know the symptoms. Luckily it wasn't a case that needed surgery or some other drastic medical procedure or his goose would have been cooked.

Father was the first member of our family to become involved with the underground movement. His World War I expertise with explosives was a big asset for the Guerrilla fighters who would regularly blow up German troop or munitions trains.

A typical raid would involve placing the charges on the railroad tracks and detonating them as the troop transports were crossing. Then armed partisans would attack from both sides of the tracks, kill as many Germans as possible and run up to their hiding places in the hills before reinforcements could arrive.

The Germans would retaliate by rounding up civilians and shooting them. In some instances they would attach cars filled with hostages to their troop trains to avoid being blown up by the partisans. However, in an ultimate act of defiance and sacrifice, the underground blew up the trains anyway.

Father was a key person in numerous such raids. He would calculate the amount of explosives needed to do a particular job and would often place the charges himself where they were likely to produce the most damage.

No one in the family knew of his involvement in these most dangerous activities. Periodically he will disappear but he always thought of a good excuse for his absence, such as going to the villages to buy wheat.

At one time the Resistance command identified a strategic target of great importance: The main railroad lines that connected Thrace and Northern Macedonia with Salonica had to go over a bridge that crossed the Strimonas River.

The river was located near the town of Seres, approximately 60 kilometers north of Salonica. Blowing up that bridge would seriously hamper the German operations since seventeen trains per day loaded with supplies and munitions crossed the river.

The underground was ordered to blow up the bridge. This mission relied heavily on my father's expertise with explosives. The charges were carefully placed but the operation was compromised by a security leak. Someone had informed the Germans and they were ready.

When the partisans arrived they ran into a trap. Before they were able to detonate the charges white flares were fired into the air illuminating the entire area. For a few seconds after each flare was fired it was like daylight exposing the partisan's positions. Heavy mortar and machine gun fire followed killing dozens of freedom fighters. It was like shooting fish in a barrel.

According to an eyewitness my father was hit by a mortar fragment in the leg and fell still holding the detonator key in his hands. He then was sprayed with machine gun fire and died on the spot. He was 52 years old and I was 12.

CHAPTER 4

Mother Takes the Reins

My mother was left a widow at the ripe old age of 42 with four children and without any means of support. Furthermore the question and the responsibility of our safety and survival weighed heavily on her shoulders.

The Family after Father's Death

When my father died, we all felt such a deep sadness that seemed to drain out of us the will to live. We were sad, afraid and uncertain about the future. We all cried a lot except my mother; She became immersed into a sober and uncommunicative mode. She went through the daily chores like a zombie, speaking very little. However mother was a strong and incredibly courageous person.

She quickly snapped out of it and took charge of the situation. She gathered all of us around her and told us that now that our father was gone we must look after each other and that things would probably get a lot worse before they got better. At any rate we all decided that we would not play the German game and that we would take our chances with the resistance.

My mother was the major factor in that decision. She was convinced from the start that the Germans were not to be trusted and that they had evil plans for the Jews of Salonica. This came in part from the fact that she was an avid short wave radio listener.

Her knowledge of multiple languages enabled her to become much better informed than the average Greek about what was going on in Europe and about the fate of the European Jews. Also, her correspondence with other women in the capitals of Europe for the purpose of exchanging stamps provided her with additional insights regarding the treatment of Jews in other countries that had fallen into German hands.

She made us all very much aware that the course we had decided to take was fraught with dangers and was irreversible. From that point on we had to act as if we were not Jews, keeping our guard up for anything or anyone that might betray us. We had to be extremely careful not to say or do anything that might give us away.

Pretending not to be Jewish meant completely disregarding all the directives issued by the occupation troops regarding the Jewish population. We decided that we were not going to register with the Germans, we were not going to tell them what property we owned or where it was located, we would not wear a yellow star nor would we obey the restrictions regarding movement, i.e. staying within the prescribed Jewish Ghetto.

This was a life and death decision because if we were caught we would be undoubtedly shot. To pull off the deception we needed new names and new papers. So one of the first things we did was to change our first names to pure Christian names and to apply and obtain new identity cards from the Greek Police.

To avoid the chance that someone might recognize us we applied for the new identity cards in a precinct located in a neighborhood that was far away from our place of residence. To qualify we had to give a fictitious address. We later found out that the address we gave and was put in our new identity cards was the building that housed the City's Philharmonic Orchestra!

The procedure for getting a new identity card required a birth certificate. Fortunately the Bulgarians had burned down the City Hall in Drama and all the records were destroyed. Thus it was permissible to substitute for a birth certificate the sworn affidavits of two witnesses that they knew us and were willing, under oath, to state that we were indeed who we said we were. Since almost all of our friends were non-Jews we did not have any trouble finding two people who were willing to provide us with these affidavits.

Thus we eventually obtained new identity cards. Fortunately our family surname was not recognizable as a Jewish name and thus did not need to be changed. Another advantage in this whole deception was our perfect command of the Greek language that made us verbally indistinguishable from any other Greek. My father's insistence that we all get educated in the Greek public schools were paying off. All these factors enabled us to pass for non-Jews and circulate freely in and out of the restricted areas without fear of being discovered.

Our biggest concern was that we would run into someone who would recognize us and inform the authorities. We had decided on a plan of action for such an eventuality if we were to be confronted with someone who knew us we would tell him that we were Spanish Nationals. We had chosen this cover because initially the Jews that were Spanish citizens were exempt from the German restrictions and directives.

This resulted from the fact that Spain was a neutral country and thus the Germans had no jurisdiction over its citizens. However, later, even that cover became inadequate since the Germans, after they had deported all the Greek Jews they could find, they began to round up and sent to the death camps both the Spanish and Italian Jews in a gross violation of international law.

One by one the Germans were systematically eliminating all the signs of the Jewish presence in Salonica. One of the ancient symbols of such presence was the Jewish Cemetery; located near the University of Salonica, where for nearly two thousand years the Jews of Salonica buried their dead.

The fascinating history of this great City, that had changed hands so many times, could be reconstructed by reading the inscriptions on the tombstones. The Germans ordered the cemetery destroyed. The marbles that covered the graves were removed and used throughout the city for the construction of air raid shelters. Then they came in with bulldozers and leveled the ground and covered it in part by pouring concrete. The rest of the area was landscaped converting it into a park. Looking at this park today no one would suspect that thousands of dead Jewish bodies lie underneath.

Defying the Germans was an act that came under severe criticism from all my father's living relatives. They had several sessions with my mother trying to dissuade her from the decision to resist. They told her that it was crazy and irresponsible to go against the German orders and that she was gambling with her life and with the lives of her children.

"The Germans will eventually catch you and all of you will be killed," they said.

Adding fuel to these arguments was the proclamation to the Jewish Community by the Chief Rabbi Koretz. He tried to allay the fears of the outraged community for the mounting anti-Semitic measures by the Germans, and in fact urged his flock to comply with the German demands and directives in order to avoid further disasters.

This counsel by such a prominent Jewish leader had a profound effect on the Jewish population of Salonica and resulted in the unnecessary death of thousands of people. If he had the courage to urge the Jews to resist instead of urging them to submit, thousands of lives would have been saved by joining the underground movement and escaping the deportation.

Rabbi Koretz was acting under German orders when he made his traitorous appeal to the Jewish congregation to comply with the directives of the authorities. He gave his speech at the main Synagogue, which was ironically located right behind our home. In fact the rear wall of our yard was the front wall of the Synagogue.

The entrance to the Synagogue was via a path that ran parallel to the right side of our lot and ended on Queen Olga Street. I was there when Rabbi Koretz spoke and I vividly remember the profound and sobering effect his message had on the Salonica Jewry. They were all gripped by fear of what the Germans might do to them if they disobeyed.

Of course no one at that time knew that the alternative was deportation to a death camp. Shortly after the Koretz declaration we woke up one morning by a thundering noise that shook our home to its foundations and to the sound of broken glass. Having served its purpose, the Germans decided to blow up the Synagogue. In just seconds another symbol of the Jewish faith and culture that had endured for centuries was reduced to a pile of rubble.

Despite the pressures from the family and Rabbi Koretz's admonitions my mother stubbornly stuck to her guns. She told the well-meaning advisors,

"Leave us alone." "I will take care of my family and you take care of yours."

"I'm sure that these animals have bad intentions for us and I am not going to help them put the noose around our necks."

All of these relatives that were urging my mother to comply with the German orders were shipped and died in the concentration camps of Germany and Poland. Not a single person in either my mother's or my father's family survived.

CHAPTER 5

The Great Famine

The days became weeks and the weeks turned into months. The conditions gradually deteriorated. There were tremendous shortages of food, medical supplies and all other materials essential to life. The occupation army was gradually squeezing the life out of the Country. Everything of value was confiscated and diverted to Germany.

Famine became wide spread. The street corners of Salonica started to become littered with people dying of hunger. Their distended bodies were full of sores from malnutrition and we could hear their horrible moans as we walked by. The German soldiers would kick them, pushing their twisted bodies into the gutter. Dozens of corpses would be collected and dumped each day with the morning trash.

Everything was rationed. Our ration coupons entitled us to a few slices of molding corn bread daily. Meat or any other source of protein was extremely scarce and found only in the flourishing black market. The invading German forces came onto Greek soil with essentially no supplies. The soldiers looked haggard and malnourished. They grabbed all the food they could get their hands on with animal voracity. I have seen soldiers order omelets in a restaurant with 12 eggs!

It did not take long for shortages to become acute and famine to start. Athens was in much worse shape than Salonica. Athens and Piraeus housed about one fifth of the population of Greece. In addition thousands of refugees from other parts of Greece as well as soldiers trying to find their way home poured into the city.

The plundering and looting by the Germans depleted the available food supplies and famine became widespread. At the same time hoarding and black marketeering flourished. The schools and Universities closed and there were no job opportunities. Because of these conditions my brother Zack returned to Salonica and we were again reunited.

They say that if you are hungry enough you will eat anything. I know from personal experience that this is not true. One day, after not having eaten any kind of meat for several weeks, my mother was able to get in the black market a piece of meat. This was accomplished by trading one of her silk blouses with the wife of the butcher.

At this time money had no value whatsoever and bartering became the main way of doing business. If you had something of value, you traded it with someone that had something you wanted. The butcher's wife wanted a silk blouse because she never had one and my mother wanted food.

When the meat was cooked and we all sat down at the dinner table with excitement and anticipation one of my brother's looked at the meat and said,

"This looks like dog meat."

From that point on no one could eat that meat and we ended -up dumping it. Ah well, what is another blouse?

The worst shortage was that of fuel. Everything combustible was in short supply. The few remaining old cars, trucks and buses that the Germans did not deem worthy of confiscating, had their engines converted so that they can run by burning wood or charcoal. It was quite a sight to see trucks driving down the road at the blinding speed of 10-15 miles per hour with someone riding in the back feeding chunks of wood into a stove like contraption.

Some Greeks that managed to buy fuel in the black market had these stove - like contraptions in their trucks but they were not connected to the engine. They were there to fool the Germans. Their trucks would approach the checkpoints at 10 miles per hour and the man in the back would pretend to put wood into the stove but as soon as they cleared the checkpoint they would gun the engine and speed away.

To make matters worse the first winter of the occupation was one of the worst winters Greece had ever seen, the thermometer dipped to subfreezing temperatures. Ice and snow covered the streets and homes. The number of dead and dying from the cold and starvation increased dramatically. The worst hit were those who had lost their homes during the fighting or bombing.

Those of us that still had homes could not warm up even though we were wearing several layers of winter garments. The hardest hit were the cities. In the countryside the peasants could always find something to burn. They also ate better because they could grow some vegetables or hide some livestock from the Germans. The city folks didn't have these opportunities. Their lives depended on whatever food was allowed to come in from the farms by the occupation troops and their traitorous Greek collaborators.

Most of the city dwellers, including us, would venture into the neighboring farms and villages with clothes, antiques, jewelry or any other personal or household items hoping to be able to trade them for a few pounds of flour, a chicken or a few ears of corn. The peasants ended up owning articles that they could only dream about in the past.

In exchange for only a few meager scraps of food city folks would trade watches, furs or other prized possessions. Lacey silk underwear and embroidered nightgowns were traded for a sac of potatoes.

The peasant women, who had never owned anything that fine, wore these garments to Church on top of their dresses. They could not believe that such luxurious items of clothing were meant to be hidden by wearing them under their clothes. They wanted every one of their friends and neighbors to see how they had come up in the world.

Every family in the city was fighting for survival, each in its own way. When I reflect on those critical days of cold and starvation I cannot help remembering, with delayed admiration, how my mother, a woman that grew up with a silver spoon in her mouth, who married a wealthy man and lived in luxury with maids and servants, made the remarkable adjustment of living in poverty and under such adverse conditions.

Not only did she learn to cope but exerted the leadership and took the decisive actions necessary to insure the family's survival.

Among other measures we dug-up most of the flowers in the garden and planted tomatoes and vegetables. We cut down a number of branches from the trees and used the wood for our stove and for cooking. At one end of the yard we had constructed a make shift chicken coop and we started to raise chickens so that we could get eggs and an occasional rooster for our table.

My mother also traded some of our belongings for a pair of goats so that we can have milk. We kept the goats in the laundry room on the third floor. Since there wasn't much grass on the cement terrace on the third floor we had to provide a daily supply of food for the goats. This meant cutting branches of trees with green leaves, dragging them up three flights of stairs and then cleaning-up the mess.

This task was assigned to me and because of that I developed a lifelong dislike to these filthy animals. Goats are mean and will eat anything from newspapers to old socks.

Since no one was working and there was no income we relied on the sale of my mother's jewelry to keep us alive. One by one her prized possessions were sacrificed at ridiculous wartime prices. Since everyone in those days was selling his valuables the proceeds of such sales were several orders of magnitude below their actual worth. Nevertheless because of the exquisite pieces my mother had, even at those depressed wartime prices, the sale of her pieces of jewelry netted enough to keep us afloat for quite a while.

I have never heard my mother utter a single word of complaint, disappointment or regret for having to part with her jewelry. I now also realize how wise and prophetic was my father's policy of buying expensive jewelry for his wife when he was able to do so.

Day by day, the situation in the occupied city worsened. There were acute shortages of everything. These shortages affected everyone including the army of occupation. There was a noticeable change in the quality and quantity of food they fed their soldiers. Increasingly one observed meals consisting of bean soup or boiled potatoes replacing the old meals of pork or chicken.

It was my first exposure to dehydrated food. The Germans began to feed their troops with dehydrated carrots that were reconstituted with the addition of water. The dry product looked like orange sawdust and tasted about the same.

The starving Greek youth would rummage through the trash cans of the Germans hoping to find a potato or anything else that was edible. When the Germans noticed that this was occurring they began to mix their trash with sand or ashes so that it would not be usable.

We were dying to retaliate for this extreme act of cruelty and one day we got our chance. The German company that occupied the large house on our lot decided to set-up a field kitchen in the yard. Part of this set up was a large cauldron, where the mess sergeant was preparing the customary bean soup. At a brief moment, when the pot was unattended, we threw in a bar of soap, and watched the result from our home, hiding behind the wooden shutters.

All pandemonium broke loose when mountains of soapsuds began to emanate from the boiling pot. Much to our enjoyment the soldiers had nothing to eat and the sergeant was chewed-out by his superior officer for his negligence. At another time we managed to pour a whole bottle of ink into their wash and ruin all their laundry. Unfortunately all incidents were not that amusing.

One evening two young boys, one about twelve-years-old and the other fourteen were rummaging through the trash cans of the German company quartered in the big house. A young German officer was on the balcony playing the violin when he spotted them. He ordered them to stop but they were too frightened and started to run.

The officer then removed his pistol from the holster and calmly shot and killed them both. He then went back to the balcony and continued to play his violin. He said that they were trying to steal his car, which was a preposterous lie. He did not show the least bit of concern or remorse for killing two innocent children.

With the food shortage becoming so critical, my mother decided to venture a trip out of the city for the purpose of trading some of our personal effects for anything edible. We had heard that in the mountain region near the town of Veria there were villages occupied by people known as "Vlahi".

These were simple shepherds that lived in those mountains for years and spoke their own language. Most of them understood Greek but their origin was Rumanian and the language they spoke among themselves was a dialect of Rumanian.

As Rumanians they were entitled to receive food rations not available to the Greek population. Furthermore, because of the remote location of their villages, they were left more or less untouched by the occupation. Located high on the mountain, the villages were linked by narrow paths accessible only by mule. Since there were no roads, no vehicles could reach them. As a result, the Germans never bothered to attempt to establish a presence there.

Because of all these reasons, the mountain people lived essentially the same way as before, a simple but healthy life, with adequate amounts of food derived primarily from livestock and the cultivation of small vegetable gardens and fruit trees. They were especially known for their dairy products: milk, butter, and a variety of cheeses.

The sheep provided them with ample supplies of meat. They also raised chickens and had fresh eggs. In the past they came down the mountain a few times a year to sell their products and buy clothes, shoes, blankets and other necessities. During the occupation even these commodities became scarce, thus the Vlahi did not venture down the mountain as often as before.

My mother and I saw this as an opportunity to exchange some of our belongings for food. We loaded two valises with my father's clothes, shoes, and winter coats and some of my mother's fancy dresses, and boarded the bus to Veria. We reached Veria late in the afternoon and tried to locate a friend of a friend whose name was given to us before we left.

After considerable amount of time and searching, we were able to locate this individual who was a Jew married to a Christian woman and hiding his identity to avoid capture. Like us, he was a fugitive trying to survive. He owned and operated a small fabric store in town and lived a quiet life maintaining a low profile and trying not to attract any unwelcome attention.

As soon as we met and without any hesitation he invited us to spend the evening in his house and offered to help us get transportation to the mountain villages. This was extremely lucky for us since they were no Hotels in town in those days and we did not have anyplace where we could spend the night. Sometimes strangers were allowed by the local people to sleep in their barn on top of the haystacks.

Fortunately, we did not have to do that. Our new friend and his wife fed us a delicious dinner of lamb and bean stew with dark peasant bread and we slept in a comfortable bed with warm wool blankets and feather pillows.

I can never forget the warm hospitality shown to us by these people who were essentially total strangers. This was typical of the ancient Greek tradition of extending your hospitality to strangers without even asking who they were and where they were going. The man played the bouzouki and my mother sang, which was a real treat.

Soon everyone joined in and for just a little while we all forgot the horrors of the war and the German occupation. The next day our friend took us to a livery stable where, after much bargaining, we rented two mules and a handler to take us up the mountain.

After securely tying the suitcases to the saddles, we mounted the mules and started our journey up the mountain. Neither mother nor I had ever before been on a horse, mule, or donkey. We later discovered that mules are particularly chosen for travel up winding and dangerous mountain roads because they are extremely surefooted.

However, they have the nasty habit of riding right at the edge of the cliff, which scared us out of our wits. The handler kept saying, "Don't look down and don't be afraid. Let the mule alone and it will choose the safest path." Nevertheless, we were convinced that at any moment we would fall down the cliff.

To maintain our courage we started to sing while holding on for dear life. We also discovered that peasants have absolutely no sense of time. We occasionally ran across someone who was coming down the mountain while we were climbing. "How long is it to the next village we would ask?" "Oh, it is not long at all. By the time you smoke a cigarette you will be there," they would reply. Two hours later, there was still no village in sight.

Finally, we reached our destination. We were greeted with surprise and cordiality. Apparently, visits from town's people were rare in these parts. They welcomed our presence there and the opportunity to acquire some of the much-needed items of apparel, particularly shoes and sweaters. Eventually we emptied the suitcases of all the clothing items and loaded them with blocks of cheese, cans of butter, salami, sausages and eggs; a veritable treasure beyond our wildest dreams.

In the evening, the village chief invited us to spend the night at his home. We were treated to a delicious dinner of roasted lamb, corn on the cob and homegrown vegetables. The home consisted of two levels. The ground floor was one huge room with a large wood-burning fireplace. In the back of the room was the kitchen.

There was no electricity or plumbing. There was an outhouse located in the backyard and washing was done with water from a well equipped with a hand pump. A wooden staircase connected the main floor with the upstairs loft, which had a bed and a couple of chairs. The wall of the loft that faced the front of the house had a large opening but no windows.

We were given that bed to sleep in, which was apparently the only bed in the house. The sheets and pillowcases were crisp, clean and hand embroidered. It looked as though this was the first time they were ever used. While we enjoyed the comforts of this bed all the rest of the family, including their livestock, slept on the ground of the floor below. This was the way that these simple folks, who didn't have much, but were fiercely proud, expressed their hospitality.

The next morning after a delicious breakfast of fresh milk, bread, butter with honey, and a plate of cheese, we said our goodbyes and thank - yous and started our descent to Veria. The next day we were back in our home in Salonica delighted with our loot. This gave us a temporary reprieve from starvation but after a short while the hunger and fear returned.

CHAPTER 6

Anti – Jewish Measures Intensify

History tells us that the first Jewish settlement in Salonica dates back to 140 BC and it consisted of Jews from Alexandria. Central European Jews settled in the city in 1376 AD and Jews from northern Italy in 1423 AD. However, the biggest influx of Jews took place in 1492 AD, during the Spanish Inquisition when Queen Isabel expelled all the Jews from Spain.

These Jews came to be known as "Sephardic". Many of them settled in the Balkans and still today speak a dialect, "Ladino", that is primarily ancient Spanish adulterated with some Turkish, Italian and Portuguese words. Initially twenty thousand of these Jews settled in Salonica but that number grew, by some accounts, to over sixty thousand.

Thus Salonica has been regarded for decades as one of the great centers of the Sephardic culture. When the Sephardic Jews first settled in Salonica, Salonica was part of the Ottoman Empire and thus under Turkish domination. Although Non-Muslims, the Jews of Salonica faired quite well as Turkish subjects and excelled in commerce and in the professions.

The Turkish officials often relied on the Jews for advise and offered them key positions in the administration. Thus a Sephardic culture flourished many years before Salonica was returned to Greece. Since the Turks did not have public schools the Jews sent their children to private schools for their education. Foreign Nationals such as the French Catholic Nuns operated the schools.

At home the Jews of Salonica continued to speak Spanish. As a result when Salonica was returned to Greek hands during the Balkan Wars of 1912 there was already an established Jewry in place that did not speak much Greek. The Jews that were once a majority in Salonica were overwhelmed by the influx of one hundred thousand Greeks that settled in the City as a result of a population exchange with Turkey orchestrated by the 1922 Treaty of Lausanne.

Because of this history the Jews of Salonica spoke Greek with a distinct accent that betrayed their ethnicity. This turned out to be disastrous in terms of their chances of survival from the German persecution. It was impossible for them to pretend to be non-Jews because their accent gave them away.

In contrast to the Jewish natives of Salonica my parents who were also born Sephardic Jews in a country that was almost exclusively Orthodox Christian had a strong ethnic Greek identification. Our family, as well as most of the few families that made up the tiny Jewish Community of about 1200 in Drama, was fully integrated into the life of the town.

Neither one of my parents was very religious. I don't remember ever going to the Synagogue except for weddings, funerals or bar mitzvahs. We did observe all the major Jewish holidays such as Passover, Rosh Hashanah and Yom Kippur, but aside from that, our lives were not different from any other of the town's residents. Ninety - nine percent of all of our friends were not Jews and the same was true of our parents. We were all the same, except now, after the invasion, we were suddenly different Despite our being a distinct minority my father insisted that all of us attend the Greek Public Schools that were almost exclusively made up of Orthodox Christian Students. The result was that no one could recognize that we were Jews by the way we spoke the language. This gave us a tremendous advantage when we decided to ignore the German orders and pretend that we were not Jewish.

The anti-Jewish measures taken by the Germans were initiated very shortly after the invasion of Salonica but intensified gradually. The Jewish Community Council members as well as other Jewish Community leaders were immediately rounded-up and thrown in prison. All the Jewish Community records were confiscated; Jewish stores were looted and closed.

The next step was the forceful displacement of Jews from their homes to make room for the housing of German soldiers. The Germans opted to have their troops interspersed with the civilian population, rather than house them in barracks, to avoid air attacks or focused acts of sabotage. To achieve this objective they first had to vacate the space.

Their first target was, naturally, the Jews. The typical scenario involved a random search, which was conducted with the help of Greek traitors who accompanied the Gestapo or Military Police to help them identify Jewish homes and apartments. When they found a home they wanted they usually gave the occupants five minutes to leave and take with them their belongings.

Anything left behind after the five minutes became the property of the Reich. Those that were unfortunate enough to face such a situation walked out holding their children by the hand and leaving everything else behind. What can anyone, after all, really take from their home under such circumstances?

One day in the early hours of the morning there was an ominous loud knock at our front door. When my mother opened the door she came face to face with an SS officer, several soldiers in black uniforms armed with submachine guns, and a Greek collaborator in civilian clothes wearing an armband with the Swastika. The civilian spoke to her in Greek and asked her,

"Who lives here?"

My mother ignored him and addressed herself directly to the officer in his language and with a loud and contemptuous voice said,

"Are you in the habit now of employing illiterate people?"

Her remarks and her audacity visibly disturbed the German. He replied,

"What the devil do you mean by such a question?"

"I am disappointed by your choice of language", she said,

"I was always told that Germans, especially officers, are courteous and polite when addressing a lady."

She then pointed to the brass plaque that was screwed onto the door where the name of the previous tenant was engraved in bold letters: Ioannis Panagopoulos (a typical non- – Jewish Greek name) and said,

"Why is this idiot asking me who lives here? Can't he read? Our name is plainly written on the door."

At that point the Greek traitor interjected "Nicht Juden" i.e. "They are not Jews."

The German officer then clicked his heels, saluted "Heil Hitler" and they all left. Thus the quaint custom of the wealthy Greeks to place engraved plaques with their name on their front door and the boldness and guts of my mother saved us from being thrown out of our home. If they had asked us for our identity cards we would have been sunk.

In the meantime life went on. The schools were open but not fully operational. We had to go into double sessions and the standards were greatly relaxed because of over crowding, hunger and lack of heat.

47

Our high school, like all the others had severe shortages of everything. At noon we were served a watery bean or vegetable soup with questionable taste and even more questionable nutritional value. We still found ourselves able to play, joke and occasionally learn.

My brother Zack was the oldest of my siblings. His personality was at the other end of the spectrum from Albert. Zack was very daring, extroverted and happy go lucky. He liked taking chances and often got into scrapes. He had a mischievous nature and liked to tease. He had nicknames for every one of us, and the angrier or resentful we got when he called us these names the more he did it. Although very intelligent he did not take his High School studies very seriously. He and his buddies had too much fun mocking the teachers and getting into trouble.

Because of all this horsing around he failed the exams in the fifth grade in High School and remained in the same class. Unable to face my father with the news he ran away from home and disappeared for a short while. Later we learned that he had boarded a Boat from Kavala and traveled to my grandmother's house in Salonica.

My father contacted his younger brother Mathew, who had connections with the local authorities and asked for his help in locating Zack. In two hours the secret police located Zack and send him back home to face the music.

He then enrolled into the University, which were a hotbed of activism and a focal point of the resistance movement that had begun to take shape and became more and more organized. The activities of the students were under constant surveillance by the police but they managed to eluded them and carry out a program of resistance. The danger excited and delighted Zack. The resistance activities suited his daring personality perfectly.

Zack was a late bloomer and despite his rocky high school days he did well enough in his University studies to win a prestigious academic award, but he never bothered to tell the family. One day, when we were all seated at the dinner table, my father said to Zack,

"What is this I heard? You won some kind of an award?"

Zack said, "Yes father I did."

My father then turned to my mother and said,

"The academic standards in this Country must be going to the dogs, if Zack won an award."

This lack of faith in my brother's scholastic ability is amusing today but I suspect it must have caused some pain to Zack at the time.

Zack and his friends, many of them also refugees from Drama, quickly became involved with the underground and its clandestine operations. In one of their missions they were ordered to case the German "COMANDANTUR", (Headquarters) and establish the number of soldiers present and the general nature of their defenses.

So they started to walk back and forth in front of the building and to take note of the number of posted guards, their routine in terms of the area each patrolled and the frequency of guard changing. Suddenly someone in the balcony started waving his arms wildly and shouting to the guards, "Arrest those men, arrest those men!" The guards moved quickly, pointed their guns at my brother, and rounded him-up as well as two of his friends.

The others took off like a light and disappeared into the crowd. At first they did not recognize the man who was shouting the orders but then, as they got closer, they saw Spiridis, the Nazi clown from Drama,

Before war came to Greece, Spiridis was the self-proclaimed leader of the Nazi party in Drama with a membership of one. He was a comical little man that no one in town took seriously. His office walls were full of swastikas, Nazi slogans, and pictures of Hitler and Goering.

Every time it was Hitler's birthday or any other major Nazi event Spiridis would sent congratulatory telegrams and dispatches to Germany and received acknowledgements that he framed and proudly displayed and showed to every one.

The people of Drama treated Spiridis with derision and ridicule, like all the other crazies in town. He was just another clown to laugh at. My brother and his cronies often visited Spiridis and pretended to be his followers. They gave him the nazi salute, called him "Mein Fuhrer" and teased him constantly. As it turned out this was a tragic mistake that almost cost my brother his life.

Spiridis was now standing on the balcony of the German headquarters, in full Nazi uniform waving a Luger pistol at them and saying, "A ha! Gentlemen who is laughing now?" "I will now teach you respect". He then ordered the guards to throw them into a room and lock the door.

The Germans, who did not know that Spiridis was a crack pot, took him seriously and based on the long term communications he had with Berlin they were sure that this was a staunch German supporter and a true Nazi. Consequently they gave him a uniform and the title of Uberstrumfuhrer and an entire floor in their headquarters. Moreover Spiridis was often called to participate in the interrogation of suspected Greek saboteurs.

Thus by an ironic twist of fate the comical little man that was the subject of derision and ridicule in Drama now had the power of life and death over my brother and his two captured friends. The fact that Zack was a Jew made matters considerably worse.

Spiridis walked into the room flanked by two goons and turned up the volume on the radio. The goons then savagely beat the trio while Spiridis watched and laughed. At some point he waved his hand and said "That's enough for now".

The underground was immediately alerted and it was decided that drastic action was needed in order to save their lives. Two operatives armed with automatic weapons waited until Spiridis left his office to go home. They followed his car, driven by a German soldier, and watched him unlock his front door and go inside.

One of them took a position at the back door. The other circled around to the front door and drew out his pistol. He then knocked on the door. Spiridis shouted, "Who is it?" "I got a telegram for Mr. Spiridis" he replied. "Who is it from?" Spiridis asked. "It is from Berlin. I think it is from Hitler".

Spiridis was instantly elated and opened the door. The resistance man pushed his way in, grabbed Spiridis by the neck, and shoved his 45 automatic against his face. He then said,

"You will do exactly as I tell you or I will blow your head off."

"Unbuckle your belt and let it drop on the floor."

"Now step back".

"Turn around slowly and walk towards the kitchen door".

"Unlock the door and step back."

"You can come in now," he shouted and the second man came through the door with gun drawn.

"Sit down on that chair and put your hands behind your back," he ordered.

Spiridis who was shaking like a leaf promptly complied.

"Tie him up," he said.

After he was tied to the chair he removed the pistol from Spiridis' head. Spiridis asked,

"Who are you? And what do you want from me?"

The partisan struck him across the mouth with his pistol. Blood began to drip out of his upper lip.

"Shut up he said. We are asking the questions here not you."

"We heard that you captured and beat-up three innocent young Greek men? Is that true?"

"No, no," said Spiridis

"I've never harmed any Greeks. Quite the contrary I help them out when they get in trouble with the authorities."

He struck him again with his weapon causing a deep gash in his left cheek.

"You lying bastard I ought to kill you right now and ask you questions later.

If you don't cooperate instantly I will start shooting your toes off one at a time and then your fingers. Nothing will give me greater pleasure than to watch you die slowly, you filthy Nazi collaborator."

Spiridis, petrified with fear and bleeding profusely quickly replied,

"I'll do anything you want but please don't hurt me any more."

"I want you to get on the phone and order the release of those boys. I don't care how you do it but unless I get word that they are free I am going to kill you one piece at a time."

"Now get on the phone and remember that my friend here will be listening on the other extension. If you say anything suspicious I will blow a large hole in your head. Also remember that both of us understand German.

He then brought the phone near Spiridis and asked him for the number of the German Headquarters and proceeded to dial the number while the other fellow picked up the extension. He then held the receiver next to Sipiridis face and said,
"Be careful what you say."

"This is Uberstrumfuhrer Spiridis speaking. I want the three Greek youths released at once. Are you questioning my authority? Yes, yes, I said at once."

That evening Zack came home. He was badly bruised but alive. He told us the story of his capture and that he was suddenly released without any explanation. Spiridis disappeared and was never seen nor heard from again.

CHAPTER 7

Trying to Cope

Adaptation to new situations is a remarkable sociological phenomenon. Even during these dark periods of enslavement we were able to find moments for laughter and enjoyment as if what was happening was just a bad dream that would soon pass. There were short periods of time when things would even seem normal and at times amusing.

One of the funniest episodes of my career as a thief and saboteur occurred one morning while I was standing in the balcony in front of my house. From my position I had a clear view of the garden and of the street. After a few minutes I observed a German truck pulling up and parking in front of the house.

A big fat German corporal then disembarked, opened the rear gate of the truck and lowered a platform one end of which was touching the pavement and the other was attached to the gate thus forming an inclined plane, which allowed for the easy unloading of supplies.

He then got in the truck and started to roll down the platform a huge wooden barrel. When it hit the ground he left it unattended and went inside the house. This was perceived as a clear opportunity for me.

I ran down from the balcony, opened the doors of the tool shed that was in the garden, rolled the barrel inside the shed, closed the doors of the shed and ran back upstairs resuming my position on the balcony. The whole operation took less than five minutes.

The fat corporal quickly returned and saw that the barrel he had just unloaded was gone. With a highly perplexed look he started to utter a loud stream of German curse words. He could not understand how, in such a short time, anyone could steal such an enormously large and heavy object and disappear from the scene.

He then looked up and saw me standing in the balcony.

"Hey you" he shouted. "Did you see any one remove a barrel from here?"

"A barrel?" I repeated, "What kind of a barrel was it?"

"A large wooden barrel" he replied.

"Are you sure that you have unloaded a barrel?" I asked sarcastically.

This infuriated the German who had a zero sense of humor.

"If I'll come up there, I'll show you how sure I am." He said, "I'll brake your head and then we will find out who is crazy."

I realized that it was very dangerous to tease him any further so I very meekly said,

"I am sorry, Sir, but I just came out on the balcony and I did not see anything."

The German uttered another string of profanity, got into the truck and drove off in frustration.

That night I ventured out of the house and into the tool shed to see what was my valuable prize. I carefully removed the lid of the barrel and discovered that it contained several heads of cabbage immersed in a salt solution. The whole family feasted on sauerkraut for the following several weeks.

Even though we were hungry and sad we would still gather around the piano and sing our old favorite songs. German soldiers occupied the houses all around us, including Grandfather's big house. We began to know many of them by name and some would come and sit with us on our balcony and show us pictures of their wives and children and talk about their towns and villages.

Like all soldiers away from home they were lonely. Sometimes they would bring us a loaf of their bread or a piece of smoked lard they called "Shinken." My mother would make coffee, without coffee and without sugar. Instead of coffee beans we used roasted Garbanzo beans and instead of sugar saccharin.

She occasionally would serve some fruit, such as figs, from the trees in our garden. One of our regular visitors was a German soldier with the unlikely name of Ernest Girl. Ernest played the violin and we often had musical sessions with him and my sister on the piano. He was a staunch pacifist and anti – nazi but scared to death that he might be betrayed.

To play the part of a tough guy he carried a huge gun case attached to his belt but if you looked inside the case it was stuffed with rags. We were sure that Ernest posed no danger to us but we still did not tell him that we were Jews. He was, after all, a German and therefore by definition he could not be trusted.

Our number of "visitors" began to multiply, That's when we decided to start a restaurant. We cleared an area in our garden and set up a few tables and chairs under the trees. Our "clients" were mostly German soldiers who were lonely and were looking for companionship. Because of our intense hatred for them we fed them all kinds of junk cleverly camouflaged to make it look good.

We never washed the dishes or glasses. If there was a remnant of sauce or salad dressing on the plate of one soldier we added food in it and served it to the next one. "Let the pigs contaminate each other and die" my mother would say. It took a lot of ingenuity and imagination on the part of my mother to find things to prepare in this "Restaurant" since food was so scarce.

Saccharin and the sap of Cherubs were used as sweeteners. Beaten egg whites were used for whipped cream. We made "Ice Cream" from fruits grown in our trees and Goat's milk. Quite often the "clients" themselves supplied us with the food ingredients and we did the preparation.

Most commonly we would get loaves of German bread, a few potatoes, or a piece of smoked pork or lard. The soldiers, most of who did not know how to cook, devoured everything that was put in front of them and were delighted to have "a home cooked meal." This also was our way of coping with hunger and staying alive.

However our business enterprise did not last very long. Suddenly one day we had a visit by the Military Police. They chased all the Germans from the premises, smashed all our tables and chairs and warned us that if we tried opening again we would be arrested and thrown in jail. They then hung up a sign "Off limits to military personnel" and left. Of course they never suspected that we were Jews.

Very quickly all of us, myself in particular, became proficient enough in German to carry out a decent conversation and it was at that time that I began my young career as a thief and a black market operator. I was no longer the innocent and naïve child that left Drama. In a short period of time I had become hardened and "Street Smart".

Every few weeks our new "friends" the German soldiers would disappear as their unit was transferred out of the area, probably to the Russian front. During that time the neighboring houses were temporarily empty waiting for a new batch of

German soldiers to be housed there. This presented a window of opportunity for my newly acquired skills as a burglar.

Because of my small size and great agility I was able to climb unto the balconies and find an open window or unlocked sliding door that allowed me to enter the house. I would then systematically remove everything that was not nailed down. Some of these things we could use and the others I traded in the black market.

My special targets were the wooden bunk beds the Germans constructed out of unfinished rough pieces of lumber. That wood was dry and made excellent kindling for our stove.

Eventually I became so adept in this and so bold that I started to enter the homes even at the times when the German soldiers occupied them. I would select a time when everybody was out on maneuvers, enter the home quickly, pick a convenient target, and run out.

I never stole anything that could be traced such as a watch or other personal effect. I usually looked for food and managed to bring home a loaf of bread or, if lucky, a piece of meat.

My favorite targets were the wooden slats that supported the mattresses in the bunk beds. I discovered that one could remove quite a few of these slats and still leave enough for the support of the mattress. However, on occasion, I would go too far and remove too many of these slats causing the soldier sleeping on the upper bunk to fall through the hole and land on his buddy below, mattress and all. The cursing that ensued was loud enough to be heard for blocks and gave us all a good laugh at the expense of the "master race".

During my clandestine activities I had made a significant discovery. The Germans had taken over a large building that before the invasion was an Italian School. In the exercise yard, that was adjacent to our property, they had built stables for their Clydesdale- type horses.

I had found out that the horses were fed corn meal. So I had decided that it would be good to steal a few sacks of this cornmeal and make bread. Since I couldn't carry the sacks on my own I decided to recruit my brother Albert for this operation and I almost got us both killed. Albert was very skeptical about the operation but he went along anyway.

After dark we crawled under the barbed wire fence and on our hands and knees traversed the wide-open area of the field until we reached the stables. We spotted the sentry pacing up and down. It took him about five minutes to go from one end of his beat to the other.

We waited until his back was turned and he had reached the point furthest away from us and ran into the stable. Sacks of corn flour were neatly stacked-up on the shelves. Thank heavens for German precision and efficiency.

We tried to remove a sack but it was much too heavy. I didn't count on that. We looked around for a smaller container but there was none. Precious time was wasting and the horses started to make noise. We were afraid the sentry might come in any minute to investigate and catch us red-handed. I tucked my shirt in my pants and tightened my belt around it. I then asked Albert to pour some of the flower through my neck opening. I then did the same for him and got ready to leave.

We slid open the gate of the stable cautiously and peeked at the outside. The sentry was nowhere in sight. This made us very uneasy. We started to slowly crawl away. Five yards and then ten, twenty and thirty. We were almost at the end of the field when all hell broke loose. Bullets began to fly over our head.

We were spotted. Sirens began to wail piercing the stillness of the night and dogs began to bark. We ran the rest of the way and managed to crawl through the opening on the barbed wire.

In less than two minutes we were up the steps and into the safety of our home.

In a few minutes the Germans had discovered that nothing was missing, attributed the incident to a false alarm and cancelled the alert. We learned the next day from our German friends that one of their comrades that was on sentry duty the night before was arrested for deserting his post to get a cup of coffee and smoke a cigarette.

As the months rolled by and the shortages became more severe we became more inventive and more skillful in the tactics of survival. The German soldiers that went home on leave brought back suitcases full of contraband for sale in the black market. The main items were Saccharine, Atabrine and cigarette paper.

Germany was advanced in synthetic organic chemistry and these products were of high quality and had great trading value. Saccharin was the main sugar substitute and thus in great demand. Atabrine was a very effective anti –malaria drug much superior to Quinine.

Greece was a tobacco producing country but there was no paper available to make cigarettes since most of the paper products before the War were imported from Finland. Consequently cigarette paper, that allowed one to roll his own cigarettes, was worth its weight in gold.

The German cigarette paper comes packaged into tiny cardboard containers that looked like miniature boxes of Kleenex. Each package contained 100 sheets of cigarette paper. One edge of each piece of paper had glue so that when the cigarette was rolled it could be licked and provide a seal to make a finished cigarette.

I became heavily involved in buying these products from the soldiers and selling them to the peasants. It was a dangerous occupation because if caught dealing in the black market by the

Gestapo one could be shot and that included the German soldier who were bringing in the stuff in the first place. However, because of my youth, inexperience and a healthy dose of stupidity I had no concept of danger. For me the whole thing became a big game and I was beginning to enjoy the adventure.

One of our favorite deception schemes involved removing all the cigarette paper out of the packages, except for the top few sheets, and replacing it with newspaper strips. We had found a way to do this without damaging the package so that you could not tell by looking at it that it was tampered with.

We then sold these bogus cigarette paper packages to the peasants who did not discover the deception until they went home. The fact that this was dishonest didn't seem to bother us at the time. Survival is a very strong instinct.

CHAPTER 8

My Baptism as a Saboteur

I began to derive a vicarious pleasure from my new status as provider of things the family needed. My mother stopped asking me when I brought something home how it was acquired. I think that she preferred not to know.

One of the crucial things for our every day existence was the ability to cook. We had found an old, small portable, kerosene camping stove, but we had no fuel for it. I decided to get us some fuel.

The Germans had converted the basement of one of the neighboring homes into a fuel dump. The fuel was used to power their trucks and armored cars. The fuel was stored in 55-gallon steel drums and into smaller canisters of the type that could be strapped on the side of a vehicle. The dump was always heavily guarded.

I began to spend time in that area trying to strike up a conversation with the sentries that were on duty. Since I was just a 13-year-old kid, probably the same age as some of their own children, they did not regard me as being particularly dangerous. Also, the fact that I was someone new for them to talk to helped break up the monotony of the hours they spent on sentry duty.

Of course this was strictly forbidden and we had to be careful not to be observed. In a short time I got to know all the guards by their first names and began working on them and trying to find out what they wanted so that I could trade for a gallon of gasoline. Eventually I began trading, swapping a dozen eggs or a pair of silk stockings for a gallon of gasoline.

I brought along an empty one-gallon tin can that said "OLIVE OIL"" on the label. The guards would let me sneak in the basement where the fuel was kept. I would then quickly fill my can from an open 55-gallon drum equipped with a hand pump and run out. The whole transaction took less than 3 minutes but it seemed much longer.

This ritual took place about once a week. One day the guards told me,

"No. We cannot let you in any more. Things are really getting tight.

The Sergeant is getting suspicious and we are afraid of getting caught."

I said "You will let me fill my can or I will tell your Sergeant that you were letting me steal gasoline for a month whenever you were on sentry duty."

I now shudder when I reflect on how reckless and stupidly dangerous this was. Here I was an unarmed young boy, a mere child, blackmailing two armed German guards who could shoot me on the spot and probably get a medal for it. All they had to say is that they saw me trying to break into the fuel depot.

I guess it is true that God protects the fools and feebleminded because the guards were frightened by my threats and they said," All right, go ahead but make it quick". As I entered the fuel dump it occurred to me that this was probably the last time I was going to be able to do this and that my gasoline-trading career was about to end.

At that point an idea began to form in my mind that both frightened me and excited me at the same time:" START A FIRE AND BURN THE FUEL". I knew that the guards, if they survived, could not point the finger at me without implicating themselves for which they would surely be shot.

So it seemed to be a pretty safe bet that I could strike a blow for freedom without being caught. I entered the basement and quickly filled up my can with gasoline. I then took out of my pocket one of those crude cigarette lighters I sold to the peasants. The lighter consisted of a flint that would give a spark when you turned with your thumb the small metal wheel located adjacent to it. The spark would in turn ignite a long cylindrical wick. The wick would burn without a flame, all you had to do to light a cigarette was to touch the tip of the cigarette to the smoldering end of the wick and take a drag.

I lit the wick, pulled it out of its housing and placed the unlit end into the spout of the gasoline pump. I could see the liquid being drawn by capillary action into the wick. Eventually the combustible fuel was going to come into contact with the burning end of the wick and the whole place would go up.

I ran out as fast as I could. A few minutes after I got home there was a loud explosion and flames shot up into the air. All pandemonium broke loose. There were sirens, Germans running wildly out of the building, which was rapidly being engulfed by fire, people shouting and the sounds of police and fire vehicles arriving at the scene.

By the time the fire fighters arrived the whole building was engulfed in flames and it was too late to save it. Eventually the roof collapsed and the whole structure caved in. Fortunately or unfortunately there were no casualties just destruction of German property, which made everyone rejoice.

Both the Greek and German authorities launched an intense investigation as to the cause of the fire. Since the fire took place at night when civilians were not allowed on the streets and the fuel depot was heavily guarded around the clock they were forced to eliminate sabotage although it was the first thing they suspected.

Everyone agreed that no one could get in and out of the basement without being spotted by the guards. The two guards on duty vouched for each other and swore that they did not see anyone in the vicinity prior to the fire. Finally a statement was released to the press, that the fire was accidental most likely due to the faulty wiring of this old building. I never told anyone that I had anything to do with that fire.

After a while my brother Albert, who normally was very cautious, decided to take a chance and get his baptism of fire, so to speak, by trading with the German soldiers. Albert was the studious kind, serious and somewhat introverted for his age.

He was clearly the favorite of both my mother and father. There were many reasons for this: He was a good student and excelled in his schoolwork, which was very important for my father. He was also quiet and did not cause any problems nor did he get into many jams. Also he got very sick with typhoid fever and almost died.

This was a major factor in my mother's special attachment to him. She had already lost one child, my sister Alice, who died before I was born at the age of nine. Nursing Albert back to health after months of being bed ridden at home forged a special and lasting kinship between them.

Albert was always very neat well organized. He had all these special odd collections of tiny glass bottles and other things like that, which he kept in a locked cabinet and did not let anyone lay their hands on it. Even as a child he was conservative, logical and careful. He was a lot more mature than others of the same age and did not take many chances.

Thus it was out of character for him to take the risk of being involved in the black market. He did so at the urging of a childhood friend of his who was already heavily involved in black market activities and offered to show him the ropes.

On his first solo attempt he approached two German sailors and gave them the pitch, "Alles Kaufen Camarad". (We buy everything). As bad luck would have it the sailors were shore patrolmen and they arrested him dragged him by the arms and took him away. His friend, sick with worry and fear, followed them from a distance.

They were heading towards the docks, which was an encouraging sign, because the German Police Headquarters as well as the Gestapo Headquarters were in the opposite direction.

The fear was that his arrest for black marketeering might lead to interrogation that would reveal his Jewish identity. The persistent tailing of the sailors paid off. The friend saw Albert get into a boat and taken to a submarine that was in the harbor. He quickly ran to our home and told us what had transpired.

My mother was instantly filled with fear and worry. Albert, her favorite child, was captured and she did not know what to do to save him. We were all in a panic not knowing what to do. Eventually we started to think of a plan. Two things became immediately obvious. First, no one but a German would be allowed to board a submarine and secondly, only a high-ranking officer could bring about Albert's release.

The non-commissioned officers ran the German Army. The higher ranks were very rarely visible. Discipline was maintained by fear. In every military unit, down to the smallest platoon, there was a nazi party member whose assignment was to listen to the conversations of his comrades and inform on them when they said or did anything that might be construed as being subversive or against the nazi party. Most often the soldiers knew who that person was and avoided making any incriminatory remarks in his presence.

The punishment was usually brutal, ranging from severe beatings to being shot for treason. One of the biggest fears of every soldier at the time was a transfer to the Russian front. Every one was afraid of every one else. I had soldiers tell me how the Russians came at night and wiped out half of their platoon and admonish me not to reveal the fact that they told me to their comrades. Some of the comrades would then tell me the same thing and ask me not to relate it to the others.

A mere Corporal or Sergeant had tremendous authority. I saw them line up the soldiers, make them lift their boots, and inspect them to see if any of the hobnails were missing or if they were properly polished. If they found anything wrong they would rake that soldier over the coals. The Sergeant would slap the soldier in the face and shout,

"You are a donkey, a pig, and a poor excuse for a soldier".

The soldier would reply "Yavol, Her Unterofficier" which loosely translated means, "Certainly, Mister Sergeant" or "It is true, Mister Sergeant."

No matter what kind of insults the Sergeant would hurl his way, the soldier standing at rigid attention would never utter a word of contradiction. Most of the soldiers were paralyzed with fear from their own people.

Given those circumstances it was a nearly impossible task for us to even locate a German officer no less ask him to help us free Albert. Bribery was the only avenue. We had heard through the grapevine that a Greek of Bulgarian decent was a German collaborator and had connections in high places. We put out the word that we needed his services and that we were willing to pay him well.

A meeting was arranged and my mother pleaded with him to help us. She told him that Albert was just a child that didn't know what he was doing and was never in any kind of trouble before. Of course not a word was said about our being Jewish. They agreed on the size of the bribe, half in advance and the other half when Albert was free.

Frederic Kakis

The next day Albert came home. He was scared but he told us that he was very well treated and also very well fed by the sailors. He did not know what they were □planning to do with him but he suspected that they were going to release him anyway, they just wanted to scare him a bit first.

In a soccer field near the outskirts of the City the Germans had instituted a makeshift "Prisoners of War" camp, which housed captured British, Australian and New Zealand soldiers. Each day the prisoners, under heavy guard, were paraded through the streets. I am not sure what the purpose of this was but I suspect it was for propaganda purposes to show everyone that the Allies were beaten.

The prisoners were clad in rags, remnants of what, at one time, used to be their uniforms. Their bodies were lean from malnutrition and black from the constant exposure to sunlight. Their shoes were worn and many had their feet wrapped in rags. Despite all this they marched and sang like soldiers without betraying the least bit of suffering or exhaustion.

Looking at them one could easily get the impression that they were the captors and that the German guards were the prisoners. Their courageous and heroic demeanor is indelibly imprinted in my memory. Even though they were captured they looked and marched like soldiers. There is something after all to the British "Stiff upper lip" tradition.

The Greek civilians had learned the daily route of the prisoners and they would make little care packages with a few essentials, such as a piece of soap or a pair of woolen socks, a scarf anything they could spare that the prisoners might use.

Then they deposited these packages right in the middle of the road, a few minutes before the prisoners would appear. When the prisoners went by they would quickly bend down and grab the package before any of the guards would notice.

On one such occasion, I decided to deliver a care package. Unfortunately, for me I waited too long and one of the guards saw me and gave chase. I run as the wind with this fat German soldier hot on my heels.

He yelled several times ordering me to stop but I was not in the mood to oblige him, besides I was sure I could outrun him. Luckily he did not try to shoot me. I jumped one picket fence and then another trying to lose my tail in the maize of back yards and back alleys.

My assailant finally caught his pants on a wrought iron fence. I can still hear him cursing me wildly as he tried to hold up his torn pants. The entire street of civilian onlookers as well as some of the guards and all of the prisoners were laughing and booing. However, I wasn't about to stop. I kept running until it was clear that I was no longer pursued and then I stopped and broke into a hysterical laughter.

CHAPTER 9

The Noose Tightens

Little by little the conditions were deteriorating. The Germans tightened the noose and were choking the life out of the country. By 1942 the measures against the Jews began to accelerate and the repression continued to mount.

One of the major signals that things were about to take a turn for the worse came on the infamous date of July 11, 1942. On that day 9,000 Jewish males were gathered on Liberty Square in Salonica allegedly to register for work assignments. They were kept in the burning sun at gunpoint without food or water for eight hours during which time they were subjected to scores of indignities such as undressing and rolling on the ground naked.

The Germans turned their dogs loose on them and laughed while they were being mauled. This was the first public example of the sadistic nature of the Nazis. Several people passed out from heat and exhaustion and fell down to the ground. Every time this happened they were viciously kicked and beaten by some soldiers while the rest enjoyed the spectacle.

This debacle sent waves of fear and alarm throughout the Jewish Community. The July 11th episode signaled the onset of conscription for slave labor. Several thousand young Greek Jews were taken prisoners and sent out of town and put to work on a road gang.

Among those captured and sent was my oldest brother. The conditions he encountered there were atrocious. The men were starved, beaten and worked until they dropped. Malaria and typhus were rampant. There was very little food or medication. Many got ill and died.

The guards were primarily Greek Policemen with a German Officer in charge. There was also a smattering of heavily armed German soldiers. When my brother arrived he asked to see the officer in charge. He was dragged into the office by two guards. The German Officer had his shiny boots on top of the desk and was leaning back on his chair smoking a cigarette.

"What do you want to see me about, you dirty Jew?' he said.

My brother replied,

"I am an officer in the Greek army and according to the Geneva Convention Officers cannot be forced to do manual labor. I am therefore asking you to relieve me of any such duties."

The German turned to the Greek Policeman and asked,

"Is what he is saying true?"

They replied, "Yes, sir, it is. His papers show that he was a Captain in the Greek Army Core of Engineers."

The German then said.

"Find something else for him to do but get him out of my face. He is making me sick."

After that my brother was assigned a job in the office keeping records of the work schedules and other such things. At the first opportunity he escaped and came home.

Meanwhile the situation in the labor camp worsened. The Jewish community feared that most of the young men that were unaccustomed to such hard labor would die or be killed. They made an appeal to the German authorities to release the men and offered to raise money to hire laborers as substitutes.

The Germans demanded the exorbitant sum of 2.5 billion Drachmas. The Jewish Community rallied around the cause and raised the money. The men were then released and returned to Salonica only to be captured again and be shipped to the death camps. The whole thing was a farce, a diabolical game orchestrated by the Germans.

As the oppression increased so did the resistance. Three major resistance organizations had surfaced: E.A.M. an acronym that stood for National Liberation Front, E.L.A.S. which stood for Greek National Liberation Army and E.P.O.N. which was the youth equivalent of E.A.M.

E.A.M. was the political arm of the resistance movement and operated mainly in the occupied cities. E.L.A.S. was the fighting arm and operated as an army from bases in the Greek Mountains. The main goal of all three of these organizations was to orchestrate acts of sabotage, to inflict casualties on the Germans, and disrupt their war machine in any way possible.

The entire resistance movement was organized and directed by the Communists. However one needs to put this into perspective in order to avoid any misconceptions and inaccuracies: 1. Despite the fact that the leadership was Communist the vast majority of the members of the resistance organizations were not. 2. The Communists emerged as natural leaders because they were the only element in Greek society that had any experience in organizing and administering an underground movement. 3. A lot of good things can be accomplished for the wrong reasons.

The Communists undoubtedly had their own agenda; however, this does not mean that they could not do a first class job in fighting the Germans and help liberate the country. In fact the performance of these underground organizations was outstanding and so was their fighting record.

Finally most of the people who joined the underground movement had their own private reasons for wanting to fight the Germans.

For many, such as the Jews, the underground was the only available refuge. It was either joining the resistance movement or surrender to the Germans and be shipped out for "labor in the east", which was the German euphemism for the extermination camps.

As part of their reign of terror, the Germans emptied the prisons of all the thieves and petty criminals. They gave them special uniforms with swastikas and turned them loose on the population. This army of thugs did a lot of the dirty work for the Germans, thus freeing their soldiers for combat. No one liked those traitors, not even their German masters. They were low-level people without a conscience or morals and thus very dangerous. They would turn in their own mother for the right price.

By the end of 1942, all the Jews of Salonica were successfully segregated into three Ghettos. To insure compliance with the residence restrictions the Germans recruited young Jewish men who were given some fancy police title and identifying armbands. These recruits then shamefully patrolled the various intersections to insure that the Jews did not leave the ghetto.

Other measures included the order that all Jewish properties and personal assets be immediately reported to the authorities. All trade unions were ordered to expel their Jewish members and all Jewish shops or businesses were closed and their contents confiscated by the Germans.

In addition, Rabbi Koretz was ordered to assist in the gathering of the Jews in the outlying areas, towns, and villages. To insure compliance, the Germans conducted surprise raids and captured dozens of Jews that were kept as hostages. At the slightest sign of rebellion, they would take a couple of dozen hostages and shoot them.

As the measures against the Jews intensified, a few hundred decided to join the partisans and fight under Greek or British command. Some of the units formed at that time were almost exclusively made up of Jews. Joining the underground movement could have saved many more Jews, especially the young.

Unfortunately, they were reluctant to do so because they felt that it was their duty to accompany their aging parents in this journey to the unknown and try to give them as much aid and comfort as possible. Tragically their sacrifice was totally in vain because the Nazis separated the young from the old even before they loaded them on the trains to the death camps.

Our family became progressively more isolated from friends and relatives. Germans now occupied most of the homes around us. The Gestapo Headquarters were located on the same block as our home and we often had to walk past that entrance. We were very much afraid that someone would recognize us and betray us to the Germans.

By removing the Jewish population, the Germans cut out one of the City's most vital organs. Everyone, even those that were anti-Semitic felt the great vacuum created by the closing of so many vital businesses, shops and services. The place was like a ghost town.

The Jewish presence in this ancient city played a dominant role for centuries and affected every walk of life. Jews made up an important part of Salonica's "intelligentsia" but also an important part of the manual labor. For example, most of the stevedores that worked on the docks were Jewish. One would often see them walking on a narrow wooden plank with 100 kilo sacks on their back loading or unloading cargo from ships or barges. At the other extreme, the Jews were also well represented among the scholars, scientists, physicians, and merchants. After they were all rounded-up their absence was widely felt.

As the oppression intensified so did the resistance. We were under orders to disrupt the German operations in any way possible. The acts of sabotage began to multiply.

In reprisal, the Germans would randomly capture civilians and hold them as hostages. After every act of sabotage, they would take any number of these hostages and shoot them in an attempt to put an end to the resistance.

It didn't work. The killing of innocent men and women only served to intensify the hatred of the Greek people for the oppressors and forged their will to resist anyway they could. Those of us who were too young to carry weapons found other ways to resist and constantly harass the Germans.

In the cities we would set fires, slice tires, disabling their vehicles, help allied soldiers, cut telephone wires and disrupt the German communications, distribute anti- nazi pamphlets and news bulletins and steal anything we could lay our hands on from their soldiers.

As if it wasn't enough to be a wanted Jew with false papers and on the run, I also became involved in these resistance activities. My knowledge of German coupled with my youth made me valuable. I was able to penetrate some rather restricted areas without arousing any suspicion, collect valuable information, and then pass it on to the resistance leadership.

One of our missions entailed the writing of anti-nazi slogans on the walls. The group consisted of a dozen or so teen-age boys carrying musical instruments such as guitars and mandolins. We walked casually in columns of four about six feet apart. In the middle of this column were two youths charged with doing the painting. One of them had a jacket thrown over his arm concealing a can of paint and the other had a paintbrush hidden in his sleeve.

Whenever there was a suitable clean wall or surface, the group would stop. Those that carried the instruments would surround the "painters" to conceal their activity, and start singing and playing the instruments. As soon as the painting was completed and on the appropriate signal, the whole group would move quickly to a new location and the process would be repeated.

A particular tune was selected as the danger warning. The most forward foursome of the group would begin to sing this tune indicating the approach of German soldiers or patrols. If that occurred, our instructions were to immediately get rid of the paint and brush and move quickly away from that location.

What made such an operation particularly dangerous is the fact that it had to be done at night. One could not very well paint the walls in broad daylight and hope to remain unnoticed. Furthermore, it had to be done at a time when there were very few people on the streets. This meant being out after curfew, which was extremely dangerous.

As luck would have it the night of our mission, when we had nearly finished and we were ready to disband and go home, our forward lookouts heard the engine noise of an approaching vehicle and gave the warning signal. The paint and brush were discarded into the street sewer and the group started to move away.

Upon turning the corner, we run smack into the spotlight of the approaching patrol car and froze in our tracks. We started to say our prayers fully expecting that we will soon be machine-gunned down. Then we heard the shouts "Alto, Alto" and we knew that it was not a German patrol.

As the armored car approached us, we realized that it was an Italian patrol of the "Carabignieri", the Italian Military Police.

We heard one of them say to the sergeant in charge, "Dio santissimo, sono bambini" (Dear God, they are children.)

With their submachine guns pointed at us the sergeant asked,

"What are you doing out so late at night? Don't you know that there is a curfew on?"

"We went to serenade our girls",

one of us replied, showing him the musical instruments.

"Ah l'amore."

Said the sergeant and they all burst into laughter.

"You present a big problem for me" said the sergeant. "If I let you go you may run into a German Patrol and they will kill you for sure. I guess we will have to escort you home but I don't ever want to see you in the streets after curfew again."

Lady luck had smiled on us again and since that night, I have high regard for Italians who even at times of war behaved as civilized and compassionate human beings in sharp contrast with their murderous German counterparts.

Public transportation in Salonica consisted of buses and trolley cars. The trolley car lines were designed and installed by a French company in the early 1900's. Besides being functional, they added a note of charm to the city with their picturesque antique design. The cars were ornate, made out of highly polished wood, red and green metal plaques and gold lettering.

They were powered by electricity obtained from overhead wires. Conductors in their navy blue uniforms collected the fares and gave the signals to stop or go. The operator was in a glass enclosure and drove the trolley, occasionally ringing a

Frederic Kakis

giant bell with a foot pedal to warn pedestrians who were attempting to cross the street.

One day I was riding on the trolley car that ran in the middle of Queen Olga's Boulevard, parallel to the seafront. This line connected the downtown part of Salonica to the trolley depot at the other end of the city and one of its many stops was near my house.

It was usually very difficult to find a seat especially during certain rush hours such as the early morning, at noon, or in the late afternoon when most people were trying to get to work or return home. During those hours people were packed-in like sardines and many rode hanging outside the cars with their feet on the trolleys steps and their hands firmly clenched around the vertical bars located on each side of the car entrance to assist people that were going in and out of the trolley.

Others, more desperate for a ride, rode on the rear bumpers of the last car holding on for dear life. The Germans had issued an order that anyone seated in a public transportation vehicle had to get up and give up his seat to any German that entered the car.

That day I was too absorbed reading a copy of the latest cheap mystery magazine to notice that two German soldiers had entered the car. When I failed to get up and give them my seat, they became enraged. Before I knew what was happening they grabbed me by the arms, lifted me off my chair and tossed me out of the moving car onto the pavement.

My body hit the cobblestones hard, I rolled forward a few times and then came to a stop. I felt an excruciating pain and then passed out. When I came to, I was still laying down on the ground. As I opened my eyes, I saw a circle of heads leaning towards me. One of them wore a Greek Police uniform and he was shouting,

"Move back. Give him some air."

78

I asked him,

"What happened?"

He said "Don't try to talk and don't move. Help is on the way. You fell out of a moving trolley car."

I felt intense pain in every part of my body but especially in my right leg. It felt like my leg was broken. I was transported to a Hospital where they x-rayed my leg confirming that it had a fracture and I was then fitted with a cast.

I recovered quickly from my injuries, and with the typical resiliency of the young, I was up and about in no time. But my emotional scars and psychological wounds deepened. I found my hatred for the Germans intensify, a feeling that still persists today over fifty years later.

At the same time, whatever little faith I had in the Divine Benevolence evaporated. In my young mind I could not reconcile the concept of the omnipresent and just God that we were taught to believe in, and the unbelievable acts of cruelty, torture and murder that took place all around me.

I did not understand, and still don't, how a just God would allow entire families of good pious people to be herded like cattle into freight cars and be shipped into unknown destinations. How a bunch of thugs, thieves, and murderers would be allowed to rob, beat, and degrade innocent people, displace them from their homes, confiscate their businesses, and separate them from their friends and neighbors.

These feelings of hatred overwhelmed me even before I knew that the ultimate fate of all my relatives was extermination. The idea of taking young children, gassing them to death and burning their bodies in an oven fills me with intense revulsion and rage, especially since, for the most part, those responsible for those heinous crimes went unpunished.

Frederic Kakis

It was a similar kind of rage that dominated my being during the occupation. Resistance was the only thing that made sense, and allowed me, and thousands of others that were made to suffer by the German presence to find some comfort in the idea that we were doing something, however small, to get even with the captors for all the cruelty and injustice that was inflicted on the entire country in general, and the Jewish population in particular.

The family decision not to follow the German commands and to join the resistance allowed me to walk proudly and hold my head high by knowing that I, and all the members of my immediate family, were able to strike some blows for freedom instead of going like lambs to the slaughter.

CHAPTER 10

Deeper into Hiding

Gradually it became obvious that our staying in our home surrounded by Germans, after all our relatives were rounded up, presented an unacceptable risk. There was always the chance that someone would recognize us, and either unwittingly or on purpose, betray us. We had already been confronted with situations that can be described as "close calls".

We would occasionally run into well meaning, but not very astute friends or acquaintances, in public places, where the risk of being overheard was very real. In a voice that was loud enough to be overheard they would express their astonishment that we were still there circulating freely when all the other Jews were captured. We usually diffused the issue by saying,

"I beg your pardon but you must have me confused with someone else."

Or "This is not my name and I don't know what you are talking about."

Fortunately, the person we were talking to would quickly catch on and say, "I'm sorry, I thought you were someone I once knew but obviously I was mistaken".

Because of all these factors, once again, we started to prepare to leave our home and seek a hiding place in a more remote area. We began to scout the small communities near Salonica for an appropriate hiding place. Finally, we settled on a suburb called "Karabournaki", located approximately 1.5 hours away from our home.

We rented a tiny home in a low-income neighborhood populated by fisherman and blue-collar workers. This was a strictly Gentile area of the city where the residents were poor hardworking people trying their best to survive and provide some sort of sustenance to their families. Because of these characteristics and the remote location relative to the city, it was not worthy of much attention by the Army of occupation.

One rarely saw German uniforms in Karabournaki. The Greek local Police maintained law and order and only half–heartedly enforced the German directives. We felt that living there, away from our old stomping grounds, would be a lot safer and the chances of being recognized by anyone a lot smaller. All we had to do now was to figure out the logistics of making the move.

It had to be done in a way that it would not attract any attention. For obvious reasons we could not bring a truck in broad daylight and load all our belongings. This would have aroused suspicions and trigger unwelcome inquiries. Consequently, we had to move bit-by-bit and as unobtrusively as possible.

This meant that we could only take things that would fit in small bags, i.e. mostly clothes and small personal effects. All of our furniture, beds etc. had to be left behind. Thus for the second time in two years we were being uprooted and had to leave, like thieves in the night, leaving behind an entire household full of personal effects.

We purchased a modicum of cheap, used furniture, just the bare essentials, and settled into our new home. Shortly after that, it became obvious that we needed a lot of things that we had left behind in our old home. The idea, of having to go out and buy again all that stuff that we were forced to abandon was very distasteful to all of us, especially to my brother Zack.

He eventually managed to persuade my mother to let us go back to the old house and remove some more of our personal effects. When we asked Zack how he was planning to transport them his answer was," by cart".

"But we don't have a cart we replied." To which he said,

"We will steal one from the Germans."

It seemed like a perfectly logical suggestion at the time. Now it seems insane.

Stealing a cart from the Germans was easier said than done. The plan was fraught with danger. Certainly getting a few pieces of furniture from our old home was not worth dying for. But, we were young, living in crazy times, and had stared death in the face several times before.

Under those circumstances, this move was no more insanely risky that some of the other things we were doing. My brother Albert and I were quick to endorse Zack's plan and started to plot the stealing of the cart.

We first had to identify a location where the Germans stored such equipment. After making a few inquiries, we discovered that all such places were heavily guarded and that our chances of removing a cart without being caught were nil.

We then changed our tactics and began to look into the possibilities of stealing one while it was in use. Not too far from our hiding place there was a make-shift produce market, under a big tent that housed an array of open stalls where the peasants occasionally would bring and try to sell or trade a few meager farm products.

On one of these occasions, we spotted a German one-horse wagon tied up on a post outside the tent. The German soldier, probably a cook, unhitched the horse, hung a feeding bag in its mouth, and went inside to get supplies. We quickly grabbed the two-wheel cart and ran like hell through the streets and back alleys.

When we got to our new home, we started to laugh imagining the face of the German when he came out loaded with supplies and saw that the cart was missing. He most likely would be on his way to the Russian front shortly after he reported the incident to his superiors.

The next phase involved the round trip to our old house. No matter how many times we considered the scenario the conclusion was always the same:

Too Dangerous! We considered every possibility but there was no way to avoid going to our house without using the main drag i.e. Queen Olga's Boulevard that also passed in front of the Gestapo Headquarters. After weighing all the pros and cons, we decided that the boldest plan was probably the least dangerous.

It consisted of the three of us pulling the cart in the middle of Queen Olga's Boulevard, in broad daylight. Our reasoning was that no German would suspect that three Jewish fugitives would have the guts to pull a stunt like that and neither would anyone else that saw us come and go.

So, we hitched ourselves to the wagon that was still painted gray, had the German insignia, and pulled it in broad daylight though the streets of Salonica.

The whole thing was insane and maybe that is why it worked. Amazingly, no one stopped us to inquire how we came to possess a German cart. Such an inquiry was sure to lead to the discovery that all our papers were fake and result in our capture. When we passed in front of the Gestapo Headquarters several soldiers, who were on the balcony, saw us and were laughing boisterously that we were hitched to the wagon. One of them yelled out

"Which one of you is the horse?" and the rest busted out into laughter. It never occurred to them to ask, "How and where did you get a cart that belongs to the German army?" If they did, we would be dead. I remember that the soldiers guarding the entrance to the Gestapo Headquarters had their vicious dogs on a leash. Zack saw them too and jokingly he told us in Greek,

"Let's go over to the other side of the street just in case they have trained their dogs to smell Jews".

By the grace of God, the mission was accomplished safely. We loaded the cart and made it back to Karabournaki without incident. In retrospect, even as I relate this adventure, I am struck with the realization of how foolhardy that whole affair was. I certainly would not have the courage to go through something like that today.

In the ensuing days life returned to some semblance of normalcy. Using fake names and false papers we registered with the local Police stating that we were refugee's from the North that had to flee from the Bulgarians, which was actually true.

Just the mere mention of the word "Bulgarians" was enough to trigger the anger of any red blooded Greek policeman and ensure a sympathetic ear. Consequently, the local community immediately accepted a widow with four children fleeing from the Bulgarian brutalities.

All of our neighbors treated us with sympathy and kindness. My mother's new name was Elpida, the Greek word for hope. My sister was renamed Maria. Albert became Alex and Zack was baptized Yannis the Greek equivalent of John.

I had to get used to answer to the name "Ericos" i.e. Eric. We had to be very careful to observe all the religious" Saint Days" that corresponded to our newly acquired names since the Greek Orthodox population celebrates name days rather than birthdays. For example, during the religious holiday that honors St. John every one named John had a celebration, invited guests and received presents. Not to observe these traditions would certainly arouse suspicions.

Survival was becoming more and more difficult. Everything was rationed. Our coupons entitled us to a loaf of corn bread, which was usually moldy and bitter and often contained indigestible parts of cellulose from the husks. Since that day of the occupation, I developed a lifelong dislike for corn bread.

With the help of our new friends, we also planted some tomatoes and other vegetables in our back yard and acquired a couple of egg laying chickens. Our fishermen neighbors, from time to time, would generously give us some fish.

This was a welcome change in our diet, which consisted primarily of vegetables and beans. I am always struck by the fact that the poorer the people, the more generous they are.

It was heart warming to see their willingness to share whatever little they had with their friends and neighbors.

In conformance with our new identities, we started to go back to school. I refrained from any resistance activities or involvement or any black market trading. Every Sunday we all went to Church with our neighbors and strictly observed all the religious holidays. Our house was regularly visited and blessed by the parish priest.

No one even remotely suspected that we were Jews and it looked as if our hiding place would serve its purpose well until one day in the late afternoon when we were all seated around the dinner table, a young boy from the neighborhood ran over to our house and knocked furiously at our door.

When we opened he said excitedly

"Kiria Elpida, Kiria Elpida"(my mother's fake Christian name) there is a German soldier in the neighborhood asking for you. We all felt a shiver of fear that we have been discovered and we were shortly going to be arrested.

A few minutes later a German soldier wearing a huge leather pistol holster on his belt started to walk down the narrow path that lead to our front door. It was too late to escape. When we came face-to-face, we recognized who it was. It was our old violin player friend Ernest Girl.

"Don't be afraid," he said, "I am not here to harm you."

We then asked him to come in. He handed my mother a bag containing a loaf of German bread and sausages and a piece of smoked pork.

"I brought you some food" he said, "I'm sure you can use it".

Then we all sat down to partake of the meal. Ernest told us that he suspected all along that we were Jews but that we had nothing to fear from him because he was Austrian and staunchly anti nazi.

"How did you find us?" my mother asked.

"It wasn't easy", he replied but he would not elaborate any further and we were afraid to press the issue.

Ernest's visits continued for a short while. Each time he came, he brought along a care package of much welcomed food supplies. His visits served to alleviate even the slightest suspicion in any ones mind in our new neighborhood that we may be anything other than what we purported to be. Certainly, no Jewish family would be visited regularly by a German soldier!

Despite the appearance of normalcy, Ernest's visits were very disturbing. We became progressively more apprehensive that others might follow him and that he may lead them right to us. In addition, the fact that he was able to find us was indicative that others, less friendly, could probably do the same.

Consequently we came to realize that our hiding place was not as secure as we originally thought and that somewhere along the line we had made a mistake and left a trail that could lead to our capture. After considerable agonizing and soul searching, we decided that it was time to bail out again and move to a more remote location, this time being extra careful not to tell anyone or leave behind any clues regarding our whereabouts.

CHAPTER 11

Finding a Safer Hideout

The person primarily responsible for planning this next phase of our escape from capture was my sister Carmen. She was a beautiful girl at twenty, slender, medium height with light brown hair and brown eyes. Carmen was very bright and an outstanding student with a voracious appetite for learning. She was able to advance a whole year in High School while Zack failed one year and was a year behind. Consequently despite the difference in their ages they ended up in the same graduating class.

She excelled not only in her studies but also in the extracurricular activities of her time such as dancing the traditional Greek folk dances. She received a number of recognitions and awards from the school for these attributes. She also had a fine operatic voice, which she inherited from Mother, and played the piano with considerable skill and dexterity.

This made her very popular in their circle of friends and classmates. Despite her superior intellect and school performance she was discouraged from pursuing further studies. She resented my parent's unwillingness to allow her to enroll at the University, a resentment that persisted throughout her life.

In all fairness to my parents this misguided notion that advanced studies were only appropriate for males was the prevailing notion of their time. Most of society held the view that a high school education was enough for young girls who should instead concentrate on learning domestic skills, playing a musical instrument, learning a foreign language and finding a husband, preferably rich. Thus both my sister and our parents were victims of the backward attitudes that prevailed.

Carmen argued that our survival required that we abandon the big cities and seek refuge in a remote area. She had a childhood friend that she remained close to all through elementary and high school who now lived on an Island in the Mediterranean. Her friend had repeatedly invited her to come for a visit. She was one of many non-Jewish friends that we trusted implicitly and knew that they were never going to betray us.

This was a major factor in our family's successful attempt to escape capture. Our friends unhesitatingly put their own lives on the line and the lives of their families to help us. For that we are extremely and eternally grateful. I have been blessed throughout my lifetime with good friends and I have learned to treasure and nurture those friendships very early, during those fateful years of World War II in German occupied Greece.

The family decision was to have my sister contact her friend, explain the precarious situation we were in and asked her if in her judgment it was safe for us to seek asylum on the island. She quickly responded that there were no Germans on the island and that the only presence of occupation consisted of a small contingent of Italians who acted more like tourists than the army of occupation.

She assured us that with a proper cover story we would be absolutely safe. Her family offered to assist us to get settled, if we decided to move there, naturally without telling anyone that we were Jews. All of the feedback about fleeing to the island we received from my sister's friend was positive.

It looked as if we could hide there in relative safety for the rest of the war. The remaining problem was how to get there. What would normally be a very simple matter, in the time of the occupation, became an extremely complex strategic maneuver.

First, we had to obtain travel permits from both the German and the Italian authorities. To do that required that all of us appear in person and that our fake ID cards and other required documents would have to stand up to the scrutiny of the officials that would issue the travel permits. We also had to give a plausible reason for the trip that would be deemed compelling enough to issue the permit. Because of the Jewish situation, many families were trying to flee the German jurisdiction and the authorities were extremely suspicious and alerted.

If all of the above were accomplished, we then had to find a vessel that was willing to take us to the island. We also had to find someone that would agree to act as our sponsor that would accept us at the other end and introduce us to the locals as his relatives, in a manner that would not generate suspicion that we were Jews seeking a hiding place.

Finally, we had to orchestrate the departure in such a way as not to arouse suspicion among our neighbors in Karabournaki. We had to avoid giving the impression that this was a permanent move. Anything else would generate a lot of unwanted questions and potentially dangerous inquiries. No one had to know why we left or where we were going. The fact that a German soldier was able to trace our path during our previous escape made us extra cautious.

All of the above had inherent major risks. Our fake papers could pass during a casual inspection but if an in depth search was to be performed it would be discovered that the address shown was fictitious. Not knowing how thorough the authorities were convinced us that appearing before the Germans to request a travel permit presented an unacceptable risk. We were afraid that it might result in delivering our entire family to their hands. Consequently, we had decided to seek the assistance of our German collaborator "friend" whom we had successfully bribed into helping us before.

The story we told him was that mother had to have a delicate operation, which may require a lengthy hospitalization and that, she needed a place to leave us until she was well enough to care for us. We also told him that the specialist that mother needed lived in Athens and that mother had a cousin there that had agreed to take us in and care for us until mother was well again.

Using his connections with the Germans, this individual, after collecting a substantial sum from my mother, was able to secure the German travel permits. When they asked him why we did not appear in person he told them that all the children were ill with malaria and may be contagious.

Getting the German permit was only half of the problem, albeit the most difficult part. We also needed to get a permit from the Italians. The Italian consulate was located on Queen Olga Boulevard, only a couple of blocks from our old residence. Since there was no other way to obtain the permit except going there in person we decided to chance it. Our biggest fear was that being in the middle of our old neighborhood some one might recognize us and accidentally or on purpose give us away.

Thus one morning we didn't go to school, we got dressed in our Sunday clothes, took the Bus to the Trolley Depot, and then rode the trolley all the way to our old neighborhood. We rode silently all the way constantly being on the alert for any surprise encounters. Fortunately, they were none.

When we arrived at the Consulate we found an enormous crowd of people who were waiting hoping to secure travel permits for their families. We stood on line for several agonizing hours always afraid that some one might spot us and blow our cover.

When our turn finally came, we were escorted into an office that had no chairs for any of us to sit down. A very young Italian officer was sitting behind an enormous desk. Behind him hung a picture of Mussolini flanked on each side with the Italian flag. He pretended to be examining some documents on his desk and for several minutes ignored my mother who was standing in front of his desk.

He finally, without looking directly at her and speaking in broken Greek said,

"Let me have your papers." While looking at the papers and still not facing her directly, he asked,

"What is the purpose of your trip?" My mother replied,

"I am ill and may require surgery. This Doctor in Athens was highly recommended to me by friends that know him as the best specialist in Greece for this type of ailment. I would like him to examine me. If it turns out that I will require surgery and hospitalization I have a cousin in Athens that can take care of my children while I am in the Hospital."

The Italian suddenly threw the papers at my mother and shouted angrily in Greek,

"You are a damned liar. All you Greeks are liars and thieves. You probably took me for some kind of fool thinking I would swallow such an idiotic story. I don't believe a word of it. Your papers are probably fake and you, most likely, are damned Jews trying to escape German capture."

Most people at this point would have caved in but not Mom. She banged her fist on his desk and in a torrent of fluent Italian shouted back,

"How dare you speak to me like this, you insolent pup. Look at me when I am speaking to you and take off your hat when you are addressing a lady. Apparently, your mother did not teach you any manners. You are young enough to be my son and I am just the person to do it, even if I have to go to your superiors."

The young officer was completely taken off guard, first because of her fluent Italian which he did not expect and secondly because of the fearless and almost defiant and menacing way in which mother stood up to him. The vast majority of people that stood before him were subservient and meek. He stood up and ordered the sentry to bring a chair. With a reddened face he stammered, "I apologize, dear lady. Please sit down and calm yourself."

After my mother was seated he asked,

"Where did you learn to speak Italian so well?" She replied,

"My grandmother, who is at this moment is turning in her grave, was Italian. Besides, before this wretched war I was a Prima Dona on the Opera stage. "

She knew how to push just the right buttons. This brought about a complete metamorphosis. The officer, sweet and polite as he could be, processed all her paper work and issued her a permit to travel. Once more mother's sheer guts and presence of mind coupled with her facility with languages saved our necks.

Thus, the first and most crucial step in planning our departure from Karabournaki i.e. the securing of the German and Italian travel permits "was accomplished. My sister's friend on the island arranged with a man who lived on the island with his mother to help us with the trip. He was to pose as my mother's nephew and tell everyone that he was bringing his widowed aunt and her children, who were refugees from the Bulgarian occupied territory, to live with him on the island for the duration of the war.

This way the locals were forewarned and they would not be surprised by our arrival and ask too many questions. Remarkably, this man, whose name was Apostolis, knew the true story and was still willing to risk his life to help us without any expectation of reward. Apostolis was an entrepreneur who made a living by bartering and trading, a fact that earn him the nickname "The Black Marketer".

Through his contacts with the local fishermen Apostolis arranged for us to be picked up in a small port in Halkidiki, named "Portes" which in Greek means "Doors". As soon as we were notified of the date of departure, we began to prepare for leaving our home in Karabournaki. It was obvious that if we all left at the same time and with an excessive amount of luggage we would arouse suspicions and unwelcomed inquiries.

We decided that it would be safer if we would split up. My mother and I would travel by bus with only a small, carry - on bag. My sister would travel by herself in another vehicle and my two brothers, Zack and Albert, would take the heavy luggage and a couple of trunks of personal effects and try to reach Portes by boat. The rendezvous point was the fishing boat anchored in the harbor.

The whole idea behind this plan was to avoid a circumstance where the entire family was captured and killed. By splitting up, we hoped that some of us would make it safely. Besides, it would be less suspicious than the whole family traveling at the same time.

For the third time in less than two years, we were forced to flee, like thieves in the night, carrying only the bare necessities and leaving behind an entire household of furnishings and personal effects.

On the specified date my mother and I woke up very early in the morning and before any of the neighbors were up left our house and headed towards the bus stop. My sister left shortly afterwards without being noticed and boarded the morning bus, but to a different destination. The plan was that she would get off at this other village in Halkidiki and then take another bus to complete the final leg of the trip.

The hardest thing to arrange was the boat trip. The removal of the trunks that contained what was left of our most precious belongings had to be done unobtrusively. If anyone in the neighborhood would witness such an event, it would amount to a dead giveaway that we were actually abandoning our home and had no intentions of ever returning.

That would have been very difficult to explain without telling the whole story. In those days such revelations would be extremely dangerous since it was impossible to know whom you could trust. Yet, that part of the plan could not be accomplished without some outside help.

My brother Zack had made some new friends, two brothers named Mihalis and Yannis. They were the sons of a fisherman who was captured by the Germans in a random raid and held as a hostage along with many other innocent civilians. He was killed by the Germans in retaliation to some act of sabotage by the underground as part of their regular ritual of executing ten Greek hostages for every German soldier that was killed by the resistance forces.

Because of their tragic loss, the two brothers had an intense hatred for the Germans and for this reason Zack decided to trust them and seek their help. Zack took a chance and told them about our situation. They immediately offered to help with the escape. They told Zack they did not want to know our final destination, this way if they were captured by the Germans and were tortured they could not betray us.

They had inherited a fishing boat from their father and they were both expert seaman and knew the territory well, having sailed in these waters since they were children. With the help of the two brothers, Zack and Albert moved the trunks and the big valises in the middle of the night and loaded them on the boat.

Fortunately, Karaburnaki did not have a heavy military presence and there were very few patrols enforcing the curfew.

As soon as everything was aboard Michalis and Yannis set sail for Halkidiki.

The night was pitch black with no stars and no moonlight...perfect conditions for a getaway. Dark clouds hung over the horizon making the boat virtually invisible unless you were right on top of it. The chance of being sighted and captured by a German patrol boat were, therefore, very slim. This served to relieve my brothers' anxiety and fear. However, these were also the signs of an impending storm as they were soon to discover.

The winds began to pick up, the waves were getting bigger, and light rainfall was coming down. In a very short time the winds greatly intensified, which necessitated taking down the sails and the mast for fear that the boat would capsize. Heavy waves began to pound the boat and torrential rain broke out.

Everyone on the boat was holding on for dear life as the huge waves tossed it up and down. Albert got violently seasick and was throwing up while at the same time trying to bail out water from the boat with a tin can. Everyone was soon doing the same thing to prevent the boat from sinking.

The two brothers, who had been in situations like this before, were giving the commands trying desperately to maintain control of the boat. All of the supplies that they brought aboard were either soaked or washed overboard. Eventually the brunt of the storm passed and the seas became calmer.

Michalis and Yannis decided to try and reach land to replenish the supplies before attempting to sail to the final destination. It is truly remarkable how the Greek sailors could find their way around without a compass and without any radio or navigational equipment. Guided only by years of experience, their knowledge of the direction of the currents and by the stars, they were able to steer a course that brought them exactly to their chosen destination. This task was even more difficult in the aftermath of a heavy storm. Nevertheless, they were able to bring the boat to a tiny port in Halkidiki called "Mihaniona".

As soon as they reached the dock, they were surprised to see a Bulgarian armed sentry who boarded the boat and at gunpoint demanded to see the papers and the travel permit. Zack gambled on the fact that he was probably illiterate and handed him a paper issued by the Germans that was a fishing permit for the boat.

The sentry picked it up and looked at it upside down and as Zack had guessed, he could not read it. It was enough that it had the Stamp of the German authorities, an eagle standing on a circle with a swastika. That seemed to satisfy him. The brothers offered him a bottle of Ouzo and told him that they needed to disembark and get some supplies. He said "O.K. you can get your supplies but you are not allowed to sail at night and you must remain tied up at the dock until morning."

In the meantime, he was eying intently the trunks and suitcases that were on the boat. Michalis and Yannis thanked him and assured him that they had no intentions to sail into the night with that horrible weather. As soon as the sentry got off the boat, they told Zack and Albert that they did not trust the Bulgarian, and they were very much afraid that if they left the boat tied up and went to sleep that the Bulgarian would come back, kill everyone and steal the trunks.

Consequently, as soon as they loaded the new supplies they released the rope and let the boat drift towards the open sea. When they were a few feet away, they used the oars and started to row frantically to get as far away as quickly as possible. The noise alerted the sentry who opened fire with his automatic rifle. "Everyone down" they shouted as they raised the sail. The boat quickly picked up speed, under the hail of bullets, and they were soon out of range. The next stop was Portes, the rendezvous point for our departure.

CHAPTER 12

A Few More Hurdles

In the meantime my mother and I independently boarded the bus to Halkidiki not knowing any of the above complications that Zack and Albert had run into. It was an aging bus, with a converted engine that burned wood, which allowed it to move at the blinding speed of about five miles per hour. At this rate, it would take us several hours to reach our destination.

The bus was crowded with people and livestock, mostly peasants traveling to and from their villages. The air was hot and stale. An overpowering mixture of malodors gave the bus a disgusting stench.

Opening the windows didn't help much.

Because of the slow speed at which we were moving, the smoke from the burning wood and the fumes from the exhaust were sucked in, making our environment even more uncomfortable. My mother wore a cheap black dress, a black scarf over her hair and no jewelry. My clothes were also worn and shabby.

We chose our clothes carefully to blend in with the rest of the passengers. We certainly did not want to attract any attention to ourselves. The road was unpaved and full of potholes, which made for a very bumpy ride. We braced ourselves for a very long and uncomfortable trip and then it happened.

We hit a large pothole. There was a loud, explosion- type noise and the truck skidded and turned on its side. All pandemonium broke loose as people were trying to climb out the windows of the overturned bus. My mother and I were seated next to a window and thus were able to get out quickly and easily.

We found out that the bus had blown a tire and broke an axle and ended up lying on its side across the road blocking both lanes of traffic. There were some minor injuries but most of the passengers were okay. My mother and I were unharmed but extremely distressed at this turn of events.

We knew there was no other bus and we also knew that by the time this one was repaired and under way, we would miss the boat to the island. The situation appeared to be hopeless.

A few minutes later, a German military convoy consisting of an open vehicle in the front carrying a German officer and five trucks with green canvas tops arrived at the scene. The officer shouted an order, "Push this piece of junk off the road, and clear the path for the vehicles". Immediately a bunch of soldiers jumped out of the trucks and began to push the bus out of the way.

Then my mother had her brilliant idea to ask the German Officer for a ride. I told her, "This is crazy, it's too dangerous, and it will never work".

She replied, "Because it is crazy that's why I think it will work". She approached the first vehicle and spoke to the German officer in fluent German.

"Sir, I was traveling with my son on this bus and I must reach Portes today or I'll miss my boat. Would you be kind enough to give us a ride in one of your vehicles?"

He looked at her with a look of admiration for her mastery of his language and said "Sorry but I cannot help you. It is against regulations to allow civilians to ride on military vehicles."

"But surely an important officer such as yourself must have the authority to make an exception." she persisted.

Surprisingly he said, "OK get into the last truck and stay out of sight. Don't open the tarp and don't try to get off until I tell you to, and if you are wondering why I am doing this it is because you look a lot like my wife."

Strangely, he did not ask to see our papers nor our travel permit! We did not need a second invitation. We quickly ran and climbed in the last truck, closing the canvas gate. In a few minutes, we were moving. Since we were riding in a gasoline-powered truck we arrived in Portes nine hours early.

Finally, the truck stopped, after what seemed to be a very long time, the canvas covering the rear of the truck was opened, and we were told to get off. We left and started to walk slowly towards the dock.

The boat to the island wasn't there yet. We decided to sit and wait in a small café opposite the dock for the arrival of the boat and the rest of our family. The gravity of the day's events suddenly hit us. For quite a while, we sat silently considering all that had transpired.

Particularly the audacity of a Jewish family trying to escape capture, asking a German officer for a ride filled us with a strange mixture of emotions. Fear that we could have been captured, self-admiration for having the guts to attempt it, relief that we got away with it, and humor in thinking the irony of the whole thing.

Finally, we looked at each other and burst into loud and uncontrollable laughter releasing all the tensions of the day in one shot. Mother said, "When we tell the rest how we got here they will never believe us".

The first person to arrive was my sister. Except for the discomfort of having to ride so many hours on those crummy buses she made it all right. She reported that her papers held up during the inspections at several checkpoints. We filled her in on our adventure and we all had a good laugh. Since we were riding in a German Military vehicle, we were waved on at each of the checkpoints and never had to show our papers.

Next, the fishing boat that was to take us to our final destination arrived at the dock. It was a lovely hand - crafted schooner named "CHRYSOULA", which roughly translated means "The Golden Girl". It was owned and operated by the Ververis brothers. The oldest brother George was the captain.

He was a stocky man of average height with short gray hair, penetrating black eyes, and a dark oily complexion. His face was deeply creased and his skin had a leathery appearance from continuous exposure to the sun and the elements. He wore a navy blue pea coat and the traditional black cap of the Greek fisherman.

Captain George was a man of few words, rather sullen and introverted. His brother Petros was taller, had a fairer complexion, blue eyes, blonde curly hair and an easy smile. His hands and face also bore the marks of having spent most of his life at sea. Petros was a lot more talkative and friendlier than his brother George.

The rest of CHRYSOULA'S crew consisted of two sailors. One of them also doubled as the "engineer" and the other was just a deck hand.

This was a large fishing vessel by Greek standards equipped with a powerful diesel engine, which was used minimally because of the severe fuel shortage. The rest of the time the boat relied on wind power for its motion.

To operate a fishing trawler you needed permission from the German Naval Authorities who usually confiscated most of the catch. However part of a catch was to the professional fishermen better than no catch at all.

Transporting passengers was not part of the deal, and I am sure that the Ververis brothers were not thrilled at the prospect of having us aboard, even though I am sure that they were well paid by Apostolis, who had told them only that we were refugees from the Bulgarians, that my mother was his Aunt and that she was coming to live with him on the Island.

Later that evening the boat with Zack and Albert finally arrived. Once again, we had all made it in one piece. We were enormously relieved and very glad to be reunited. We loaded our belongings onto the CHRYSOULA with the help of the crew and boarded the ship.

Captain George ordered us to go below and stay out of sight. He was curt and authoritative causing us some anxiety. Fortunately, his brother Petros lightened our spirits by saying, "Don't mind my brother. He is always grouchy but his bark is bigger than his bite. I f you need anything just ask me and I will be glad to help you."

Captain George announced that he was planning to get under way early in the morning. We all said good night and went below. We found a bunk and laid down on it fully clothed. The crew slept on deck under the stars. Exhausted and overwhelmed by the day's events and rocked by the waves we soon fell fast asleep.

We were awakened in the early hours of the morning by noises on deck. Captain George was preparing to shove off. All of a sudden, we heard heavy footsteps and voices that sounded like German. It was enough to put us in a state of panic even though our papers and travel permits appeared to be in order.

We had visions of being captured at the last minute after we had come so far. Fortunately, it was just a routine check by the shore patrol checking the boat's papers in insure that it was properly registered with the local German Naval authorities and that the captain had secured the permit to sail and leave the harbor.

George produced all the documents and handed them to the leader. He examined the documents and asked,

"Is this your entire crew?"

"Yes, Sir" captain George replied.

The German then shouted "Alles in ordnung" i.e. everything is okay.

"Go and bring us back lots of fish".

Our heart skipped a beat as the patrol left. We were glad that they did not ask if there were any passengers and did not search the boat.

Within minutes after the patrol left, we were finally under way. Our destination was the island of SKIATHOS located in the Aegean about 150 miles south of Halkidiki and about 250 miles south of Thessaloniki. SKIATHOS belongs to a group of tiny Islands known as SPORADES. The four major populated Islands in that group were SKIATHOS, SKOPELOS, ALONISOS and SKYROS. There was a second village in SKOPELOS named GLOSSA.

These Islands were primarily known for their production of olive oil. Apparently, the climatic and soil conditions were ideal for growing Olive trees. SKYROS, which was the southernmost and largest of these Islands, was also known for the manufacture of a very unique style of home furniture. The Islands also had an ample supply of fruit trees and an abundance of fish and seafood.

As soon as we were far enough from land and into the open sea, Petros came below and told us that it was okay to come up on deck. It was a damp and chilly morning and we really welcomed the hot cup of coffee that Petros gave each of us, although it was made up without real coffee and without real sugar. Roasted garbanzo beans or Chicory was used as a substitute for coffee and saccharin was used as the sweetener.

Captain George was an excellent seaman and knew these waters like the palm of his hand. He had sailed in this area since he was a child on his father's boat, and he was familiar with every tiny landmark and every current. He was at the helm most of the time, only occasionally relived by his brother. Petros took charge of the sails and gave directions to the crew.

In a very short while, the sun came up warming our bodies and lifting our spirits. We were free, alive, together and on our way to a new, and hopefully, better place.

CHAPTER 13

Skiathos: A Bit of Tranquility Amidst the Horrors of War.

I will never forget the first time I saw the outline of Skiathos as our boat entered the harbor. Amphitheatrically built on the sides of two adjacent hills were rows and rows of white homes with cobalt blue doors and shutters, their red roofs shining under the rays of a brilliant, almost blinding, sun. Interspersed were the churches with their blue domes and their steeples rising above the outline of homes, their crosses pointing to the bluest sky I had ever seen.

The deep navy blue color of the sea, that is so uniquely characteristic of that part of the world, presented the eyes with a sharp color contrast to the whiteness of the scene. Along the entire shore, almost touching the deep blue waters, were dark green pine forests with their windswept branches brushing against the golden sand of the beaches The harbor, full of fishing boats of all types, sizes and colors, added an extra dimension to this vision of loveliness. The entire image resembled the canvas of a famous impressionist artist.

As the boat got closer and closer we began to get a better look of the dock. Along the horseshoe shape waterfront there were stores, cafés, and restaurants. On the right side of the boat, projecting straight into the water was a tiny island with a large, official looking, building on it. Surrounding the building was a tall stone fence.

Outside this fence there was a path partly covered by pine trees and other luscious green vegetation. The entire outside perimeter consisted of huge boulders partly immersed in the seawater. Growing wildly between those rocks there were huge cactus plants whose large flat and thorny leaves projected into space like the palms of some giant creature.

We later learned that this tiny island appendix was called the "Bourzy" and was a remnant of an ancient fort that guarded the entrance to the harbor from foreign invaders. The Bourzy was connected to the main Island by a narrow path at the entrance of which was a marble statue of the famous Modern Greek author "Papadiamadis" who was a native of Skiathos.

The building at the Bourzy had undergone several transformations through the years that included its use as the City Hall and later as a High School. At the time of our arrival it was used as the barracks and the Headquarters of the small contingent of Italians that were the official occupation troops in Skiathos.

A concrete pier projected out of the waterfront allowing the smaller boats to dock. The larger boats were anchored further away. All of these boats had little wooden skiffs equipped with oars. These skiffs were used to load and unload passengers and supplies to and from the anchored vessels.

Captain Ververis, with the skill of those that have performed the same task thousands of times, entered the harbor and maneuvered the boat into position zig zagging in between the vessels that were already there. He finally dropped the anchor and launched the skiff that would take us to the dock. We boarded the small craft and one of the crewmembers assumed a standing position at the stern and using only one oar, that he vigorously rotated and simultaneously moved back and forth, propelled the boat forward towards the dock.

I had never seen anyone move a boat with a single oar before and I watched with fascination the movement of the oar in and out of the water creating a propeller-like whirling of the sea. When we finally reached the dock an Italian soldier who asked to see our papers confronted us. Judging by his appearance we were reassured that this was going to be a piece of cake.

He was dressed in light gray army pants but he wore sandals, an unbuttoned white civilian shirt and no cap. If it weren't for the small pistol buckled on his belt one could take him for just another Greek fisherman. The control was brief and perfunctory and we were allowed to leave the dock and step foot on the soil of Skiathos.

Waiting for us was our "Cousin" Apostolis and my sister's girl friend Irene. For the sake of any curious onlookers we put on a show of embracing and kissing. Finally we loaded our belongings to the waiting donkeys and started climbing up the hill to Apostolis' house.

The road leading to the house was paved with odd shape flat stones that looked like a giant jigsaw puzzle. The roads were divided into two halves. Both the right and the left half were slopped towards the center thus forming a natural trough. This construction permitted rain water as well as water from domestic use to drain via the center of the road downhill and eventually into the sea.

All the houses along the way had a fresh whitewash. This included the front steps and the portion of the sidewalk in front of each house. As we learned later applying the whitewash to all these areas was part of the daily housekeeping chores of each housewife.

The house where Apostolis lived was typical of most of the homes on the Island: mostly one-story structures with very thick walls covered with stucco. The more affluent of the residents lived in two story homes. The walls were whitewashed inside and out with lime.

Small windows with wooden shutters kept the sunrays out. That, combined with the thickness of the walls, provided good insulation keeping the interior shady and cool during the hot summer days and warm during the winter months. A large wood-burning fireplace provided the only means of central heating.

Skiathos did not have electricity in those days and no interior plumbing. Candles and oil burning lamps provided light at night and water came from wells or hand operated pumps located outside. The kitchens were large and equipped with stoves that burned wood or wood charcoal. A large assortment of pots and pans was available along with the necessary utensils.

The pots and pans, for the most part, were made out of copper platted with tin. Also there were some iron pots and several sizes of glazed pottery casseroles.

Most of the glasses, dishes etc. were also made out of glazed ceramics by local craftsmen. The homes had high ceilings and good sturdy roofs made out of red, Spanish style, ceramic tiles.

The chairs were made out of hand carved wood with decorative woven straw seats. Most of the tablecloths, napkins, towels, bedding, and other cloth materials were made out of brightly colored yarns dyed and woven locally.

These Islands were well known for their crafts and one found an amazing assortment of attractive and decorative furnishings inside those rather plain and primitive homes. Tables of several sizes and shapes were present as well as chests, sofas and colorful ceramic flowerpots and vases. The beds had metal springs, cotton mattresses and feather pillows. However, for the most part, the bathrooms consisted of "outhouses" located in the back yard.

The Islanders made their own soap from oil and potash and used it for washing clothes and everything else that was dirty, including them. A prominent feature of each home was a large, commercial size, brick oven located in the yard. The oven had a dome of bricks and mortar and a flat surface constructed with rocks and cement. A metal door allowed access to the interior. The heating was provided from a compartment below that was designed to accommodate large pieces of firewood.

The oven was capable of baking several 15-20 pound loafs of bread at a time. The reason for this, as we discovered, was that each household baked enough bread not only for their own use but also for all the immediate neighbors. This local custom allowed each family to bake only a few times a year and still enjoy a regular supply of freshly baked bread.

Apostolis was a middle age, medium build, heavy- set man with jet-black hair and eyes. He had bushy eyebrows and a dark olive, almost black complexion. His appearance was foreboding, like a person you would not want to mess with. His ready smile softened this tough exterior and inspired confidence.

When we reached the home we were warmly greeted by "Kiria Zoë", (Mrs. Zoë), Apostolis mother who invited us to sit down and, as per the local custom, offered us "Glyko" which is a spoon full of homemade fruit preserves and a glass of cold water. This ritual was, and to a large extent still is, traditional in every home one visits in most towns or villages of Greece. It is a sign of welcome and an extension of their hospitality. Coffee or other beverages are also often used and offered to visitors but in war times they were in extremely short supply.

Apostolis was single and lived at this home with his widowed elderly mother who adored him because he was her only child. They were themselves at one time refugees having originally fled from Asia Minor.

He made a living by trading in any type of commodity he could lay his hands on, which earned him the nickname "the black marketer".

As we found out later Apostolis was at one time a member of the Communist party in Greece but after years of beatings and torture in the hands of the secret police he finally signed a declaration denouncing the party. From that moment on he was ostracized and could no longer participate in their activities.

As I have mentioned earlier in this story the Communist party in Greece had assumed a position of leadership with regards to the liberation movement. Thus Apostolis found a chance to become re-involved by joining the underground resistance organization known as EAM, which stood for "National Liberation Front". As a ranking member of this organization in Skiathos it was incumbent upon him to do anything in his power that would damage the Nazis. Which explains, in part, his willingness to help our family even though he was putting himself at risk. The underground movement welcomed and protected anyone that was fleeing from the Germans and was willing to fight for the liberation of Greece.

After the initial amenities were over a tentative plan of action was discussed for the initial period. It consisted of the following: We were to stay with Apostolis and his mother for a while until the local people had a chance to meet us and get used to our being there. No one outside Apostolis, his mother and my sister's girlfriend would know our real story and identity.

We were warned not to trust anyone and keep our mouth shut. We were to tell anyone who asked that we were refugees from the Bulgarian occupied region of Greece and had no place to go except our cousin Apostolis. Anything else would not only put us at risk but Apostolis and his mother as well.

We should try to become integrated into the local scene, go to Church regularly and try to make friends among the local residents. Later when things had normalized we would look for our own place of residence. In time each member of our family would be introduced and invited to join the appropriate local resistance unit.

That night we went to bed and for the first time, in a long time, we felt safe and slept soundly and peacefully. After a hearty breakfast of delicious brown natural wheat bread, butter, feta cheese, and honey we set out to explore the Island.

Skiathos was a hilly Island with many densely wood areas, mostly pine trees, and several dozen beautiful beaches. These beaches were, for the most part, not accessible by land since there were no roads or paths leading to them. The only way to reach most of them was by boat.

Fortunately almost every family on the Island had some kind of boat. In a very short time I was able to meet and become friends with several young boys my age and participate in their activities. I particularly enjoyed the wood chopping expeditions. We would jump on a boat and go to one of the secluded beaches for a swim in the clearest waters I have ever seen.

After spending most of the day on the beach we ventured into the forest and chopped down the dry branches of the pine trees and collected pinecones, which we then loaded on to the boat and brought home. The supply of firewood was always welcomed.

The northern part of the island was always windy. The beaches were wild, rocky and full of boulders. Whatever sand there was, was coarse and mixed with round pebbles sometimes as large as a melon. The seawater was cold and the currents treacherous. Only the most adventurous and highly skilled swimmers dared to bathe in the northern beaches.

In contrast the other beaches consisted of fine golden sand and the pine trees grew almost to the edge of the water. The sea was usually calm and much warmer. Lying on these huge sunny beaches alone without any other living soul in sight one had the eerie feeling of being in the Garden of Eden.

The western side of the island was separated by a narrow straight with the mainland, an area known as the "Pylion". This mountain range was a stronghold of the resistance. The main reason for this was the topography. The Pylion terrain was such that it did not allow the mobilization of troops armed with heavy weapons, such as artillery, or mechanized units.

The villages along the mountain sides were connected with narrow goat paths that only one soldier at a time could climb. There were no roads to support armored vehicles or tanks. Trucks to carry the troops and their supplies, or even smaller vehicles, were also totally useless in those roads.

Other than walking and climbing, the only other way to get up these hills was on horseback, or better yet on mule back. For this reason the enemy's superior numbers and equipment were not of much use in such a terrain. A simple machine gun, strategically placed, could prevent the Germans, almost indefinitely, from climbing to the top and attacking the guerilla hiding places.

The resistance-fighting pattern consisted of short hit and run operations. They could never match the German forces in terms of numbers or equipment in a protracted battle. What usually happened was, the underground selected a target such as a convoy or a munitions train.

They mined the road or placed explosives on the railroad tracks and when the fireworks started they launched a surprise attack from both sides of the road. They blew up as many vehicles and killed as many Germans as they could, and then ran like hell up to the safety of their mountain strongholds.

These tactics continuously harassed the Germans and kept their soldiers busy exacting a heavy toll in terms of life and supplies while there were little or no casualties on the part of the freedom fighters. Periodically the Germans, out of sheer frustration, would launch a concentrated effort to clean up the resistance strongholds that resided in these mountains.

They would surround the base of the mountain with soldiers covering the entire perimeter. They would then start to move these troops in a coordinated and synchronous fashion up the sides. The Partisans called such a move the "Combing". "They're combing us again," they would say while retreating to higher and higher ground.

The Germans would eventually reach some of the villages along the way and find that only women, children and very old men were there. They would capture a woman and attempt to interrogate her.

"Where is your husband?" They would ask.

"I don't know" the woman would answer. "He abandoned me".

The interrogator would then shout an order,

"Take the first child and shoot him."

After they shot her child in front of her eyes they would ask again,

"How is your memory now? Do you now remember where your husband is?"

Then they would proceed to shoot the next child and the next and finally the mother and throw a grenade and blow up the house. The truth was that the wives did not really know where their husbands were at any one time because they were moving around. All they knew was that they were fighting with the resistance. But even if they did know, they were not going to betray them to the Germans.

These atrocities were common in those days and they were not committed by a hand- full of fanatics, such as the SS or the Gestapo, but by ordinary foot soldiers under the lame excuse that they were just obeying orders. Entire villages were decimated in those raids and burned to the ground but to no avail. The fighting continued and finally the Germans would give up the search and leave.

Attempts to reach the guerilla hiding places from the air were equally futile. The dense forests and hundreds of caves provided safe cover so that nothing was detectable from above. Sometimes they would try to bomb these positions but they never hit any real target.

The Germans had installed antisubmarine nets across the narrow straights from the Pylion all the way to Skiathos to prevent the freedom fighters from receiving supplies by sea. The nets were kept in place by buoys anchored at regular intervals. These buoys stretched out like the beads of a giant necklace across the water during the entire distance between the island and the mainland.

My friends and I would often venture to swim across these straights by resting along the way on those buoys. It was nonetheless a daring and hazardous undertaking, which made it that much more attractive. It usually took several hours to reach the other end by swimming and resting, swimming and then resting some more.

During one of those times, as we were ready to attempt to swim across we spotted a boat headed in our direction. We knew from the general shape that it was not one of the local fishing boats. At first we thought it was a German patrol boat and we considered making a run for it, but on further reflection we decided that the boat was too close and we were probably not going to make it. Besides, we were not doing anything that might get us in trouble. As the boat got closer we realized that it was not a German boat.

When it reached the shore several figures dressed in black and carrying automatic weapons jumped out and motioned us to get closer. A young man, who seemed to be the leader of the group, then spoke in English and we realized that they were British commandos on a mission. Communication was difficult since none of us spoke English and they did not speak Greek.

Finally one of the commandos started to speak German and I was able to translate. They asked us if there were any Germans on the island and we assured them that there weren't any. They were very interested in the nature of the fortifications along the coast and whether or not the Germans had placed any mines between the Pylion and Skiathos.

We told them that when we swam across resting on the buoys we could see that there were heavy cables suspended there, but we couldn't determine what was hanging at the other end. They offered us chocolates and cookies. They also gave us several tins of food and then said goodbye and left.

After their departure we tried to open one of the cans but we did not have a can opener. We finally got it open by using the tip of an old bayonet. It contained smoked bacon slices wrapped in a roll on wax paper. We left the can on the ground and went to get some firewood to start a fire so that we could cook it and eat it. When we got back it was covered with millions of ants.

I still remember how upset we all were, but we were not about to discard such a rare delicacy. We took the can down to the sea and immersed it in seawater to drown the ants. It must have worked because when we finally cooked it and ate it, it was delicious and no one got sick. Maybe this rumor of getting severe abdominal problems if you eat ants is a lot of hogwash after all. At least in war times I can attest that eating a few ants is perfectly safe of course they were washed and cooked

The next day there were several loud explosions that shook the island. We later determined that the commandoes blew up part of the fortifications in the channel. This was the last time any of us attempted to swim across to the Pylion.

CHAPTER 14

A Restless Time of Uncertainty

In the fall of that year, one of my new friends, a fourteen-year-old comrade, talked me into a venture that almost cost both of us our lives. On a tiny island, a couple of miles from the entrance to the harbor, there was a lighthouse. The lighthouse was there to warn the passing vessels to steer clear of the treacherous rocks below. That spot was the scene of numerous shipwrecks in the past when skippers battling the rough seas ended up scuttling their ships on the rocky bottom.

During the war the lighthouse was abandoned. The lighthouse keeper took off and disappeared. My friend had found out that the lighthouse keeper had been raising rabbits, which after he left were running wild on the tiny island and had multiplied like crazy because there was an ample supply of vegetation and water. He thought that this was a good time to go rabbit hunting. He took the small boat from his uncle's fishing trawler and persuaded me to go along.

All we had with us were two burlap sacks and a dog. After a couple of hours of rowing we reached the lighthouse. We pulled the boat out of the water and turned the dog loose. The place was indeed infested with rabbits. The dog would chase them and with one snapping motion of his powerful jaws would choke them.

At no time at all our sacks were full of dead rabbits. We then turned our attention to exploring the island and the lighthouse. We climbed the spiral staircase to the top and were fascinated by the assemblage of mirrors and lenses and the reflection of the sun's rays from their surfaces. We continued our exploration looking into old trunks that still had some of the clothing and personal effects of the lighthouse keeper.

We were so engrossed in what we were doing that we did not realize that the weather had changed. The sea became choppier. The waves got higher and dark clouds began to accumulate on the horizon. It was time to get out of there and head for home. We loaded our loot and the dog on the boat and began rowing away towards Skiathos.

The heavy sea was tossing the tiny boat around like a walnut shell. Suddenly a heavy wave lifted us up and slammed the boat unto a rock. The boat began to fill with water. The two of us and the dog jumped into the water and began to climb onto the rock, dragging the boat behind us with the rope that was attached to the bow.

Fortunately the top surface of the rock was relatively flat and we were able to get on it and eventually, with the help of the swells, also drag the boat entirely out of the water. We were then able to inspect and assess the damage. There was a hole the size of an orange at the bottom where the wood came into contact with the sharp edge of the rock with which we had collided.

The boat was certainly not usable the way it was, and we had no tools with us or any suitable materials for repairing the damage. The situation looked pretty grim. Then I had an idea. Using a rock I unfastened the rear bench of the boat. We then pounded a piece of the boat's rope with a heavy stone until it became a pad of hemp large enough to cover the hole in the bottom. We then secured it in place by positioning the broken bench on top of the pad and nailing it to the bottom of the boat.

We put the boat in the water and climbed back in. Our crude repairs did not seal the leak but slowed down the water infiltration considerably. Thus, with one of us sitting on the bottom of the boat and continuously bailing out the incoming water and the other one rowing frantically, we started our way back. In the meantime it started to rain; first a mild drizzle and later a heavy downpour.

After three hours of battling the sea and the elements we finally made it to the dock without drowning. We were wet, tired, hungry, and scared but this was only the half of it. Standing at the dock with his hands around his waist and sopping wet was my friend's uncle, foaming at the mouth with anger.

"Were did you go? And who gave you permission to use my boat?" He asked.

Not waiting for an answer, he took out his belt and whipped us both within an inch of our lives. I will never forget that beating as long as I live.

For many years many of the Island's residents took to the sea seeking a better future. Those that did not want to make a living by fishing went to Piraeus, the port adjacent to Athens, to attend technical schools that prepared them for a career in the merchant marine. If they successfully completed their studies and passed all the exams needed for the license, they signed up with a shipping line and went out to sea aboard various types of ships.

Many worked on tankers and others on cargo ships. Thus, when Greece was occupied by the Germans, a number of the Skiathos residents found themselves in a strange port at some distant part of the world, blocked from returning home and became separated from their families for the duration of the war, i.e. for several years. But even prior to the occupation those who had chosen to have a career in the merchant marine were absent from home for long periods of time returning home very infrequently.

There was usually a very close correlation between the ages of their children and the home visitation dates. The separation, which lasted for months at a time, was extremely hard on the families, especially the wives who ended up for the most part raising their children by themselves. Eventually, after they felt that they had saved enough money to retire, the sailors would leave the ship for good and settle on the Island.

Their homes were full of souvenirs and fine household products they had collected from all around the world, that included crystals, fine china, silks, and other valuables. One could often encounter some of these old timers in the local taverns sipping wine and telling fascinating stories about the exotic lands they had visited and the adventures they had while sailing around the world.

Often facts became enriched with fiction and each time a story was told it varied somewhat from the previous telling, but to those of us listening it didn't matter. The tales were always interesting and transported us, however briefly, to an exiting make-believe world that took our minds off the hard times we were enduring.

Another of our favorite pastimes was singing. Our "Choir Director" was a young man who had been away to school and while there he joined a choir. He was thus able to learn a few songs and pick up enough pointers to start our local singing group. A number of us who liked to sing joined his choir.

I had inherited a good singing voice from my mother and taught myself to play the guitar. I thought joining the choir would be fun and it was. After a lot of coaching and numerous rehearsals we became quite a formidable singing group. In the warm summer months, under the brilliant stars one could hear our voices serenading the girls and evoking the wrath of the parents.

We became so popular that even the Italians, who had music in their blood anyway, started to join us and sing with the group. All of the resistance songs were based on haunting and beautiful Russian music. The lyrics were in Greek but the melodies were clearly Russian.

Most of these songs lent themselves well to choral singing. Thus part of our repertoire included the patriotic songs. It was amusing to hear the Italians, who frequently joined our singing group, sing these songs that spoke of "breaking the chains of tyranny and liberating the country from the barbarians". They either did not know what they were singing or did not care.

At any rate the Italian "occupation" of Skiathos was a joke. The small contingent of soldiers that were stationed there was almost forgotten by their own leadership. Gradually the soldiers, who were not great on discipline to begin with, began to look and behave more like the local fishermen than the army of occupation.

They still stood guard and all that but the rest of the time they wore civilian clothes and went fishing or bathing on the beach. One could frequently hear them singing their beautiful Neapolitan tunes in the stillness of the night.

Life in Skiathos for our family was, in many respects, a lot better than before and in some respects worse. It was no doubt a lot safer with fewer chances of being identified and captured and certainly there was a lot more food available than on the mainland so we were not starving. On the other hand we were a lot more isolated, stripped of all things familiar including friends.

There were no schools and zero opportunities for cultural or intellectual stimulation. There were no movies or theaters not even radios, magazines or newspapers. The physical amenities and creature comforts had deteriorated to the lowest level in our lives. We had no furniture of any kind, no cooking utensils and just the inventory of clothes and shoes we had brought with us.

Little by little our financial resources, including my mother's jewelry, were depleted and there was no opportunity for any of us to earn any real income. Furthermore we could not live with Apostolis indefinitely and we had to find our own home. My mother was able to get a little income by knitting sweaters for the richer ladies in town or embroidering for prospective brides. She also started giving French lessons to a few daughters of the wealthy families on the Island.

We certainly could not afford to rent a place, not that there were many such places available anyway. After an exhaustive search we found an old abandoned ruin that had no known owner. It must have been empty for a long time because it was completely cannibalized of anything movable. It had no doors or windows. The roof was missing several shingles and the wooden floor inside had a gapping hole in the middle that allowed the wind to blow into the house.

Since the "house" did not seem to belong to anybody that was living on the island at the time we decided to move there and establish squatter's rights. With a lot of hard work and scrounging we were able to make the place half way livable. Sympathetic neighbors gave us a modicum of simple furnishings. We closed the openings as best we could. An old blanket was laid on the floor covering the hole and whenever the wind blew it curved up like a sail. After a lot of scrubbing, patching, and whitewashing the place was still substandard as homes go but it was ours and it was free.

The back yard had an outhouse, a water pump and the traditional large oven. Our food consisted primarily of things we collected from the land and from the sea. Fish that we caught ourselves or we obtained from the local fisherman by working on their boats. Fruits and olives were available from the trees on the farms all around us. There was so much there that no one minded our gleanings.

We dug up the earth around our palace and planted vegetables. We also started to raise chickens that provided us with a supply of eggs. We learned to eat and value any kind of food that was edible, from the backside of the black sea urchins to the sweet prickly pears that grew in the wild cactus plants around the Burzy. They were also all kinds of wild fruits and berries in the countryside ready to be picked.

For any services performed by any of us we usually got paid in olive oil. We then traded this oil for other necessities, especially flour. The wood for cooking and keeping warm came from the abundant pine trees in the area, which we chopped ourselves. My mother was an absolute magician when it came to preparing a meal with these meager ingredients and under such primitive conditions. We were alive and relatively safe but at the bare existence level.

I was quite happy with this existence. For the first time in a long time I was able to be footloose and fancy free the way other children of my age were. I didn't have to go to school and I had very few other restrictions. After all we were on an island. Where can one go on a small island? It was nearly impossible to get mixed up in any kind of real mischief because everybody knew everybody else and there was no place to hide.

I was having a ball with this newfound freedom and little or no responsibilities. I was happy to walk around the beach barefoot, go for a swim in the crystal clear waters, play with my friends and take long walks exploring the countryside and enjoying the abundance of tasty treats along the way. It was a very basic and hard lifestyle, a far cry from our previous life of comfort, but one I was nonetheless enjoying because I had never experienced it before. But not everyone in the family felt that way.

CHAPTER 15

To Athens and Back

My brother Zack, who had been admitted to the Medical School at the University, was anxious to pursue his studies. My brother Albert, who was always very studious, was upset for not having the opportunity to go to school. There was absolutely nothing for them to do on the Island. The idleness and boredom was eating them alive.

After many heated discussions my mother finally broke down and consented to Zack and Albert leaving. She was not comfortable with the idea of their going to Athens and being separated from the rest of us. She also knew that it would be difficult to become established there and pursue their studies.

Everyone and especially my mother recognized that this was very risky but finally yielded under the pressure and said okay. with the proviso that if things didn't work out they would immediately return to the safety of the Island. One of the reasons that she relented was that Athens was under Italian and not German control and it was well known that the Italians, despite pressures from their German allies, had still not implemented any anti-Jewish measures.

Zack and Albert packed their suitcases and arranged with a local captain of a fishing boat to take them as far as Evia, a large island like land mass located near and parallel to the eastern side of the Athenian peninsula. Evia was located approximately half way between Skiathos and Athens That was as far as they could plan their trip. They had no way of knowing how they would make it the rest of the way to Athens but hoped that they could somehow hitch a ride.

We embraced each other and as we stood on the dock-waving goodbye I had this awful feeling of gloom not knowing when or even if we would see each other again. Captain "Koukias", a veteran of these waters, stood at the helm with an unlit half of a cigarette hanging from his lower lip and wearing baggy black pants, a remnant of the Turkish-style attire, that was typical of the garb worn by those Greeks that came from Asia minor. Without any compass or any other navigational aid he steered the vessel straight for Evia

The trip was long, tiring and uncomfortable but otherwise uneventful. Upon arrival they had to go through control by the Italians who checked their papers and searched their luggage. When they opened Albert's suitcase they found an album in which Albert had neatly pasted his entire collection of caricatures of Mussolini that had appeared throughout the entire Greek-Italian conflict in Albania in various Greek newspapers and magazines.

The Italians were not amused. They became angry and started shouting threats and obscenities at both of them. Continuing the search they found a textbook that was used to teach English. That did it. They were both arrested and locked up in a small room with no doors and windows and left there for several hours. Zack was furious. He told Albert

"If we ever make it out of here alive I will kill you!"

Finally an Italian officer came in and began to interrogate them. He kept asking them over and over again where they were going and why they were learning English. Zack told him to please forgive Albert because he was just a child and didn't know what he was doing, he didn't mean any harm etc. The interrogator was apparently a fascist and was greatly offended by the way the caricatures in Albert's collection portrayed the great "EL Duce" and he wasn't buying any of their explanations. He used his riding crop to hit them in the face several times during the interrogation while he shouted,

"You will tell me the truth or I'll beat you to death."

After about an hour he got up and said

"I am leaving now but I will be back and you will tell me everything or I will see that you rot in hell."

When he left the room their faces were cut up and bleeding. Zack used his handkerchief and put pressure on the wounds to stop the flow of blood. Their injuries were painful but superficial.

Thank God the Italians were not up to par with their German allies in the art of torture and interrogation. Nevertheless they were both very apprehensive about what was going to become of them. To complicate matters further Zack had hidden in the lining of his jacket a passbook that he needed to re-enroll in the University, which had on it his real name. Fearing a thorough body search he retrieved the booklet and was looking for a way to get rid of it. Unfortunately there was no place to hide it in that room.

The walls of the room were made with wide wooded planks vertically situated and nailed to the studs. The planks were not close enough to touch thus there was a little space between them. Zack quickly regained his composure and decided to push the booklet through these cracks hoping that there was some dead space between the walls or that the room next door would be empty and no one would see the booklet as it penetrated through the wall. When nothing happened after a few minutes he gave a sigh of relief and began to conceive a daring plan.

The essence of this crazy plan was that they would ask to see the German commandant. Albert agreed that this was a good plan. What they were banking on was that the Germans didn't have much use or respect for their Italian allies and that the German commandant may not be as outraged with the Mussolini caricatures as the Italians were. Furthermore they were both counting on their knowledge of German to create a friendlier atmosphere.

As soon as the Italian returned Zack said to him

"We demand to see the German commandant of this post. We will only talk to him."

After a number of heated exchanges, the Italian finally relented and escorted them to the office of the German who was the officer in charge. He was an extremely young man with blond hair and blue eyes wearing a summer navy uniform with short white pants and a white shirt. The Italian had a brief conversation with the German giving him a briefing on this case and placed on his desk the album with the caricatures of Mussolini.

After the Italian left, the German started to leaf through the album and began to laugh hysterically. My brothers started to talk to the officer in German explaining that there was no malice intended and that the book was just a childish prank. He was impressed by their command of his language and asked,

"Where did you learn how to speak German so well?" Zack replied

," We had a German grandmother that did not know Greek and the only way to communicate with her was for us to learn German."

Thus he was able to build another bridge with the young officer. The German looked at him and said,

"Do you know why the Italians are holding you? They think that you are spies. But I think that you are too stupid to be spies. Get the hell out of here and be more careful in the future about the things you and your kid brother carry with you." He then called the guard and said,

"Let these two genius master criminals go."

The guard opened the gate and let them out of the compound just as a Greek truck carrying produce was chugging along. They jumped on it and got out of there before he changed his mind.

Zack and Albert picked the worst possible time to go to Athens. The City was in the midst of the worst famine of the war. There was absolutely nothing to eat, not even on the black market. The German army was experiencing crushing defeats on the Russian front and was in total disarray.

Facing severe shortages of their own, they squeezed every drop of blood from the Greek population. One could sense how desperate things were by looking at the ages of the soldiers of occupation. Increasingly the troops used for this purpose consisted of younger and younger kids and old men. The more regular army was in combat assignments.

As their desperation level increased so did the their brutality. Disenchanted with the lack of cooperation by their Italian allies the Germans increased their presence in Athens and little by little began to strip the authority of the Italians and to enforce their own reign of terror.

The schools were either closed or functioning at the lowest possible levels because of the severe shortages of equipment, supplies and above all teachers. The University was the hot bed of activism where more time was spent in planning sabotage missions than acquiring knowledge. The authorities recognized this and tightened the screws.

There were numerous raids and arrests in an effort to crush the resistance. The lack of fuel had grounded almost all Greek vehicles thus the only way to get around was to walk.

Whatever little public transportation existed was running on erratic and undependable schedules and was dominated by the army of occupation. Medical facilities were stripped of anything useful to support the nazi war effort. People were dying like flies and a general mood of depression was hovering over the capital.

Albert's plan was to work part time at the drugstore that belonged to a cousin of our good friend Dr. Papas who owned the drug store in our hometown of Drama. He was also planning to go back to school and to try to complete his education. Papa's cousin did offer Albert a job, however, he could hardly make a living himself, because there wasn't much left in the store to sell and there were very few buyers. Therefore what he could pay Albert was very minimal.

Furthermore getting from the drugstore to school was a major problem because of the severe shortage of public transportation. It involved a long walk through some rough and dangerous neighborhoods. Finally finding a place to stay for both of them was problematic. Zack enrolled at the University and was immediately recruited by the resistance organization and started to participate in miscellaneous acts of sabotage and disruption of the nazi operations.

The resistance had intensified its assaults inflicting severe blows to the enemy. Everyone was sensing that this was no longer the apparently invincible fighting machine that first invaded the Greek soil. All of the reports from the front indicated that the Germans were getting a severe beating by the Russians and that their armies were on the run.

The BBC was broadcasting the relentless bombing of Berlin and other key German cities, breaking the back of the nazi war machine. The news made the resistance fighters bolder and more aggressive. This in turn brought about more reprisals in the form of capturing innocent civilians as hostages and killing them indiscriminately.

There were daily reports of executions. Despite the apparent successes at the front, the beast was not yet ready to die and the reign of terror continued for a much longer time than anyone had anticipated. In the process hundreds of heroic freedom fighters and entire populations of innocent people gave their lives for their country.

This was indeed the worst possible time to be in Athens. Security was tight. Everyday, when it was not expected, policemen, traitors in German uniforms or the Germans themselves would set up road blocks and stop people at random, checking their papers. The probability of Albert or Zack being stopped at one of these checkpoints was quite high. Their fake documents could not stand up to close scrutiny and could result in their arrest and execution.

By comparison Skiathos looked infinitely more attractive. Both Zack and Albert were rapidly coming to the conclusion that it had been a mistake to come to Athens and they should perhaps consider returning to the island. As it turned out the decision was made for them. During one of the secret meetings of the resistance held at the home of a young Greek doctor, Zack met about a dozen comrades of both the male and female persuasion.

The leader described their mission, which was to go out and sabotage the communications in some of the buildings that the Germans had set up headquarters. He had diagrams of the streets, the buildings, the location of the telephone control boxes and the position of the sentries.

When he finished explaining the plan of action he ushered them to the dining room. On the table there was a pile of handguns of every size and description along with the required ammunition. He then ordered each one to pick up a weapon of their choice from the table and load it. He also asked them to take along some extra bullets or clips. The instructions were not to use the weapons unless there was imminent danger of being captured. Some of those in the room were handling a gun for the first time in their lives.

To an untrained observer that group of saboteurs walking along in the late afternoon hour looked like any other normal pedestrian traffic. It was impossible to know that these young men and women who were walking along holding hands or having their arms around each other were somehow related or members of the same unit. The whole thing looked very casual and normal.

Zack, with three others, a girl and two boys a few years younger than he, was at the point. They were talking casually and walking slowly as if they were just out for an evening stroll. Suddenly, around the bend of the road they ran smack onto a German checkpoint. Two military policemen wearing helmets and armed with submachine guns ordered them to stop. As the Germans approached they could see their horseshoe plaques that hung from the Policemen's necks fluorescing in the dusk.

"Papier Bitte" one of them said. At that point the youngest male panicked, pulled his 45 automatic pistol out of his pocket and emptied his entire clip killing both Germans instantly. The whole thing happened so fast that the entire group was stunned. Other German soldiers began to run towards them from further down the street.

By that time all pandemonium broke loose. Everyone had drawn his weapon and was firing wildly in the general direction of the soldiers without having an identified or specific target. Then they took off and began to run, scattering in every direction, as they were instructed to do, jumping over fences and backyards and disappearing in the back alleys.

Many of the local residents opened their doors and let them in to escape capture, and miraculously, no one was. The next day the German controlled Greek newspapers reported that a major group of commandos attacked and killed two unarmed German soldiers who were ready to go on leave and were celebrating their last night in Athens.

The participants in this operation met the next day at a predetermined home to report the incident to the resistance leadership. They were officially reprimanded for disobeying orders and using their weapons prematurely but unofficially everyone was happy that two of the enemy soldiers were dead. Zack was told that he and those in his group that were directly involved in the shooting were too hot and should not stay in the city any longer than was absolutely necessary. He was ordered to get back to Skiathos and then go to the Pylion and join the Guerrilla fighters that were operating in those mountains.

A week later Albert made it back to Skiathos this time without any incident. Since he was just a boy he was able to obtain the necessary travel permits without any major difficulties. Zack was in an entirely different predicament being on the wanted list and an adult he was faced with many more complications, as we shall learn later. His return to Skiathos required a very elaborate plan full of danger. Because of this his return took a lot longer to our great dismay and anxiety.

Albert and I joined the EPON, which was the youth branch of the liberation movement. We had regular meetings and training sessions on the care and use of weapons and on the handling of explosives. We were taught how to assemble and disassemble guns with our eyes closed and how to use grenades and how to kill sentries with piano wire.

I am happy to say that I never had to use that skill, although many times in my latter life I was greatly tempted. Concurrently with the "military" training, we received indoctrination on the values of communism and heard the party line in every weekly meeting. Most of my young comrades and myself had neither the education nor the intellectual capacity to grasp the significance of any of this Communist propaganda.

Thus the attempts to convert us were largely wasted. The idea of doing something concrete to hurt the Germans, on the other hand, was very appealing and exciting and boosted our self-esteem. Being in that wonderful in-between age, no longer children and yet not quite adults, we looked at our involvement in the resistance movement as some sort of great adventure.

Our enthusiasm was based in our search for significance and our desire to belong to a group that took us seriously. In a way the driving force was similar to what makes young people today join gangs. Our youthful idealism found a creative channel for its expression.

Under the umbrella of this resistance organization we felt important, wanted, and secure. . Of course all of this, at first, was highly theoretical because in Skiathos, at the time, there was nothing to resist. The most dangerous thing I was asked to do was to broadcast to the people of Skiathos the latest news about the conduct of the war that we got from the daily broadcasts of the BBC.

I did that at night from the hills just above the town using a hand- held large conical megaphone. This earned me the nickname "To Houni" which loosely translated means "The Funnel". The only other persons, besides the Greek inhabitants, that could hear me were the Italians that either they did not understand the nature of the communication or did not give a damn because they never made any attempt to capture me and put a stop to the nightly broadcasts.

Albert, now sixteen years old, was a lot more introverted, more mature, and more scholarly than I at thirteen. Without being flamboyant he was extremely intelligent, informed, and much more practical and realistic than I. He was able to see things for what they were, not as a great adventure but as a great misfortune for our family and for the country as a whole. He was willing to do his part to fight the Germans but did not look upon our involvement in the conflict as a game.

Because of our age difference and the fact that he was naturally more conservative, he was more keenly aware than I of the risks we were taking. Also he missed our old life in Drama with all its comforts much more than I did. Above all he was lonely, because he had very little in common with the local youths of his age with whom he was not intellectually or culturally compatible.

He attended the weekly organizational meetings of the EPON just as I did and complied with all his assignments but he was too smart to swallow all of Communist inspired rhetoric that they threw at us. Albert and I both understood that listening to the propaganda was the price we had to pay for having the protection and security that belonging to the resistance afforded us.

Also we welcomed the opportunities to pay back the Germans for all the suffering they had put us through. It was difficult for everyone, to understand why the Germans singled out the Jews as the primary targets of their brutality. It was particularly incomprehensible to us, who by virtue of our upbringing, did not think of ourselves as being any different from any other Greek youngster.

Consequently, we were filled with rage for having to go into hiding, to abandon our home, not once but three times, and to have to live with fear and with false identities. The magnitude of this injustice made us strong and forged our will to resist and to survive.

By virtue of the narrow-minded notions of the time, my sister Carmen was forced to assume a low-key role in the chain of events that preceded our move to Skiathos. Although she was very attractive and highly intelligent she was restricted by the customs of the day from developing her full potential. She had inherited my mother's operatic voice and musical talent. She was regularly taking voice lessons from a famous Italian voice coach whom my brother Zack mischievously had nicknamed "La perra catholica" i.e. the "The catholic bitch."

She also took several years of piano lessons and became quite accomplished in both singing and playing the piano. This made her very popular with the young crowd. It was also a real source of pleasure and enjoyment for the family. Being close in age to Zack, they moved in the same circles and had a lot of common friends.

My sister also was very well read and highly proficient in her studies. She excelled in school and was able to graduate one year earlier than her age group. Her major regret and disappointment was that my parents did not let her pursue advanced studies at the University. With that bottled up inside her, she found herself in the grip of war and brutality that temporarily sidetracked her.

She worked tirelessly helping my mother and the family through the difficult times setting aside temporarily her own ambitions and aspirations for the future. Joining the underground gave her the chance she was waiting and hoping for. She became heavily involved with the resistance organizations. Suddenly she was able to find a channel for asserting her individualism and her own suppressed search for significance and self-actualization.

The underground was the first opportunity that women had to become liberated and achieve some measure of equality. Women in the resistance were not only allowed but also encouraged to develop their own leadership potential. Their voice carried equal weight as that of men. It is easy to understand that in such an environment, my sister, who was very bright, articulate, and well educated would quickly ascend to a high leadership position.

Also her idealism and her own suppressed desire for independence and feelings that she had about being denied opportunities made her an easier target for the Communist indoctrination that we were all subjected to. She quickly became very popular with the people in the National Liberation Front and was finally able to assert her independence.

She became quite infatuated with a local teacher who was a dyed- in- the-wool Communist and a very eloquent and persuasive speaker. Most people, when listening to him, became mesmerized. After all, to any naïve young person that did not have much life experience, the Communist doctrine sounded extremely attractive. Liberty and equality, peace instead of war, no exploitation and no discrimination, all these ideals on the surface appear to be lofty goals worthy of support.

My sister bought the whole package and could not wait to fly away from the nest and go out there and preach to the masses about the oppression of the working class and the need to have all the "Proletariats" unite. This was her chance to save the world and nothing would stop her.

One day she announced that she was planning to leave the island with this teacher and go to the mountains where the real fighting was going on.

It was obvious that she was determined and at the age of twenty she was old enough to decide her own destiny. My mother made a few futile attempts to dissuade her but finally she gave up. The next day we said goodbye and my sister left us for an unknown destination.

Zack had not yet made it back from Athens and we had no news from him.

With half the family gone we continued our struggle to survive in the island. We were progressively and increasingly isolated from the rest of the country with the shortages of crucial supplies becoming acute, in some instances critical. My mother became depressed and reclusive saying very little and going through the motions but her old vitality had left her and suddenly she appeared a lot older.

I am sure that the uncertainty of our situation was heavily weighing on her shoulders. Albert tried to give her support and comfort but I was too involved with my own activities to be of any real help, a fact that I now deeply regret.

CHAPTER 16

The Nightmare Returns

When I woke up in the morning and looked out I saw the red German flag with the black swastika flying over the Burzy and a cold shiver went up and down my spine. I got dressed quickly and ran down to the wharf to see what was happening. The Italians were gone. They disappeared overnight and we never found out what happened to them.

German sentries were posted to the entrance of the Burzy. Two German gunboats equipped with machine and anti-aircraft guns were tied up in the dock area. Armed sailors stood guard while others were going about their duties. The Germans had turned on their loudspeakers and were broadcasting a series of directives. "Achtung, Achtung…" the words echoed in the quiet of the early morning hour bringing back a flood of bad memories and re-igniting the old fears.

I was seized with panic realizing that the honeymoon was over. With the Italians gone and the Germans taking over the occupation of Skiathos, I was certain that we were about to relive the terrors of Salonica: the hunger, the uncertainty, and the constant threat of being discovered and captured.

Our safety bubble had burst and I was very worried about the effect the news might have on my mother. I hurried home to tell her what I saw. Amazingly, I found my mother reassuring me instead of the other way around. When I told her that the Germans had come back she said,

"Don't worry. We have beaten them before at their game and we can do it again. Stay calm and focused. No one knows or suspects us here and there are no Jews on this island. There is also a strong resistance organization present that had been preparing for months for this eventuality. All we have to do is stay calm and this too will pass."

There was a lot of truth in that statement. Unlike our previous predicaments, we were no longer alone facing the oppressors. Our lot was now intimately connected with the rest of the people of Skiathos. We were better prepared than ever to take whatever the Germans would dish out and we were counting on the leadership of the resistance to guide us through this difficult period.

The Germans announced the immediate implementation of a number of changes:

All of the directives issued by the Italian command were now null and void.

All identity cards and fishing permits had to be reissued by the German authority.

All boats must be properly registered and could not leave the harbor until that process was completed.

All firearms and short wave radios must be surrendered immediately. Those that failed to do so would be shot.

A night curfew was to be instituted at once.

These directives created an enormous logistics problem for the Germans. First, the occupying force consisted of sailors, not Gestapo agents, or Military Policemen. The sailors were not trained in intelligence work or police matters and had no experience in enforcing such sweeping mandates. But, even if they did, they did not have enough personnel or knowledge of the local scene for the task at hand.

Just to process the hundreds of boats that needed to be licensed required many more people than they had. Furthermore, Skiathos had no Greek Police Force. Consequently, the goal of issuing an identity card to each one of the three thousand residents, without any help from a local authority, was highly unrealistic and in fact unfeasible.

The Germans must have realized that too because they abandoned their attempts to enforce it. Finally, there was a big communications problem because the Germans sailors did not speak Greek. To screen all the applicants for the permits that they required would take forever without the help of interpreters.

They would definitely need to involve Greeks that spoke German to read and translate the official Greek documents and to help them screen the people who were requesting different permits for their boats and for themselves.

The underground leaders saw in this situation a unique opportunity to infiltrate the Germans and help the liberation movement. Besides my brother, my mother, and myself there were only two other people on the island that spoke German. One was a retired high school teacher, nicknamed "the professor", who had studied in Germany before the war, and the other was the director of our choir, Vassilis Natsos.

All of us belonged to the local resistance. Our orders were to approach the Germans, become friendly with them, and gain their confidence. We were then to offer our assistance as interpreters to facilitate the screening of all the fishermen and boat owners with the registration and licensing of their boats. Our ultimate objective was to obtain licenses and circulation permits for boats belonging to the ELAN, the Navy branch of the resistance forces.

We were also ordered to steal blank forms and an official stamp so that phony documents could be forged for agents of the resistance operating in the area and for escaped allied prisoners of war who were trying to find there way back to their units in the Middle East.

Finally, we were to gather whatever information we could about their patrols, the nature of the fortifications along the chain of islands in the Mediterranean, the location of their minefields or anything else that might be of use to allied intelligence. This was quite a tall order and we had no idea of how we would go about implementing it.

The Germans set up shop in one of the commandeered local establishments that was located on the waterfront. It was a small building used before the war as the office for the Harbormaster. The same building also housed the Customs office. It contained a large front room with a walkup window, two additional offices, a storage room, and a latrine. The storage room had no windows.

No one was allowed inside this building except the sailors on duty. The business was transacted through the walk-up window in the front. Long lines of local residents, mostly fishermen, with their documents on hand lined up from the early hours of the morning waiting to get their permits so that they could move their boats and resume their fishing.

This was essential to their survival and to the survival of their families. Without fishing, most of the residents of the island would starve.

It was not difficult to gain the confidence of the sailors that were charged with this impossible task. They were caught between a rock and a hard place. The process of screening without anyone interpreting was frustrating and excruciatingly slow, but their superiors were not interested in excuses; they wanted results. As soon as we made it known to them that we were bilingual, we were drafted.

We took turns and each of us spent a few hours a day at this post, interpreting and translating documents from Greek to

German. Ironically, most of the local population who were not aware of our true mission thought of us as collaborators and treated us either with derision or with the silent treatment.

Some tried to bribe us so that we could help them get their permits faster. Others openly threatened us or showered us with insults. I hated that part of the mission and felt helpless because we were not at liberty to explain that we were under orders from the resistance to do what we were doing. As the days rolled by, we became progressively more familiar with the routine.

We cultivated the friendship of the key people and very quickly, we were on a first name basis with the sailors that were handling these clerical tasks. In order to help them with their duties it was of course necessary to allow us to be inside the office. The first part of the mission, getting the boats used by the resistance registered and licensed, was not very hard.

The sailors spoke just a few words of Greek and could certainly not translate any Greek documents or determine their authenticity. They relied entirely on us.

Stealing blank documents or official stamps, however, was an entirely different matter. All the documents were kept in a metal cabinet in the storeroom. After office hours, both the cabinet and the storeroom were locked and the officer in charge of the operation, Lt. Wolfgang Bruger, had the only keys. To separate him from his keys, even for a few moments, seemed to be impossible. Furthermore, we were constantly being watched. After office hours, the place was locked and an armed sentry was posted at the front. For a while, taking anything out of this building, without being caught, looked hopeless.

It was clear what stealing the documents required: getting past the sentries without being spotted, gaining entrance to the locked building, unlocking the storeroom and the metal cabinet, and then leaving with the forms undetected.

There was simply no way that this could be accomplished. After considerable agonizing over our dilemma, we finally came up with a plan. The plan was bold and very risky but it looked as if there was no other way to carry out our mission. It called for the stealing of the documents in stages.

After several days of observation, we noted that both the storeroom and the metal cabinet were unlocked during business hours but only the Germans were allowed to go in and out. Our plan called for one of us to sneak in the storeroom remove a bunch of the blank forms and passbooks and hide them temporarily in some other spot still inside the storeroom itself. Having done this, that person would, at the appropriate moment, run out of the storeroom without attracting attention.

This had to be done quickly and for this we needed a diversion that would bring everyone out to the front room for a few minutes. We decided that at an opportune time, the professor would set the wastepaper basket on fire, which was bound to attract the attention of the sailors.

At that exact moment, I would sneak into the storeroom. Vassilis would be the lookout in the hallway outside the storeroom and signal me that the coast was clear and that I could run out of the room without anyone seeing me.

One day we got our chance. Lt. Bruger went out for a few minutes leaving just the sailor-clerks behind. This gave us the opportunity we needed. While the sailors were temporarily busy with the fire I got in the storeroom, grabbed a bunch of documents from the cabinet, and threw them in a metal bucket that was used to mop the floors. I then covered the bucket with a dirty rag and ran out of the storeroom.

The entire operation took less than three minutes. The professor was apologizing profusely to the sailors for throwing his cigarette butt in the waste paper basket. He told them that he was sure the cigarette was out when he tossed it in, but apparently, it was not completely out.

Thus phase one of the plan was done. Phase two was more complicated and a lot more dangerous. At exactly 5:00 PM every day, the C.O. would order the staff to put everything in the cabinet. He would then lock it, walk out of the storeroom, and lock the door.

Following that everyone would leave the building and he would secure the front door and then leave himself. This routine never varied. In the morning the procedure was reversed. Our plan called for one of us to hide in the storeroom and remain there overnight.

Vassilis who was the most agile and athletic of the bunch volunteered. At 4:50 PM, he entered the storeroom, at a moment when no one was looking, and laid down, flat on his back, on the floor behind the counter. The officer with unfailing German punctuality came in shortly after, locked the cabinet and the storeroom, with Vassilis inside, and walked out.

When all the noises had subsided and he was sure that everyone had left for the day, Vassilis got on his feet, flicked on his flashlight and retrieved the forms from the mop bucket. He then stripped to his waist, distributed the forms into two folders, and taped them on his body with black electrical friction tape.

After he made sure that the folders were securely fastened, he replaced his undershirt, his shirt, his sweater, and his jacket. The garments completely concealed the folders that were underneath. When all the preparations were completed, he sat down and tried to get some sleep waiting for the morning when the storeroom would be unlocked.

The next day, at exactly 9:00 AM, like clockwork, Lt. Bruger opened the building and let all the staff in. He then proceeded to the storeroom, unlocked the door, walked over to the cabinet and unlocked it. He then stood in front of the counter for a few seconds that looked like a lifetime to Vassilis, who was on the floor directly behind the counter, holding his breath.

Luckily, he then turned around, walked out, and headed for his office. Vassilis jumped up on to his feet and followed him out of the room just a few seconds later. Suddenly, Bruger came out of his office again and bumped into Vassilis in the hallway.

"Where did you come from? He asked I didn't see you come in."

"I was in the latrine," Vassilis replied "Is there anything I can do for you?"

Burger said, "No. Just go about your business."

Vassilis stayed there for the entire day with the documents strapped to his body so as not to arouse any suspicions. Later on, we met with the resistance leaders and turned over everything to them.

Thus, another part of our mission was accomplished, which was fortunate because most of the boat registrations and the issuance of permits were completed and soon there will be no compelling reason for us to hang around the office. Stealing an official stamp so that it could be used to falsify documents was impossible.

The Germans where the only ones who handled the stamps and they never left them lay around. Even if we could steal one of their stamps, its disappearance would be discovered immediately and the finger of suspicion would be pointed directly to one of us. Consequently, we abandoned that idea.

Instead we proposed to our leadership that if they had some particular person that they were trying to get documents for to use the forms we stole, fill them out completely and then send someone to the walkup window and hand us the papers.

We would then try to sneak them in with the whole pile of papers that needed to be stamped. This way it would look like a routine transaction similar to all the others and there was a good chance that the clerk would stamp the papers without much scrutiny.

However, this could only be done on rare occasions. If it were frequent, eventually, we would be discovered.

The last part of the mission, the gathering of intelligence, was not very fruitful. Skiathos was not an important enough post for storing any information that had strategic value. The sailors manning that post did not know much; consequently, there was not much information we could gather that would be of any real value to the war effort.

CHAPTER 17

The Capture of "Milliouni"

Our vigil over the operations of the German authorities in the Island continued despite the lack of any spectacular discoveries. The only information we were able to get had to do with the schedule and itinerary of the patrol boats. This was prepared on a weekly basis and occasionally it would be left on someone's desk for a few minutes, long enough to take a peek.

Whenever that happened we reported it to our command, which in turn, informed the allied submarines in the area by short wave radio. From time to time, using binoculars, we were able to observe from the top of the hill a torpedo hitting a German boat and cutting it in half.

The sea would subsequently wash to the shore dead bodies of Germans as well as various types of equipment and supplies. On these occasions the partisans would dispatch a unit to go down to the beach and remove anything that appeared to be useful.

This included the clothes, boots and even socks and underwear from the corpses. The resistance fighters at that time did not have their own uniforms or shoes. All their clothing and gear, including their weapons were things that they got from the Germans they killed.

At one time, the sea washed out on the beach a large quantity of five-gallon tin cans. When we opened them, we found that they were filled with a dark maroon colored substance that looked like wood shavings. None of us had ever seen anything like that. The substance in these containers swelled to a bloody pulp when water was added to it.

Someone suggested that these cans contained dehydrated ground meat. However, we did not even want to venture a guess as to what kind of meat it was. The stuff looked disgusting and no matter how starved we were for protein none of us would try to cook that mess. The whole shipment was dumped back into the water and we let the fish eat it.

At night, we continued to broadcast the news with the cardboard megaphone. However, with the Germans present this task became a lot more dangerous. Armed German patrols combed the area at night and would shoot on sight anything that moved. To minimize the risk we adopted the following policy:

The broadcast time would vary each day and instead of one, we would have three different people broadcasting from different locations. Each would only broadcast one third of the news thus minimizing the time on the air and the chance of being discovered and captured or shot.

As a further precaution the sequence and the location of the post that each of us would broadcast from, would not be determined until the last minute and only the three of us would be involved in the selection.

We decided to select randomly by the tossing of coins. By this system, it was impossible for any one to have any advanced knowledge or betray us. These nightly activities drove the Germans crazy and made them offer a reward for our capture.

One fateful evening the broadcast was interrupted by the sounds of machine gun fire. The next day we saw the bloodied body of one of our comrades hanging from a lamppost on the wharf. The bloodstained megaphone was still clutched in his arms.

The German patrol apparently ran into him, killed him, and hanged his body as an example to others. The next night someone else took his place and the broadcasts continued.

With most of the registration and licensing of boats completed, our presence at the German control station was no longer needed. The professor continued to make an appearance there from time to time primarily to resolve isolated language problems and help the local residents.

After the killing of our comrade, the authorities tightened their grip on the island. There were more patrols at night, more surprise raids and more arrests. Those arrested were beaten and tortured in the hope that they would reveal to the Germans the names of the resistance leaders and their hiding places.

Most of those arrested had no clue regarding the resistance. Everyone in the movement used a pseudonym, never their true name, and only the top leaders knew the meeting locations. Consequently, the interrogations did not help the Germans. No one would speak and a few died during the interrogation.

The rest of the hostages were shot. The resistance moved their operations further up into the hills, using the huts that were in the olive groves as temporary quarters. To minimize the chances of discovery the meeting locations were constantly rotated and only a few people knew the locations.

The German patrols never ventured too far from the town primarily because they did not know what strength the underground had in those hills and they did not have enough troops to mount an all out offensive.

In retaliation for the killing of all these innocent civilians, it was decided to mount a strike against the Germans.

Two individual units of the resistance armed with submachine guns and grenades would launch a simultaneous surprise attack on the gunboats docked at the harbor. The attack would involve a concerted land and sea operation. A third unit would blow up their antenna temporarily paralyzing their communication.

The attack took place in the early morning hours when most people were asleep. The island was filled with the sound of the explosions and gunfire. In a matter of minutes, the two boats were in flames and sinking. The German radio room was blown to bits. Sailors were running out of their barracks in a panic, half dressed, trying to get organized and pursue the attackers.

There was a lot of shouting of commands and indiscriminate firing of rifles at the direction of the burning boats. A couple of the freedom fighters were wounded and were carried away by their retreating comrades. By the time the Germans got over the shock to organize a counter attack, the guerillas had retreated into the hills.

The attack stunned the Germans. In the entire time of their occupation of Skiathos no one had as much as fired a single shot at the Germans and certainly there was no evidence of any armed resistance in the past during the Italian occupation of the island. The Germans were thus lulled into a false sense of security and did not expect such a massive raid and the large loss of men and equipment that resulted from it.

They were completely unprepared. However, they quickly got over their initial shock; they regrouped and repaired their communications. They then radioed for reinforcements. The next day several boats arrived loaded with German infantry and arms. Their mission was to comb all the hills and capture the resistance fighters, cleaning up their nests once and for all.

In the meantime, boats evacuated all of the fighting men that were in the hills across the channel into the safety of the resistance strong holds of the Pylion. When the Germans cautiously climbed up the mountain roads, they encountered zero resistance and found no trace of the guerilla fighters.

A few days later they returned to the town empty handed and reported that there were no longer any fighting units in the hills. The next day they got into their boats and left, leaving behind just a few sailors as the occupying force.

The German occupation troops left Skiathos just as suddenly as they came without any previous warning. In their place, they left a Greek "administrator". He was a German collaborator, originally from Salonica, by the name of Dr. Fokas. Apparently, the Germans, who were already losing the war, could no longer afford to have their sailors tied-up, occupying an island with no real strategic value.

They consolidated and maintained only one post in the Island of Skopellos and were using this command post as the hub for controlling all of the Islands in the Sporades. Fokas was a pathetic creature trying desperately to look authoritative by waving his pistol around and periodically when he was drunk firing his weapon indiscriminately and frightening the residents of the Island.

Despite his tough rhetoric he was really a very frightened man realizing that the Germans were losing and some day soon, they might pull up stakes and leave him behind to explain to the resistance his traitorous actions. To bolster his position Fokas imported a few other Greek hoodlums from Volos, members of the traitorous "Security Regiments" organized and used by the Germans to do their dirty work.

These thugs were armed, dangerous, and totally devoid of conscience. Unfortunately, Fokas being from Salonica knew my father's family and that we were Jews. On his orders, my brother Albert and I were arrested, severely beaten, and interrogated by Fokas for hours. He was trying to make us confess that we were Jews hiding out.

When he did not get what he wanted he threw us in Jail. When our capture became known my mother was sick with worry and fearing for our lives, she decided to go see Fokas and plead with him to release us. Fokas told her straight out that he knew us and that he was aware that we were Jews. He played a cat and mouse game with my mother trying to trap her by speaking to her in "Ladino" the dialect used by the Jews of Salonica.

After several hours it was obvious that Fokas was not about to release us, and that he was planning to turn us in to the Germans at the appropriate time to gain further favors from his masters. A more drastic approach was needed. Apostolis arranged for two armed guerillas to pay a visit to Fokas at his home late at night.

Apparently, they were able to convince him that if he would betray us to the Germans his days were numbered, and there was no place he could hide. The resistance would find him and shoot him like a dog. Apparently, he was scared enough because the next day we were released without explanation.

The absence of any real military presence on the Islands encouraged further acts of sabotage by the resistance. In retaliation for the hostilities, the Germans intensified their dragnet. German gunboats blockaded the entire complex of the northern Sprorades islands.

Many of these gunboats were confiscated Greek fishing trawlers outfitted with weapons. It was extremely difficult and dangerous to attempt sailing in or out of this area. The Germans maintained an iron grip stopping and searching every vessel large or small.

Food shortages became acute especially in the categories of meat and grain products. The German patrols systematically looted the fishing boats of their cargo. Thus, the islands were robbed of their most vital food, fish. Occasionally a boat with supplies would get through the German blockade, usually by bribery.

When that happened the local residents would trade 10 kilos of olive oil for one kilo of potatoes or wheat!

The principal person responsible for orchestrating and implementing the blockade that was starving the Islands was a high-ranking German Naval officer by the name of Adler. The inhabitants of the islands better knew Adler by the nickname "Milliouni". He acquired this nickname because his patrol boats would often request and exact a ransom of one million drachmas to allow a fishing boat to get through.

Adler's headquarters were in the neighboring island of Skopellos. He had the reputation of being a ruthless and sadistic individual. He was a loyal member of the nazi party and a personal friend of Adolph Hitler. The underground leadership received a request from the British Command in the Middle East to capture Adler alive and to turn him unharmed over to the British.

Apparently, the Germans had captured a British General and they were planning to negotiate a trade, giving them Adler back in exchange for their man. The underground took up the challenge and started to plan the capture of "Milliouni". First, they planted a member of the underground as the engineer in Milliouni's gunboat. Then they arranged a meeting between Milliouni and a beautiful divorcee who lived in Skiathos and instructed her to become friendly with Milliouni.

As predicted Milliouni fell for her. After a number of rendezvous' in Skopelos, she invited him to visit her at her home in Skiathos. This was part of the underground's orchestration for the capture of Milliouni. At the designated date Adler's gunboat arrived in Skiathos and docked at the south end of the wharf, exactly opposite the vegetable store of Marika, the fat lady of Skiathos. Marika weighed about 400 lbs and was one of the local landmarks and curiosities.

Despite her enormous bulk, she was able to move quickly when she had to and had a sharp eye for details. Nothing that was going on the dock ever escaped Marika's attention. The resistance had recruited her to keep watch and notify them as soon as Adler's boat would arrive.

She was also ordered to observe and report the number of German sailors, their disposition, and the type of military weapons they had on board. Mihalis, the Greek engineer, was instructed to wait until Adler had disembarked and was on his way to visit his girlfriend and then create a diversion that would keep the sailors on board occupied and distracted at the time that the resistance units were planning to attack and capture the vessel.

On the day in question, Marika signaled the arrival of Adler's boat. She reported the crew consisted of six German sailors and Mihalis. One of the crew was on sentry duty manning the large machine gun. Two of them were busy mopping the deck and polishing the brass fittings. One was busy polishing his shoes and the remaining two were armed with submachine guns and were moving back and forth from one end of the deck to the other.

Adler came out of his cabin dressed to kill with his white summer dress uniform that consisted of white shoes, white socks that came just below the knee, short white pants and an ornate silver belt. Hanging from the right side of the belt there was a small dress sword. His chest was covered with numerous multicolored ribbons and decorations. Hanging from his neck with a light blue satin ribbon was the equivalent of the German Navy cross.

On the left side of his waist there was a leather holster containing a Luger pistol. He wore the traditional white navy captain's hat with the gold braid and on the shoulders of his short sleeve shirt were the navy and gold stripes indicating his rank. One must admit that Adler presented a very dashing figure indeed.

As he stepped out of his cabin, the sailors on deck came to a rigid attention. Adler turned around, gave a military salute to the flag on the mast, and disembarked. He walked slowly and unsuspecting through the narrow back streets heading for his girlfriend's home. The home had been under surveillance for several hours.

As soon as Adler arrived and went inside, the resistance units took their positions and surrounded the house with armed soldiers. At the appropriate moment, they sent word to the units on the wharf that they were in position. This was the signal to attack and capture the gunboat. Mihalis partially disassembled the engine and yelled out to the sailors on the deck to come down and have a look because there was something wrong with the engine.

The two roving sailors descended to the engine room leaving on deck only a sentry on the machine gun, the cleaning crew, and the sailor that was polishing his shoes. On a signal from Marika two resistance units came barreling down the side streets and opened fire killing the sentry.

The other three sailors surrendered at once. The armed guards in the engine room heard the shots and immediately suspected Mihalis' complicity. One of them lifted a heavy wrench and attempted to smash Mihalis' head. At that precise moment a resistance fighter, who was coming down the stairs to the engine room, saw what was happening and emptied a whole clip of ammunition, completely severing the German's arm. The other sailor threw his weapon on the floor and raised his hands in surrender.

In the meantime, Adler heard the shots inside his girlfriend's house and probably guessed what was happening. Using the same megaphone that we used to announce the news, I was ordered to inform Adler that the house was surrounded and that there was no chance for escape and to ask him to come out with his hands up. Following this warning Adler upholstered his Luger put it to his girlfriend's head, and told her:

"Find me a way out of here or I will blow your brains out."

The only part of the house that was not guarded by resistance units was the hill directly behind the back yard. The reason for that was that the hill was so steep that it was considered impossible for anyone to climb without assistance or special equipment.

Nevertheless Adler, to everyone's surprise and amazement, was able to climb it and thus temporarily escape the dragnet around the house. The girlfriend alerted the troops outside that Adler had escaped and they immediately started to give chase. I will never forget that scene.

Adler ahead running frantically towards the dock, the armed resistance units running behind him, and behind them, almost the entire village, armed with sticks and agricultural tools also running in a wild frenzy shouting "Death to Milliouni".

Adler's big mistake was that he thought his boat was still in the harbor. That is why he was running towards the wharf. When he got there, he realized that the boat was already captured but instead of surrendering, he jumped in the water and started swimming away towards the open sea.

It was of course a futile effort, since there is no way you could escape from an island, no matter which direction you swam. When the resistance units reached the dock, Adler had swum a fair distance from the shore. With his luger still in his hands, he began firing towards the dock injuring two of the resistance fighters.

There was a great temptation to take him out, however the orders were to capture him alive. Using machine gun fire, the resistance fighters began to fire in a tight circle around Adler's position in the water. At that point, he stopped swimming because had he continued he would swim right into the path of the machine gun fire.

A group of resistance fighters boarded a small boat with an outboard motor and headed towards Adler's location in the water. When they reached him one of the men raised his rifle butt and tried to hit Adler in the head. He missed and hit the side of the boat breaking the rifle in two which was just as well for if the blow would have reached its target it would have probably cracked his skull and killed him invalidating the whole operation.

They fished Adler out of the water, tied his hands behind his back, and brought him to the dock where an angry mob of men, women and children wanted to lynch him and make him pay for the months and months of starvation and misery that he was responsible of inflicting on the Islands through his naval blockade.

He was obviously frightened by this scene and began to shout

"Ich nicht Milliouni" which means,

"I am not Milliouni".

He was thinking that he could fool the people in believing that they had the wrong man. In fact, no one had any doubt of who he was and if it were not for the orders to deliver him to the British in one piece, he would have died an ugly death in the hands of the frenzied mob.

As it was, two rows of armed resistance fighters, one on each side, protected him from attack. The people had to be satisfied with spitting on him and shouting obscenities.

Within a few hours, under heavy guard, Adler was transported across the Island to the side facing the Pylion. From there he was moved by boat across the narrow straights to the seaside village of St. Johns. The captured gunboat was already there and in the hands of the resistance. A special resistance unit escorted him to a secret rendezvous and turned him over to the British commandoes.

The operation was thus successfully completed. The many months of planning had finally paid off. The big question now was what would be the German reaction to Adler's capture. There was no doubt in any one's mind that there would be repercussions. The only question was what kind and how severe.

We did not have to wait very long to get the answer. The next day the Germans arrested the Mayors of the three towns, Skiathos, Skopelos, and Glossa and sent them, on a German vessel, to the Pylion to meet with the resistance leaders and negotiate the immediate release and return of Adler. They threatened terrible reprisals if their demand was not met.

The resistance answered by seizing the boat and taking the crew prisoners. Two days later, when it became evident that their attempted diplomatic mission had failed, we heard the characteristic noise of the diesel engines as three German patrol boats headed for Skiathos.

Vassilis Natsos and I were ordered to meet the Germans as they disembarked on the pier and find out what their demands were. In retrospect, I now realize that this was a suicide mission that only a totally insane person would undertake. It was very probable that the Germans would shoot us on sight rather than speak to us.

However, at the time, the orders made perfect sense, and with the stupid courage of the young, we went down to the wharf and waited for the arrival of the German gunboats. As soon as they were tied down a young naval officer jumped down from the boat onto the dock came over to us and said:

"It is no use to try to lie to me. I know that our commander was captured on your Island by the resistance forces two days ago. Before leaving Skopelos, he filled the customary travel plan indicating his planned itinerary that included the point of departure, the route, the destination, and the time and date of his return.

The fact that he never came back to base tells us that both he and his boat were captured on your Island. Under any other set of circumstances, he would have sent us a radiogram. The boat with the Mayors also disappeared, which confirms our suspicions. We are here to deliver a final ultimatum. If our commander is not released and returned unharmed in three days, we will come back and burn your Island to the ground. We will also burn Skopelos and Glossa. "

At the point Natsos said to the German

"Do you have matches?"

I was petrified with fear. I told Natsos in Greek,

"Shut up you fool. Are you trying to get us both killed? These are murderers. They have no sense of humor."

The German said angrily to Natsos,

"What did you say?"

Fortunately Natsos was able to back peddle quickly and said,

"I asked you if you had any matches because I want to smoke a cigarette."

The officer handed him a book of matches and told us to deliver his message and to see if we could gather the people at the church square so that he can warn them personally of the dangers of not meeting the German demands. We took off and immediately started to spread the word to anyone we met to flee as fast as possible or else run the risk of being shot.

We had heard of another instance where the Germans gathered the entire population of a Greek village at the square stating that they wanted to talk to them, and after they were gathered, they opened machine gun fire and killed them all.

After a while the gunboats left but there was no doubt in anyone's mind that they would return and carry out their threat. This event triggered a massive exodus from the main village to the olive groves up in the hills. Every able man, woman and child quickly packed some items of necessity and the family heirlooms, loaded them on horses or mules and headed for the huts in the olive groves that were normally used as temporary residences during the olive harvest.

Since we did not own an olive grove or a hut, we arranged with some neighbors to set up a tent on their property. So we gathered our meager belongings, abandoned our house again, such as it were, and headed for the hills along with most of the inhabitants of Skiathos. The only people that stayed behind were those that were too old or too sick to move and a few hard heads that stubbornly refused to believe that this was a real threat.

It was ironic that the old tent that was part of my father's World War I memorabilia, the same tent that my mother had asked him so many times to get rid of, along with his other "Junk", was now our home.

The next day, in the predawn hours, we heard the ominous thuds of the diesel engines that signaled the impending arrival of the German patrol boats. From the vantage point of the high hills, we were able to use our binoculars and get a good view of the forces of destruction. At least half a dozen boats arrived loaded with Germans and Greek traitors in nazi uniforms, the infamous "Security Regiments" from Volos.

The initial phase involved extensive looting of the homes and businesses. From our hiding place, we could hear the shots that could only mean one thing, the Germans and their murderous Greek thugs were killing anyone they met during the looting who had the misfortune of remaining in the town.

After several hours, there were loud explosions from dynamite and grenades. Finally they boarded their vessels, moved back a few yards, and opened fire with their deck guns, mortars and machine guns leveling all the homes and stores that faced the water. Huge flames and black smoke rose up to the sky and were visible for miles.

Apparently, the Germans were making good on their promise to destroy the Island. Finally, the boats left and an eerie quiet settled over Skiathos. Fortunately, the Germans did not venture any further out than the main town. Perhaps they were afraid that they might encounter heavy resistance in the hills and thought it wiser to leave right after they finished their dirty work.

If they had gone further up the mountain, the death toll would have been much higher since there were no armed resistance units in the hills for some time, and the scared mass of civilians that had escaped would have been no match for the German troops.

After it became evident that the Germans were gone for good and were not returning, we began gradually to make our way back into the town. The images of death and destruction were truly devastating and have remained indelibly imprinted in my mind forever. Every living thing that had remained behind in town was dead, not only humans but animals as well.

The streets were littered with corpses and carcasses of dead dogs, cats, goats, horses, mules, and donkeys. Their decaying bodies lying in a pool of blood, bayoneted to death covered with swarms of flies. Many homes were still smoldering and others were completely burned. The streets were covered with broken glass and hundreds of personal articles that the looters had not deemed worthy of stealing and simply tossed them out of the windows.

Frederic Kakis

Broken furniture was scattered all over and everything from mattresses to tables were floating in the bay. Blackened ruins had replaced the beautiful sight of the picturesque white and blue homes along the waterfront that one normally encountered when entering the port of Skiathos. It was an ugly and grotesque picture like the smile of a beautiful woman that had most of her front teeth knocked out.

Following the return, we took up the sad task of burying the dead and cleaning up the mess. The whole island was united by the adversity and it was heartwarming to see neighbors of reaching out and helping one another in the common effort to rebuild their homes and their lives. The news soon reached us that Skopelos and Glossa had suffered a similar fate to Skiathos.

Fokas left the island with his masters and we were finally free from any type of foreign occupation. However, the war was still going on and the Germans were still not too far away. The blockade continued and the famine intensified, but there were many signs pointing to the conclusion that the end of the war was near.

The Russian counter - offensive was in full bloom inflicting many casualties and destroying the German military machinery. The Germans were on the retreat and were decimated by the bitter winter and their inability to supply their soldiers with food and ammunition. The occupied Soviet territory had nothing of use because the Russians, at the time that the Germans were advancing, burned their villages to the ground rather than surrender them to the enemy.

The surrender of the Axis powers in North Africa was also a devastating blow to the Nazi war effort. The era of Italian predominance in the occupation of certain areas of Greece was also coming to an end. After the Allies landed in Sicily, Hitler was convinced that the big Allied invasion would be in Greece. He ordered the build-up of massive reinforcements and sent Rommel to Salonica to make one last desperate stand.

CHAPTER 18

Talliarina

Towards the end of the occupation the local resistance units were concentrating into a new phase: Saving and transporting Allied soldiers. With the capitulation of Italy, many allied prisoners of war previously held by the Italians were turned loose. Others managed to escape on their own. Most of them were from Australia and New Zealand.

Both groups were in danger of being recognized and recaptured. The risk was great because they could not speak Greek and had no papers, money, or appropriate clothes. Because of this, they could only roam around for a little while before running into some one who would recognize them and turn them in.

The orders from the resistance command were to find the escapees, supply them with food and shelter and hide them until such time as they could be provided with false papers and transport by boat to Asia Minor. From there, they would find their way back to the Middle East and rejoin their units.

The main routes of transportation for the escaped allied soldiers involved both land and sea segments. To fully understand the plan one must inspect the map of Greece. Such an inspection would reveal that the town of Volos is almost equidistant from Salonica and Athens, the two main centers where the Germans, and the Italians had respectively established prison camps.

Thus, the first stage of this operation involved the safe conduct of the escaped prisoners of war from the two centers just mentioned to Volos. The second step involved transporting them by boat to Skiathos where they were to assume the identity of Greek fishermen and be provided with appropriate clothes and forged documents.

The third step involved the transfer by sea to the island of Skyros where the local resistance would hide the prisoners, and wait for the opportune time to transport them past the German blockade to the Island of Lesvos were the local resistance would take charge, and provide them with safe contact to the town of Mitilini which is located just a few miles from the Turkish border.

The logistics of carrying out such an operation were horrendous and full of risks. Finding the soldiers before the Germans did was by itself a big challenge. Getting their trust was another challenge. Finding families that were willing to risk their lives to hide the escaped prisoners was also very difficult and so was the task of transporting them at night past the German patrol boats undetected.

Both the Nazis and the Turks heavily guarded the straights between Greece and Turkey. There were also minefields, treacherous rocks, and other natural obstacles. To navigate safely through all these in the darkness and without special equipment and remain undetected required uncommon nautical skills and a lot of luck.

The land route was no less dangerous. All means of transportation were regularly scrutinized with checkpoints in all the major routes. In addition to the military, Gestapo agents were also roaming around, asking questions, and inspecting the credentials of travelers in all the railroad and bus stations. Finally, there were also the Greek traitors who were the hardest to fool and thus the most dangerous.

The resistance leaders responsible for these operations had to be very smart and very inventive in order to be able to successfully implement their mission. In one case, they were able to get the escapees past the German checkpoint by faking a funeral procession and placing the Allied soldiers in the coffin. In other instances, they dressed them as women or as shepherds crossing the checkpoints with an entire flock of sheep.

For security reasons no one in the underground knew the entire route. In this way if they were captured and tortured they could not reveal anything beyond their own limited involvement in the escape plan. For those of us in Skiathos we only knew that we were to provide the escapees with false documents and provide them with safe conduct to Skyros.

We did not know where they came from or where they were going next. Getting the permits and the false identity papers turned out to be the easier of the two parts of our assignment. The transportation to Skyros was the hardest because of the multitude of German gunboats patrolling these waters.

Since most of the fishing is done at night, it was not unusual to see fishing boats in the area after darkness. However, if a boat were unfortunate enough to be spotted by a German patrol boat they would be boarded and questioned. Under these conditions, both the appearance of the crew and their papers must be convincing enough to pass inspection.

Obviously, this was no job for amateurs. The resistance selected the most experienced sailors for these missions, people who were actually professional fishermen and had spent most of their lives at sea. From the calluses on their hands to the weather beaten faces they were unmistakably seamen and thus not likely to arouse suspicion.

The problem came in providing a suitable disguise for the allied soldiers most of whom were blond with blue eyes and fair skin. For this reason they were kept below and out of sight, even though they had the proper documents. During one of these operations, a German patrol boat near the Island of

Skyros spotted the fishing boat that was transporting two Australian soldiers.

As the patrol boat began to speed towards them the Captain told the crew to fill their pockets with grenades and be ready for action. One of the crewmembers was ordered to climb the mast and pretend that he was fixing the sails. He was armed with a submachine gun. The captain had his hand in his pea coat and was clutching an automatic pistol.

The Australians were below the deck and were advised of the situation. The captain's intention was to bluff his way. As the patrol boat got closer, a young German naval officer with a megaphone in his hand ordered the captain to stop his engine and get ready to receive a boarding party. The Captain kept shouting "Den Xero Yermanica" i.e. "I don't understand German".

The officer finally repeated his command in broken Greek and the Captain complied with the order while at the same time he told his men to be ready to open fire at his command. The German boat came along side and the officer, along with two armed sailors, jumped on board the Greek boat. He was holding a German luger pistol in his hand, which he pointed towards the Captain and demanded to see the boats papers and permits.

The Captain reached in his pocket with his right hand and handed him the papers. The other two-crew members were squatting on the deck in front of a pile of fishing nets pretending to be mending and repairing the nets while being closely watched by the two German guards.

They had not yet spotted the third crewman that had climbed the mast. He was shielded from plain view by the sails and the night darkness. The officer finished the inspection of the papers and was apparently satisfied, however, he still kept his pistol pointed at the captain and asked him in his broken

Greek what he was doing fishing so far away from his base i.e. Skiathos.

The Captain replied that they did not catch any fish there and thus decided to try their luck a bit further away. The German then asked,

"What is below?"

The Captain replied, "Just sleeping bunks and fishing equipment".

The German then said "Stand aside, I want to have a look."

As he started to go down the wooden ladder, all hell broke loose. The Captain shot him in the head at the same time the sailor from the mast started spraying the deck with machine gun fire taking out the two German sailors while the other two crew members began to throw grenades in rapid succession into the adjacent patrol boat.

Within seconds there was an enormous explosion and the patrol boat disintegrated and started to sink. In no time at all the sea had swallowed the patrol boat and the firing stopped. The Captain ordered the crew to throw the dead bodies overboard and clean up the mess.

He then continued on his course towards Skyros. They were not always that lucky. There were several reports of missions that failed because the resistance crews that were manning these boats had been captured or killed by the Germans.

The master organizer of the entire escape operation in Skiathos was a young resistance woman known to everyone by her pseudonym "Taliarina". Taliarina had single-handedly organized and managed the entire network; She found safe houses, planned the escape routes, and recruited Greek fishing boats willing to transport the escapes.

Not only did she supervise the entire operation but also frequently went on the missions herself. The Germans were frustrated and angry by Taliarina's successful rescue of the former POW's. They put a high price on her head and publicized it widely. Apparently, someone finally betrayed her.

She was captured in Skiathos while eating in a local taverna and was sent to DACHAU, the infamous concentration camp. Taliarina somehow survived the camp and after the liberation came back to Skiathos only to find that the right wing Greek government that was in power at the time regarded her as a Communist and gave her no recognition for her wartime efforts. However, the Governments of Australia and New Zealand sent a special delegation to Greece and presented Taliarina with the highest medal these countries award to civilians.

This exceptionally heroic figure of World War II died in poverty and in obscurity without ever receiving the praise from her countryman she so richly deserved. Taliarina was credited for saving the lives of over three thousand allied soldiers. Those of us who witnessed her heroic deeds will honor her memory forever.

With the virtual absence of any occupation forces in Skiathos life began to settle into a routine. In the absence of any tangible enemy presence all local operations were greatly curtailed. Some of the older and more experienced partisans left the Island and went to Pylion to join the fighting ELAS units.

What was left in Skiathos was a nucleus of older men who were members of EAM that provided guidance and direction to the rest of us and served as the link with the higher levels of the resistance echelon. They also continued to conduct the weekly indoctrination meetings where we were taught the Communist party line. The youth organization, EPON, was suddenly left with very little to do in terms of resistance activities.

I still continued to transmit the news about the war with my cardboard "megaphone" and report on the advances of the

Allied troops as soon as we heard about them from the BBC news bulletins. The landings in Sicily, the Allied invasion in Normandy and the defeat of the Germans in Stalingrad were received with great rejoicing and renewed hope that the terrible war was rapidly coming to an end and that liberation was very near.

Because my voice was changing I was eventually replaced as the main announcer by girl operatives. The leadership had decided that girls' voices carry further and would be more audible. Thus I found myself with very little to do and so did my brother Albert.

Looking for things to eat became central to our existence as shortages of food intensified due to the tighter grip exerted by the German patrol boats on vessels attempting to break their blockade and bring supplies to the Island. Daytime fishing inside the harbor produced a modicum of small fish. We also became adept in spearing small octopi among the rocks and digging up mussels and sea urchins.

We found out that if you carefully turn the sea urchins upside down you can scoop out a small amount of an edible, orange colored, substance. Other sources of food included "prickly pears" that grew on the cacti around the "Bourzy", figs from the trees surrounding the local Olive groves and wild fruit and berries that were found growing in abundance up the hills of both sides of the mountain paths. One of the wild plants found in the hills produced a fruit called "Coumaro". It was a yellow/orange spherical shaped berry the size of a small apricot. Coumara had a very sweet taste, which meant that they contained a significant amount of sugar.

Albert, who had a very sharp scientific mind and superior intelligence, formulated a plan of action and submitted it to the resistance leadership for approval. It was a very simple plan: Set up a still and get Ethyl Alcohol from the distillation of "Coumara". The alcohol produced can help the resistance

169

efforts by using it as a fuel and as incendiary device for sabotage purposes. His plan was approved.

As soon as he got the green light the whole EPON organization got behind the project with the zeal and enthusiasm of youth and in no time at all a large still was constructed from available large copper Kettles and pipes crudely put together but functioning sufficiently well to distill large amounts of coumara into alcohol.

Teams of volunteers would comb the countryside with baskets and bring their load to a central point where they were loaded on donkeys and transported to the still. Not all the alcohol produced was used for the war effort; for we soon discovered that it made a pretty good tasting beverage. As a result some unforgettable parties and celebrations took place where for a little while we forgot the horrors of war and were singing and dancing till all hours of the morning.

I now find it amazing that in the mist of starvation and death people still found time to laugh and to have a good time. I think that this is a testimonial to the resilience of human beings and their capacity to overcome unbelievable odds and suffering.

The success of the project with the still led to other activities that kept the local EPON members busy and helped the fight against the enemy. A coalition of young resistance fighters and older scientifically trained members of the EAM was formed for the purpose of a coordinated effort to produce weapons, explosives and other materials useful in the fight against the Germans.

Among the elder advisors and leaders were the local doctor, a pharmacist, and some chemistry and physics teachers from the local Schools that ceased to operate because of the war. Albert with his natural inclination and interest in science became heavily involved in this effort.

Among the products that this group came up with were explosives, crude timing devices and detonators and a variety of makeshift weapons. Pipes were converted into crude rifles capable of firing a single bullet. "Grenades" were constructed from metal cans containing bolts, screws and nails. When exploded they did enough damage to cause severe injuries to a sentry or other enemy soldier and take them out of action.

Every piece of scrap metal was used and fashioned into some type of weapon or explosive device. Some of these were truly ingenious: for example a pair of saltshakers that will explode the minute you inverted them. Another device consisted of two incompatible chemicals kept apart by glass that would shatter when thrown. Upon contact the chemicals produced copious amount of a lachrymator thus functioning as a tear gas Grenade.

A more deadly device was a container separated in two chambers by a metal divider. One of the chambers was filled with a cyanide solution and the other with acid. As long as the cyanide solution was on top nothing would happen, however, upon inversion, depending on the thickness of the partition and the strength of the acid eventually the metal would be eaten up allowing the chemicals to mix. At that time deadly cyanide gas would be released killing all those in the immediate vicinity.

I don't know how effective these devices were in actual combat or even if they were ever used. What I know is that it provided my young comrades and me with a constructive channel for our energy and gave us a sense of purpose during a period when it would be easy to become demoralized and discouraged.

From all the available information it was clear that the fate of the war had turned and that a victory for the Allies was inevitable. It would be now a matter of time before we were liberated. The trick was to stay alive until that happened.

CHAPTER 19

Zack's Return

After the killing of the German patrol in Athens, Zack became too hot to remain in the City. The German police and the Gestapo had launched an intense investigation for the capture of those involved. It was only a matter of time before someone would talk. This would be disastrous not only for Zack but also the underground organization as a whole.

Zack's orders were to report as soon as possible to the ELLAS units that were fighting in the mountains. More specifically, he was ordered to go to the Pylion and join the 27th ELLAS Division. The 27th was one of the more famous fighting units in the underground because of its many victorious engagements with the enemy.

To accomplish this he had to return to Skiathos. As simple as that may seem on the surface, it was fraught with danger. Getting back to Skiathos required a whole new set of fake documents, securing the necessary travel permits from both the German and the Italian authorities, finding transportation and successfully going through several checkpoints and controls along the route.

Zack decided to seek the help of Tassos, a former high school friend from Drama, who was the secretary of the Greek Maritime Union. Tassos was able to provide Zack with papers showing that he was a sailor in the Greek Merchant Marine and a member of the Union. His passbook would show that he was a native of Skiathos who became stranded in Athens after the freighter that he was sailing with came to the port of Piraeus for repairs.

Actually there were several vessels in the Piraeus shipyards that were, in fact, trapped in Greece by the advent of the war and the subsequent German invasion. That made this scenario plausible, at least on the surface.

To complete the deception Zack bought a used navy pea coat and a Greek sailor's cap at thrift store and let his beard grow. He put on an old pair of pants, a white heavy wool turtle neck sweater and some old shoes. When he finished dressing, he really looked like a bum or, better yet, a sailor down on his luck

The disguise was good enough to fool anyone. He tested it on Tassos who at first failed to recognize him. Zack then decided to tackle the hardest job first, i.e. getting a travel permit from the Germans. He knew that if he succeeded and fooled the Germans, the Italian authorities would be a piece of cake since it would be unlikely for them to deny a travel permit to someone that had already been granted a similar permit by the Germans. After a few days of fearful hesitation and many rehearsals with Tassos, he decided to chance it and go get the permit.

The headquarters of the German Police were in a dark gray building on Constitution Square. A huge wooden "V" was suspended from the balcony on the second floor, a symbol the Germans adopted from the British to signify VICTORY. Also draped over the balcony was a large red and white German flag with a black swastika in the middle.

Two armed guards flanked the main entrance to the building. The guards came to attention and presented arms each time a German officer went in and out of the building or even when a staff car with officers drove by. As Zack came closer to the building, he became increasingly apprehensive.

His youthful daring that has gotten him out of several scrapes in the past somehow did not seem to adequately prepare him for such an ordeal. For the first time in his life, he tasted fear. Stories of German brutality were already quite widespread. The beatings and tortures of captives in German hands were a familiar scene of the occupation.

Many of these beatings took place inside the very building he was about to enter. As he approached the entrance, he turned back twice. Finally, he decided that he had no choice and went inside. As he entered, two German soldiers grabbed him immediately and frisked him for weapons. Having found none, they escorted him to a small office.

An SS sergeant in black uniform was seated behind the desk. He had an armband with the swastika on his left arm and a dueling scar on right cheek. His hair was very light blond, almost like an albino and he wore thin gold rim eyeglasses that hung from the tip of his nose. The silver buckle on his belt had the inscription "GOTT MIT UNS". This translates "God is with us".

A huge black leather pistol holster hung from his belt. He let Zack stand in front of the desk for several minutes before acknowledging his presence pretending that he was looking closely at a document that he was holding. He finally looked up and said in broken Greek

"Why are you here?" Zack immediately replied in German

"I am here to apply for a travel permit, herr unterofficier."

"So you speak German, very interesting. Where did you learn our language? Are you a spy?"

Zack replied "No, sir. I am just a poor seaman who is trying to get home. I have learned German from my mother who was an opera singer."

"Your application states that you are from the Island of Skiathos. Why didn't you try to go home before?"

Zack said, "At first I was trying to get a job locally but I was unsuccessful. No one wants to hire a broken down seaman with no experience and then I got very sick with malaria and almost died."

"How long were you at sea?"

"A little over three years", Zack replied.

"So you were never in the army?"

"No, sir. People in the merchant marines are exempt from military service."

Then all of a sudden the German said:

"Let me see your hands".

A cold shiver went up and down Zack's spine. This was a request he did not anticipate and he was not prepared for. He stuck out his hands and the German got up, walked around the desk, and examined Zack's hands. He then slapped him hard across the face and said,

"You are a liar. These are not the hands of a seaman. You don't even have a single callous." Zack with tears streaming down his cheek said,

"I was not a deck hand. I was a radio operator."

"Is that so?" said the German,

"Then you wouldn't mind tapping something for me in Morse code?"

Zack's heart sank. There was no way out. He knew nothing about the Morse code. The only thing he could do was to carry out the bluff to the end.

"I'll be happy to", he replied and started to tap on the wooden desktop with a metal key.

"I am sending out a distress signal," he said.

"Did you understand it?"

The German who fortunately had also no clue about the Morse code said angrily

"Of course I did. What you think I am, an idiot?"

"No, sir" Zack said

"I think you are a very clever fellow to put me through the test."

"Do I get my travel permit now?"

"Let me have the documents." The sergeant said.

Zack handed him the papers. He took out an official stamp from the desk drawer, stamped and dated the permit and handed it back to Zack.

"Thank you, sir. May I go now?"

"Yes, yes, get out of here."

"Heil Hitler" said Zack and walked out.

He had to exercise all the self-control he could muster not to start running. Instead, he walked slowly down the flight of stairs and exited the building. As he turned the corner, he began shaking like a leaf once the realization hit him of how close he had come to being discovered and killed. Suddenly the war was no longer the big adventure he contemplated as a young man.

It was instead a real life and death struggle, a game of matching wits in order to survive another day.

The next step was to get the permit from the Italian authorities. Zack decided to postpone this until he had taken care to change the appearance of his hands. He was sure that the wireless operator story was not likely to work a second time. For a whole week he was digging holes in the garden with a pick ax until the palms of his hands were raw with blisters.

In a few more days his hands would no longer give him away. When he felt ready, he walked over to the Italian "Carabigneri" office. It was totally unguarded. He entered into an area that looked more like the waiting room of a medical office than a military police headquarters.

They were several Italian soldiers in uniform behind a counter. The place was full of people everyone talking loudly and gesticulating at the same time. There were piles of papers everywhere. The place was an unbelievable mess.

There was a sharp contrast between this office and the icy cold and antiseptic German Headquarters. Zack elbowed and pushed himself to the head of the line and gave his permit application to the soldier behind the counter. After the experience with the Germans, he was fully prepared for tough questioning.

To his surprise, the Italian asked him no questions. He took his papers, stamped them, and handed them back without as much as giving him a single look. Zack walked out greatly relived but also strangely deflated, feeling a little like a prizefighter that trained long and hard only to have the fight cancelled.

Well, the hardest part was done. He could now relax and plan the return trip. He decided to do it in stages. First, he would try to get from Athens to Halkida. From there, he would cut across Evia to the eastern shores and try to catch a boat to Skiathos.

He boarded a bus from Kifissia, a suburb of Athens, early in the morning and started his journey.

The bus was full of Greek peasants returning to their villages after selling their wares in the big City. Men, women, children, and some small animals were all packed into this tiny bus. The stench emanating from the close proximity of the many sweaty and dirty bodies and the livestock was unbearable.

Furthermore, the oppressive heat and lack of ventilation made breathing difficult. There were no seats left and Zack had to travel standing up until they finally got out of the City and some of the passengers disembarked. The bus was propelled by a coal gasification engine at the maddening slow speed of 5 to 10 miles per hour.

All of a sudden the driver saw some commotion up ahead and stopped the bus. German military policemen in motorcycles with sidecars were directing traffic. They held red colored paddles that looked like ping-pong rackets with long handles and were stopping all civilian traffic to allow a German military convoy to go through.

After all the armored cars and trucks carrying soldiers went by, they started to move again. The military policemen in their motorcycles were running back and forth along the road like sheepdogs gathering and protecting the flock. They wore helmets and goggles, had submachine guns strapped across their chest and large silver half moon shaped plates hanging from a chain around their neck with the words "military police" engraved on them.

Shortly after the military column began to move, there was a loud explosion a short distance away that shook the bus. Flames and smoke shot up into the sky and were visible for miles. The sounds of machine gun fire followed and all pandemonium broke loose.

Apparently, the underground staged an attack on the German column whose lead vehicle went over a planted land mine and blew up. The civilians that were caught on the road came out of their vehicles and were scattering in every direction. Shouts were heard in the crowd," run, run, the Germans are taking hostages".

Zack grabbed his sack and started running towards the cover of the wheat fields as fast as his feet would take him. He ran non-stop for several miles not daring to rest even long after all the sounds of shooting had stopped. Finally, he was exhausted and fell down on the ground in the middle of a field protected from view by the tall growing plants.

He lay there motionless listening for any sounds of pursuers. Not hearing anything, he felt reassured. Apparently, the Germans had either captured their quota of civilian hostages or were searching in a different direction. To be safe Zack decided not to make his move until darkness.

He was hungry, thirsty, hot, and exhausted. He took off his shoes and shirt and decided to try and take a short nap to regain his strength. He closed his eyes and he was quickly asleep. The sound of barking dogs woke him up with a start.

He looked up and saw the rising sun. Apparently, he was so tired that he had slept through the night until the next morning. He cautiously stood up and looked around. He saw a flock of sheep in the distance being chased by a couple of large dogs. As they got closer, the dogs left the flock and started to run towards him.

He remembered what he was told during the resistance training sessions, "If you are being chased by sheep dogs DON'T RUN. Sit on the ground and wait." Apparently being down to the level of the dogs frightens and confuses them so they will not attack you.

On the other hand, if you panic and start to run they will catch up to you and tear you to pieces. There is no way that anyone can outrun these dogs. Zack sat on the ground. The dogs came within a few feet and stopped.

They were menacing him by circling around and growling with their terrifying sharp teeth. It was an ominous situation. Fortunately within minutes the Shepherd arrived on the scene. Zack shouted to him,

"Will you please call off these damned dogs?" The Shepherd, an old man with a white beard, complied and Zack stood up.

"Thank you. I thought for a minute that I was a goner." Zack brushed himself off. "You may be wondering what I am doing here. I ran away from the Germans yesterday when I heard they were taking hostages."

"Yes, I saw the explosion and I heard the gunshots. You must come with me to the village. You will be safe there."

"Do you have anything to eat? I have not had any food for nearly two days," said Zack.

"I have some bread and some goat cheese. You are welcome to it, my son," said the old man.

Zack gorged himself on cheese and bread and washed it down with several tin cups of sheep's milk. He thought that this was one of the best meals he had ever eaten.

They started slowly up the side of the mountain allowing the sheep to graze along the way. After several hours, they reached the village and drove the sheep into the coral. By the time they were through with all the chores, it was already dark.

The old Shepherd took Zack to his home where his wife and several children were seated in front of a large fire. They immediately got up to make room for the guest. The Greeks have a tradition of being hospitable to strangers that goes back hundreds of years, since the ancient times. They do not ask the stranger any questions.

They simply extend their hospitality. Zack was served a delicious meal consisting of lamb stew and lentil soup which they washed down with several glasses of "Retsina", a white local wine that is aged in pine barrels. As a result the wine has a distinct resin flavor, hence the name retsina.

To a foreigner the wine tastes awful. It is like drinking alcoholic turpentine but the natives have acquired a taste for it and they love it. After supper, they made a bed for Zack in the loft while the rest slept on the floor below. The bed had clean sheets and blankets, probably the only set the family possessed. The loft extended into a balcony that had no doors.

As Zack was lying down on the bed he could see the night sky filled with millions of bright stars. It was a majestic sight. Feeling warm and safe, and still tired from his recent ordeal he fell asleep quickly and slept uninterruptedly until morning.

The sound of roosters crowing woke him up. He went out in the yard and washed himself with cold water pumped from the well with an iron hand pump. After he finished, he went inside. Everyone was already up and tending to his chores.

The Shepherd handed him a cup of mountain grown tea and a plate with two slices of freshly baked brown bread still hot from the oven. The bread slices were covered with butter and honey. This simple breakfast was common through the entire region.

After they ate, his host explained to Zack that the only safe way to get to his destination was to go from village to village.

He could always find a mule or a donkey to ride or transportation on one of the wagons the peasants used to carry their farm equipment and supplies.

And so it was, that Zack began his slow journey to Halkida. Sometimes riding and sometimes walking from one village to the next until his feet would no longer carry him. Based on his meager resources he should have never made it. However at every turn there were peasants that took a liking to a young man wanted by the Germans and were willing to extend their hospitality, give him shelter and share with him whatever food they had. The kindness of these simple people was truly overwhelming.

After arriving in Halkida, Zack opted to depart for the east coast of Evia as soon as possible. Halkida was a fair size town and as such more dangerous than the tiny villages in between. It was best to keep moving if he was to avoid capture. The next morning he hitched a ride on a truck that was leaving Halkida with a load of produce.

They were stopped twice along the way but his papers passed the scrutiny of the police and there was no incident. The truck left him a few kilometers from the seaport village of "Agios Apostolis" i.e. "Saint Apostolis". From there, he had to walk the rest of the way, which took several hours.

He entered the village, as it was getting dark. Not knowing where to go he headed for the local "Taverna" hoping to get some leads on boats going to Skiathos. The taverna was noisy and so full of smoke that you could hardly see. The men were smoking and drinking heavily. Their glasses were full of the dry red wine typical of that region.

Everyone was talking loudly at once and making plenty of gestures. To the inexperienced observer it looked more like a fight than a discussion. But that is the Greek way. As soon a Zack entered, there was a momentary silence as each of the men present was examining him and giving him appraising looks.

Zack sat on one of the barrels and ordered a "Katostaraki" i.e. 100 ccs. of red wine. He attempted to strike a conversation with one of the patrons seated on his right. It was a large man with blond hair, blue eyes, and an enormous mustache. The feature that captured your attention was his huge hands. He wore seaman's clothes and a seaman's hat.

He told Zack that his name was Panos and that he was the captain of a schooner that smuggled olive oil from the Islands and traded it in the black market for wheat, corn or for a few sacks of potatoes. He was planning to sail the next morning for the Island of Skyros, the largest Island of the Sporades complex, and the same group of Islands that Skiathos belonged to. Skyros was known throughout Greece for its fine furniture made of hand carved wood. Wood carving was a skill that was passed from one generation of local craftsmen to the next.

A few drinks latter Zack was able to convince his new friend to take him along on the trip, but first he wanted to know if Zack was in any trouble with the authorities and if he had the required travel permits. Zack told him that he was just trying to get home. He asked to see the permits and Zack showed them to him. Apparently convinced he said,

"Be on the dock at 6:00 AM prompt. We sail on time, with or without you."

In the morning, they set sail for Skyros. Captain Panos was at the helm shouting orders to the crew. The boat, named "Christina" was about 50 feet long, had two masts and an appropriate complement of sails. It was a beautiful craft, graceful and elegant, completely made out of wood.

It was painted white and had the sleek design of hand made boats that preceded the invention of fiberglass. All of the unpainted wood of the deck and railings was covered with high gloss spar varnish. It looked more like a pleasure craft than a fishing schooner.

Bellow the decks were several bunks, a galley, and a head. Right after the bow there was a large cargo hull full of potato sacks and other supplies. The sea was calm except for a mild northeasterly wind that gave the sails enough power to move the boat forward at a reasonable speed, all and all a beautiful day for sailing in the Mediterranean.

Zack was on deck stripped to the waist enjoying the sunshine and the cool breeze. He was totally relaxed and the rhythmic sway of the boat was lulling him to sleep. Suddenly one of the lookouts shouted,

"Craft off the starboard bow, closing in fast".

The captain uttered a loud curse and said, "It must be a patrol boat. Get your guns ready, we are in for fun and games." Zack was instantly alarmed.

"What do you need guns for? He asked. Aren't your papers in order?"

"My papers are in order", said the Captain," but we have to be ready for a fight in case they want to board us and conduct a search."

"Let them search", said Jack. "What will they find except a few sacks of potatoes?"

"A few sacks of potatoes and the two Englishmen" the captain replied.

"What two Englishmen?" said Zack, completely taken off guard.

"The two escaped prisoners we are hiding under the potato sacks," said the Captain. A bolt of fear went through Zack when he heard these words. Of all the rotten luck, he had to get a ride in a boat that was involved in the Underground Railroad for rescuing escaped allied prisoners of war and providing them with passage to Turkey.

"They're getting closer", shouted the crewman.

"Get the grenades ready," yelled the Captain, and when they get on top of us, wave and smile."

Within minutes, the German boat was within shouting distance. A German naval officer, holding a conical metal megaphone, gave the order to stop and be boarded. The Captain cupped his hands, yelled back,

"Sorry, I don't understand German", and with a muted voice told the crew to keep waving and smiling.

The German repeated the order in Greek and the Captain told the crew to start taking down the sails to show that he was complying. A few tense moments went by as the Christina slowed down and the German boat got closer. The Captain of the patrol boat and two armed German sailors were getting ready to board.

There were three more on deck, one at the helm and at least one more below in the engine room. After boarding, the German officer asked to see the ships papers. Zack spoke out and offered his help as a translator. This seemed to calm the Germans. They examined the papers and returned them to Captain Panos.

"Alles in ordnung" i.e. "Everything is in order."

The German officer ordered the sailors to search the quarters below. While he began a slow walk around the deck, Captain Panos followed closely behind. They made an almost comical pair, the Greek giant towering a couple of feet above the puny German. The officer, continuing his probe, opened cupboards and lifted the lids of storage boxes but there was nothing inside other than sails, ropes, and fishing nets. When he came to the Cargo Hold he asked,

"What are you carrying?" "Just a few sacks of potatoes," Captain Panos replied. At that point, the German took his pistol out of the holster and was getting ready to fire into the cargo hold when Captain Panos struck him a powerful blow, knocking the pistol out of his hand, while at the same time placing his powerful arm around the German's head in a tight stranglehold. The sailors below heard the commotion, started to run up the stairs, and came face to face with the crewmen who had drawn their weapons.

Those on the Patrol boat opened fire wounding one of the Greek sailors and killing another. "Order them to lay down their arms or I will snap your neck like a twig," said Captain Panos. "Do as he says", shouted the German. "Cease fire". In a matter of a few minutes, all the Germans were tied and gagged.

Captain Panos ordered his first mate to take some crewmembers and deliver the captured boat and the prisoners to the nearest resistance units, while he would continue his trip to Skyros. After taking down the German flag, and painting over the insignia, the two vessels went on their separate courses. The Christina stopped after a while for a burial ceremony for the dead sailor who was then slipped into the sea.

Following the incident with the patrol boat Zack felt safe in explaining his situation to Captain Panos who was obviously a member of the underground. Captain Panos assured him that he would get all the help he would need to get safely to Skiathos from the resistance organization in Skyros, and that he would personally put him in touch with the right people.

They arrived in the beautiful port of Skyros without any further incident. After a brief inspection of their papers by the local authorities, they were allowed to disembark. The next day Zack was introduced to the local resistance leaders who made all the necessary arrangements for his transportation to Skiathos by fishing boats via the neighboring Island of Skopelos. Four days later Zack was finally home.

After resting for a couple of days in Skiathos from his adventurous trip from Athens, Zack put on some old Army clothes and a pair of leather boots belonging to my father's memorabilia from World War I, packed a duffle bag with a few sweaters, underwear and woolen socks and started on his journey to the mountains.

The parting was highly emotional because we were all aware of the danger of being in the mountains as part of a fighting unit but we all did our best to hide our feelings behind a humorous façade. We were telling Zack how lucky he was to be able to see some action and that now that we knew he was up there we would no longer be afraid of anything. We would even leave our front door unlocked, provided it had a lock to begin with.

After a simple embrace my mother told Zack to keep his feet dry and his head covered.

"I know you will do the right thing and come back to us safely."

Zack,, now a man of twenty three, then walked out of the house and started down the cobblestone path on his way to the dock. We were not sure when or if we would see Zack again.

CHAPTER 20

Zack Joins the Fighting

The first step was to arrange transportation. This meant finding a boat that was willing to brave the German patrols and give him passage to the Pylion. It turned out that the only craft available was a small rowboat. Fortunately, it was a dark night with lots of cloud cover and virtually no moon. His companion was a young man named Andreas.

Andreas had a bushy head of tightly curled black hair, very dark black eyes, and an easy smile. His skin was brown and shiny with leathery appearance, the result of having spent countless days in the bright sunshine of the Mediterranean. Andreas, like his father before him, was a professional fisherman.

Andreas knew these Islands like the palm of his hand. He was familiar with every inch of coastline and all the places where a small boat could hide and escape detection. He also knew all the currents and how to navigate by the seat of his pants i.e. without a compass simply by observing the stars and the familiar landmarks. For this reason he was often used by the underground for transporting people to and from Skiathos.

The tiny boat was invisible on dark nights especially if the sea was rough and could slip by undetected by the German patrol boats. With his expert handling of the boat, mostly by rowing, Andreas was able to reach the beach of the tiny fishing village of "Saint John" in the Pylion. Saint John was located directly across the straights and opposite of the island.

The trip was amazingly short and without incident. As soon as they disembarked a man who was the prearranged "synthesmos" met them. This Greek word was coined to identify a guide designated by the resistance whose job was to take a particular person from point A to point B. It literally means connecting or tying two things together. When the B destination was reached another "synthesmos" would take over and provide escort from point B to point C and so on and so on.

No one knew the entire route; this way if captured he could not reveal the operation even if he was tortured. The man approached them as they got on the sand and said "I am called "Yeros" (which translates into "the old man") and I was ordered to escort you to the next point on your journey. It is best that we get started right away".

As soon a Zack was turned over to his guide, Andreas got back on his boat and started to row back to Skiathos. They walked, mostly in silence, along the steep mountain path for several hours, making only small brief rest stops. The "old man" moved up the mountain with amazing speed and agility. Zack, who was much younger and in much better shape, had a hard time keeping up.

Finally, they reached their destination: the town of "Tsangarada". Tsangarada was a small resort town where, before the German occupation, the wealthy Greeks went in the summer for a vacation to escape the sweltering heat of the cities. It was characterized by a number of natural springs that brought to the surface of the ground a stream of cold, wonderful tasting water.

Distributed throughout the town were fountains and marble troughs where water ran continuously from the bowels of the earth. Men and beasts alike stopped there to quench their thirst and drank out of the same trough. In addition to the artesian wells, Tsagarada was also noted for its lovely aristocratic homes and spacious, beautifully landscaped gardens.

One of these mansions housed the headquarters of the local resistance. Zack was taken and left there by his guide. The CO, who was a colonel in the regular army before the war and was put in charge of this resistance unit, greeted him. He was a tall man with gray hair and mustache and gray, penetrating, eyes.

His uniform was a hodge-podge of three different armies, Greek, Italian, and German. Two bands of machine gun bullets criss-crossed his chest. He wore a highly polished pair of officer's boots that he had most likely removed from a dead German. His trousers were Italian and his Jacket and cap Greek. He greeted Zack warmly and inquired about his journey. He then asked him how much military training and experience he has. Zack replied that he had completed the Officer's Candidate Military Academy but had no battlefield experience.

"That's good enough", said the Colonel. We need officers badly, especially educated people who can teach and lead the men."

"I want you to go and take command of a machine gun company."

"These are fighting men that we have grouped together because they said that they know how to handle machine guns. However, we need an officer to organize them and make them combat ready. That is your job. Do you have any questions?"

"Where are these people?" said Zack. "And how do I get there?"

"They are in a small village on top of the Pylion Mountain whose name you do not need to know right now. You will get there on foot, but there will be people all along your route who have been instructed to help you reach your destination."

"How will I know or contact these people?" asked Zack.

"You don't need to contact them. They will contact you. It is safer this way. Good luck."

As Zack started climbing up the snowy mountain paths, it became increasingly more difficult to carry all the stuff he took along with him when he left Skiathos. It was impossible to walk uphill in the snow with a heavy load. Mother had provided him with a whole bag of goods, even clean sheets for his bed. He slowly began discarding his belongings along the way until he was left with only a heavy sweater and a blanket.

When he finally arrived at his destination, it was night. There were no officers present and no one seemed to be in charge. He observed a dozen or so men busy preparing food.

Most of them had long beards and were dressed with a strange combination of military and civilian clothes. They knew that Zack was to be their new CO but did not seem to be either concerned or overly impressed. They greeted him politely but without observing any military protocol. It was obvious that Zack had his work cut out in order to transform this bunch of unkempt, dirty and unruly men into a disciplined military unit capable of carrying orders.

Zack and the Resistance Fighters

"So you are the new captain," one of them said.

"I hope that you last longer than your predecessor."

"What happened to him?" asked Zack.

"He got killed during the last raid."

"What are you men doing?" asked Zack.

"We are preparing our evening meal," the man replied. "Headquarters supplies us with the staples and we do the cooking here."

"What are you eating tonight?"

"We are eating soup made out of wheat and barley."

"May I have some too? I have not eaten anything since we left Tsangarada," said Zack.

They pointed him to the end of the line where he picked up a tin container and filled it with soup from a large boiling cauldron located on the fire in the middle.

"I don't have a spoon," Zack said.

One of the men picked up a spoon from the dirty pile of dishes licked and handed it to him saying

"Here. Use this."

The gesture filled Zack with disgust but his hunger overcame his reluctance. He wiped the spoon with his handkerchief and dipped it into the soup. While eating, a tremendous explosion shook the mountain. The men did not seem particularly alarmed. One of them told Zack,

"Don't worry, you will soon get used to the noise. It is due to the explosion of the land mines we planted on the road yesterday. In the morning we will go and see what damage we have done to these German bastards."

After the meal, the men remained clustered around the fire smoking cigarettes, talking, or singing sad patriotic resistance songs. Most of these songs were Russian melodies with Greek words and as such were mostly in a minor key beautifully expressive and melodic. Eventually the place quieted down and the men fell asleep right there in the open air with their arm as a pillow and any covers they could find.

Zack unrolled his blanket and tried to get some sleep. However, his mind was preoccupied with how he would shape these men into a combat ready unit and he had a hard time falling asleep. He finally dozed off only to be awakened by more loud noises from the distant explosions. The rest of the men did not even stir. A man in a sergeant's uniform who was holding a pair of binoculars finally awakened him.

"Captain. Do you want to see what damage we have done?"

Zack took the binoculars and adjusted them to his eyes. He could see clearly that several armored vehicles had been destroyed and two trucks were on fire. There were bodies scattered all over the road and teams of German soldiers were at the scene attending to the wounded and clearing the area.

"We wait until they finish and leave before going down to see for ourselves what was the result of our sabotage effort", said the sergeant.

"What do you do the rest of the time?" asked Zack.

"We just sit and wait for orders", he replied.

Zack spent the next couple of days talking to the men and becoming familiar with the situation. It quickly became obvious that he had a lot of work to do. The men were totally uneducated and illiterate. They were peasants from villages located in various parts of Greece and had zero knowledge of geography or map reading.

They did not even know where they were. Furthermore, their age discrepancies and diversity of backgrounds made any meaningful communication very difficult. The only thing these men had in common was their Greek ancestry and the desire to fight the Germans. Each one of them had horror stories to tell about personal losses and pain inflicted by the invaders.

The constant idleness caused by long waiting periods between missions also contributed to their unrest. Petty arguments and in - fighting would erupt almost on a daily basis. Zack was a natural leader. He took command of the situation and began shaping this conglomerate of men into a military unit.

He first interviewed every man and made a folder for each. The folder contained all the pertinent information regarding the age, the educational level, the region that each person came from, their civilian occupation, and any previous military experience. He then organized them into platoons based on similar backgrounds and origin.

The next step was to designate people as non commissioned officers and put them in charge of these units, thereby establishing structure and creating a chain of command. The older, more experienced men were put in charge and were given a list of activities and a schedule.

These included guard duty, calisthenics, and keeping the equipment and the compound clean. Those with technical skills such as carpenters, plumbers, bakers, cooks, and car mechanics were assigned to appropriate duties. Zack then instituted regular lectures where he personally taught the troops basic geography of Greece, how to study a map and how to assemble, disassemble and care for their weapons.

He found some manuals on machine guns, gave his men daily instructions on the various parts of these weapons, and taught them how to use them effectively. He found an abandoned schoolhouse and moved the men inside where they would be more protected from the elements. A large wood-burning fireplace provided the heating on the cold winter nights.

The men began to enjoy these nightly lectures. They had a natural curiosity and a lot of common sense that made it easier to learn and to learn quickly. They began to act and perform as a unit and to develop an "esprits du corps".

After a short period of time, Zack received orders from the regimental headquarters to move the unit to another location because the intelligence had learned that the Germans were getting ready to launch an air and mortar attack against the compound.

Orders usually came by courier although there was a crude but functioning field telephone system in place that was obtained from the Italians. It consisted of one man generating power by seating on a bicycle and pedaling furiously while the other operated the equipment. In this way, it was possible in an emergency to communicate not only with headquarters but also with the other resistance units.

When the order to move came Zack had the men load the machine guns on mules, pack up all the tents and equipment, and start climbing the Mountain. It was cold and it started to snow making the move difficult. While on route, Zack came face to face with a tall blond man riding a white horse.

He was dressed in an officer's uniform with the insignia of a colonel. He was a dashing figure of a man looking majestic on top of the horse. Zack thought he was seeing St. George. He asked Zack

"Where are you going?" Zack replied

"I was ordered to move my machine gun company to a new location because there is an eminent attack by the Germans."

"My name is "Pylioritis" said the rider and I am the high ranking officer and the Divisional Commander for this region of the Underground. If there is anything I can do for you let me know."

"Thank you, comrade Colonel," said Zack.

"It is I who should be thanking you. Now carry on and good luck to you, my son."

Zack stood motionless in the snow for several minutes. He could not believe his eyes that he actually met and spoke to Pylioritis who was a legend among the resistance heroes.

When they finally reached their destination the snowfall had intensified and it was bitter cold. This is when Zack's admiration for the Greek Shepherd reached the highest level. One of these "Mountain men" offered to start a fire. Zack first thought the man was crazy.

"How can you light a fire in the middle of a snow blizzard?" he asked. The man said,

"Don't worry. I do it all the time."

Within a few minutes with just a piece of flint and some dry kindling he produced from a small leather satchel, this Shepherd had a roaring fire going. Zack ordered the men to built their tents around the fire, to cover the weapons and the equipment with canvases and release the mules. Considering the circumstances, they were actually quite comfortable.

Life in the new location was much harsher than before for several reasons. First, they were higher up in the mountain and thus more isolated from any type of contact with other people. Secondly, there were no towns or villages nearby and as result no structures existed that could be used as shelters to house the men and to be protected from the elements.

Consequently, they had to live in tents and sleep along side their animals with no creature comforts of any kind. Such basic things as bathing or washing clothes were not possible. The worst problem of all was the lack of water.

Unless they happened to be in a location that had a natural spring or there was snow on the ground, they had no water. The daily routine was to dispatch a couple of people to fetch water from below. These men were chosen by lot and were loaded with all the empty canteens, which they filled at the nearest water source.

This way each man had one full canteen of water every day that he used for drinking and for all his personal needs. These daily trips were dangerous, for the further down the mountain one went the more likely it was that he might run into some trouble from the enemy patrols.

Food came from the division by mule. Everyday mules arrived with huge loaves of bread and other supplies such as cheese, dry beans, potatoes, corn, and various other farm products indigenous to the local area. Before dispensing it, the food was divided into portions, which could never be made exactly equal.

Drawing lots to avoid any arguments about the size of each portion, therefore, was the chosen method of food allocation. Meat of any kind was extremely rare unless they were near a village that had sheep or goats. Eggs and milk were only fed to those who were wounded and were in the Hospital.

The main thing that stood between the men and starvation was the fact that most of them were mountain people and were very skilled in the art of living off the land. These peasants would often trap or kill various types of animals such a rabbits, turtles and even snakes and knew how to cook them.

To avoid detection and capture they were constantly on the move but always at the high elevations where it was difficult to attack and not readily accessible from the ground. The German's superior numbers were useless in such a terrain because it was not possible to mobilize large numbers of soldiers through the narrow goat paths and certainly impossible to move any vehicles or heavy weapons up the mountain.

Attack from the air was also ineffective because the cover provided by the trees and thick vegetation made for poor visibility. Whenever the Germans attempted to bombard the area, the bombs fell in the forest and never hit any of the troops that had taken cover. The rugged terrain provided a safe place to hide between raids.

Things had thus settled for a while to a dull and hard routine, which involved lots of training sessions and activities aimed in assuring that the men were fit. The nightly lectures continued and Zack enlisted the help of others, such as a former elementary school teacher, to help him provide a very basic education to the partisans.

The military resistance operations also had become routine. They consisted of isolated acts of sabotage and destroying enemy vehicles by the strategic placing of land mines at crucial roads and bridges. This way there was a constant interruption of the German supply lines without much risk on the part of the resistance. The game plan was to keep the Germans stirred up so that they would have to maintain troops for local control, troops that otherwise would be available for fighting in the various fronts against the allies.

The news that everyone was waiting for came suddenly. The Germans were once more attempting to clean up the resistance strongholds by a massive mobilization of troops around the entire perimeter of the mountain with orders to move up in concert and smash any partisan positions they may encounter along the way.

All previous attempts at "combing" resulted in the killing of civilians and the burning of villages along the way, but failed to inflict any real blow to the Resistance movement. The guerilla fighters simply moved to higher ground until the Germans retreated. Zack received orders from the regimental headquarters to get his machine gun company ready to engage the Germans.

He was told that he would be receiving further instructions as the Germans came closer. All these weeks of training were finally going to pay off. The men were elated with the news and

Frederic Kakis

eager to get into the real fighting. The machine gun nests were placed in strategic positions at every path or crossing that led up the mountain.

Zack deployed his men and took a position in the command post from where, using binoculars, he could observe any troop movement up the Mountain. He soon spotted the Germans who were approaching cautiously. They had with them police dogs thinking that the dogs would be able to flush out the resistance fighters.

When they were close enough to spit, he ordered his men to open fire. There was a slaughter. Bodies of soldiers and dogs were dropping like flies all over the place from the machine gun barrage. It caught the Germans totally unprepared for such organized and fierce resistance.

They retreated, regrouped, and attacked repeatedly. Killing the German soldiers with the machine guns placed where they were was easy. The German casualties were mounting. After three days, they finally gave up. They withdrew and retreated all the way down to the town of Larissa. One could observe with the binoculars the long line of soldiers coming down the mountain carrying their wounded on stretchers.

The Germans were gone for now, but not without inflicting, in retaliation for their defeat in combat, heavy casualties among the civilian population in the villages along the way, burning homes and destroying property.

Zack received a minor wound on the leg from a mortar fragment and was sent to the hospital for a few days. It was his first experience with an ELAS "hospital". It was really a house where several beds were placed in the available space and a number of good-looking young girls from the villages were the nurses. There were doctors available but very little in terms of instruments and supplies.

200

The most severe shortage was the medications. The entire inventory consisted of aspirin, quinine, Atabrine, and sulfonamides for infections. Strips of boiled sheets were used for bandages and alcohol or alcoholic beverages for sterilization. There was a small amount of chloroform and ether for anesthesia.

Zack was put in a bed next to a German soldier whose truck hit a land mine and he had gone crazy from the explosion. He was laughing and shouting, telling everyone how happy he was to be there. Zack tried to talk to him but he was not coherent and did not say anything that made sense. The hospital stay was actually a pleasant interlude where Zack enjoyed the chow and the nurses and had a chance to sleep in a real bed. After three days, he was released and returned back to his outfit.

It was now summer and everything was blooming. The fields were full of wheat and other crops and the mountains were green. Living in the mountains became much easier. For one thing, they no longer had to contend with the bad weather and finding game and other types of food became easier.

It also became easier to launch periodic strikes against the Germans. The raids intensified. A hit and run pattern was employed. A train would be derailed, a road would be mined or bridge would be blown-up and a surprise attack would take place, The partisans hit the Germans hard from both sides of the road and ran for cover up the mountains before any reinforcements could come.

The German superiority in terms of men and equipment was totally ineffective in this type of hit and run tactics. Zack's outfit was by now a seasoned fighting unit, a far cry from the unruly mob he encountered just a short while ago. Zack was also more knowledgeable regarding the operation of the resistance and learned to work in concert with other units in planning and executing missions against the enemy.

All the strategic planning and all the orders came from the headquarters. They coordinated the entire effort telling each unit when to move, where to go, what position to hold and defend, and when to attack. Orders came by courier or pre-designated signals such as flares of different colors.

The raids usually involved receiving information from headquarters about the German movements with orders to attack and inflict as much damage and casualties as possible. The men then came down the mountains and requisitioned wagons, horses and mules from the villages along the way to carry them and the equipment. In most guerilla units only officers were allowed to have and ride horses, but there were some cavalry units where everybody was mounted.

When they arrived near the target area, they disembarked, hid the wagons and the animals, and preceded the rest of the way on foot. At the site, they placed their mines or charges and hid on both sides of the road waiting for a German column or a train that was loaded with munitions or troops to arrive. As soon as the first part of the convoy would pass they would detonate the charges and open fire.

The element of surprise was the most crucial factor in these operations. When enough damage was done, the order to retreat was given and the men ran to the place where the wagons were hidden and escaped up the mountain before the Germans had a chance to mount a counter offensive.

In one such operation, there was a coordinated attack on a German column transporting men and munitions. Zack's unit was prominently featured in that raid inflicting major damage and casualties with their machine guns. After the initial surprise wore off the Germans were able to regroup and started to return fire. Then they began to fire their mortars and the number of dead and wounded among the freedom fighters began to multiply.

At that time the order to retreat was given by firing a green flare. The cavalry units were the first to leave the battle scene and escape to the mountains after retrieving their horses from their hiding place. Zack's company used their machine guns to give cover and they were the last to leave. At the end, most partisans had left and they were on their way up the mountain.

Zack and his sergeant were among the last stragglers. They began to run furiously through the fields towards the foot of the mountain where their horses and carts were waiting, when all of a sudden they ran into a wounded resistance fighter who was laying down hidden from view by tall wheat. He was bleeding profusely. He asked Zack,

"Am I badly hit?"

Zack looked at the man's back and saw a gaping hole made by a mortar fragment. If the wounded man could see the extent of his injuries, he would have probably died of fright.

"Nah," said Zack. "It's just a scratch. I am sure you will be up and around in no time at all. Let's see if we can get you out of here."

"Do you think you can stand up?" Asked the sergeant.

"Yes, comrade".

Zack told the sergeant to grab one of the man's arms while he grabbed the other and they tried to stand him up. This was a big man weighing at least 200 lbs. After they took a few steps, it became obvious to Zack that the man could not walk or support his own weight and that he and the sergeant could not possibly carry him all the way to the foot of the mountains where the horse and carts were hidden.

The deck was stacked against them; the dawn was near making it difficult to hide and the Germans had sufficiently recovered to mount a search for members of the underground.

They were using police dogs to track down and flush out the attackers. Zack could hear the dogs barking at a distance and it was just a matter of time until they would all be captured and killed.

He set the man down, put a temporary dressing on his wound, and told him, "We will have to leave you here for a little while until we can get some help. We need to find a peasant with a horse or a wagon and come back for you. If we continue carrying you we will not make it and we will all be killed."

The man started to cry and said,

"No please don't leave me here to die. You will never come back for me. Please, please don't leave me here alone."

Zack said, "We will come back and get you. I give you my word, but I don't have time to argue."

They left the man in a wheat field fully hidden from view by the tall vegetation and began to run. They soon spotted a peasant with a wagon pulled by two oxen and started shouting,

"Stop, help. Stop, help".

At first, the peasant started to run away but he finally stopped. Zack asked,

"Why were you running away from us?"

The man replied, "I was frightened by your appearance".

Zack and the sergeant looked at each other and saw that they were covered with blood. They quickly explained that the blood belonged to a wounded soldier they found and that they needed his help to transport him to their lines.

"The peasant said, "OK but we must hurry because the Germans are closing in".

They mounted the cart and they began retracing their steps. This was one of the most frightening experiences in Zack's life. When he set the man down in the middle of the wheat field, it was late at night and in his desperate fight for time he neglected to note any particular landmarks that would make it easy to find the location.

Now that daylight was approaching every wheat field looked like any other wheat field and he could not remember the exact location of the wounded man. They began to scan frantically while the sounds of the dogs were getting closer and Zack knew that if he did not find him soon he would have to abandon him lest all their lives would be lost. Fortunately, they stumbled on to him, they loaded him on the cart and covered him with hay, and they all ran like hell up the mountain.

CHAPTER 21

Zack Victim of "Free Speech".

Because of the Communist leadership the resistance movement had copied a lot of the rituals from Communist Russia. One of these rituals was a regular meeting where the various resistance members, regardless of rank, were allegedly encouraged by the commanding officer to speak out on any issue they wanted. They were told to speak freely without fear of recriminations and that the purpose of these meetings was self-criticism and self-appraisal.

On the surface, this might appear to be a very useful thing. Actually, appearances were deceiving. If anyone was foolish or naïve enough to say anything critical about the leadership he lived to regret it. During one of these meetings that Zack had attended, one by one, various resistance fighters got up and told the assembly about their successes in combat against the Germans and the rest applauded loudly.

It looked more like a mutual admiration society where they were patting each other in the back than a self-criticism session. When it came Zack's turn to speak, he got up and complained that the real fighting man in his command did not have uniforms or proper shoes while the desk clerks at headquarters were all well dressed and equipped.

A friend of Zack's sitting next to him who knew the real score, was urging him to shut up, but Zack would not listen. In his youthful idealism, he truly believed that he could speak freely without fear of punishment.

The next day, Zack, who was now a seasoned combat company commander and a veteran of many engagements against the Germans, received orders to report to the supreme ELAS headquarters for all of Greece. The news was disconcerting to him because he was well adjusted where he was and he had earned the respect, admiration, and affection of the men under his command. Furthermore, the orders never gave a reason or explanation and the uncertainty added to his anxiety and apprehension.

As usual, he was not told where the headquarters were. His instructions permitted him to reach the first point in his itinerary from which he would be escorted to the next and so on. In this way if he was captured, he could not reveal his final destination and neither could anyone else. To his misfortune when he reached the first point in his journey, he found the town deserted.

There seemed to be no one around. As he wandered through the streets he ran into an old man who told him

"Get out immediately because in one hour this place will be full of Germans. We got word that they are coming to kill us and to burn our village. Just follow me and I will lead you up the mountain. Please hurry."

They started to climb the mountains as fast as their legs would take them and they soon reached an armed resistance unit who gave them asylum.

For the next few days Zack continued his journey from one point to the next until he finally reached the ELAS supreme headquarters. It was located in the central part of Greece in an area at the top of the mountains known as Karpenisi.

Karpenisi was where those fierce fighters called "Evzones" came from. Evzones were recognized by wearing a distinguishing short white kilt called "Foustanella", long white stockings and leather moccasin type pointed red shoes with a large blue and white pom-poms at the tips. They were tough and brave warriors and because of this, they joined the Police Force. Most of the Greek policemen came from that part of the country. In almost every home in the villages of Karpenisi, one could find on the mantle a picture of a young man in a policeman's uniform.

In order to reach the ELAS headquarters Zack had to travel on foot several hundred kilometers of mountainous roads and paths. During his journey, he was greatly impressed with the scope and extent of the resistance movement. In every little village along the way, there was an ELAS office that provided direction as well as food and shelter.

He was amazed by the number of small villages that Greece had with the local peasants raising goats or sheep and essentially living off the land.

Karpenisi was full of high-ranking officers, generals and known political figures that left Athens and had joined the resistance movement. Many of them were officers in the regular Greek army who decided to do their part in liberating the country from the Germans.

Shortly after his arrival, Zack went into a house that had been converted to an officers club to get some food. When he entered, he came face to face with a man in full Colonel's uniform. The man looked at him and said,

"Zack , what on earth are you doing here?"

He was Mr. Moskovitis who was, before the war, my father's old partner in one of his business ventures, a movie theater in Kavalla.

Zack replied, "The real question is not what am I doing here but what are you doing here?"

208

Moskovitis explained that as an officer in the regular army he thought it was his duty to enlist in the ELAS and try to do whatever he could to get rid of the Germans. Zack told him about the plight of our family and his own involvement with the resistance. He explained that he had not found out yet why he was ordered to report to the general headquarters but that he was going there right away to find out.

Moskovitis told him to stay still and that he was going to find out for him because as a ranking colonel he had direct access to the ELAS command. He returned shortly afterwards with a big smile on his face and told Zack.

"I found out why you were ordered to report here. You have been decorated and received a promotion. You will be sent to Arta, (a town in a region of Greece called Ipiros), to take charge of a unit located near the forces of Zervas.

There is a rumor that Zervas has been doing some funny business with the Germans and ELAS was getting ready to move on him and clean him out."

Zervas was an army officer who became the leader of EDES (The National Republican Greek League), an organization that was the right wing counter part of ELAS/EAM. Zervas had strong and long-term ties to such right-wingers as General Plastiras and the former Greek dictator Pangalos. Their political philosophy was one that embraced a deep hatred for the Communists. Ironically they were at the same time strongly anti-royalists.

Despite the fact that EDES was formed as a resistance organization, its supporters saw it more as a vehicle for opposing King George of Greece rather than the Axis. Zervas himself was too slow to show much enthusiasm for any kind of fighting. Although EDES was formed in the autumn of 1941 Zervas did not leave Athens till the summer of 1942.

He was a poor leader running a loose organization with friends and relatives in the key positions. Shortly after his arrival severe infighting ensued among his staff who were accusing each other of collaborating with the Germans. Zervas was overweight and a hypochondriac, nevertheless he managed to convince the British that he was the only viable alternative to ELAS who upon the defeat of the Germans was sure to turn Greece to Russian domination.

Because of his anti Communist crusade and rhetoric, he managed to get twice as many supplies of arms and ammunition and most of the financial support from the British. Among other things, he received a shipment of 24,000 gold sovereigns to take to the hills. Most of the airdrops in his first five months with the resistance were for his benefit. EDES was only one sixth of the size of ELAS and their role in the armed resistance against the Germans was negligible.

When Zack arrived in Arta, he went straight to headquarters and reported for duty. The commander was a colonel and the exec a captain who was also the expert on communism and the one that gave the indoctrination lectures to the men. He was a simple person with no pomposity and actually quite a likeable chap. He and Zack became friends. He told Zack,

"You were actually sent here to be punished for speaking out at a meeting, but now that you are here we can use you". The Germans seemed to have abandoned this area and there is not much resistance activity, but I think that you have earned a rest.

I need you to train men to become non-commissioned officers. We have a critical shortage of Corporals and Sergeants who can lead the troops. You can help us fill that gap."

Zack said "If you think that I can help, that's okay with me."

Thus, Zack learned that the previous commander at the Pylion who presided at the "self criticism" meeting was the one responsible for his transfer to Ipiros.

Because of Zack's statements at the meeting, he pegged him as a troublemaker and when the Central Command asked for young officers to be used as trainers, he saw his chance to get rid of him. In retrospect he may have been responsible for saving Zack's life by effectively removing him from the hard fighting zone.

Zack got started immediately. They gave him an office next to the Doctor for the Regiment who was responsible for the care of nearly two thousand men! Zack got quickly immersed in his new duties with his usual zeal and enthusiasm and was enjoying this break from the hard life of the mountains. The food was good; he had a horse, and a comfortable bed to sleep on.

Then one day, the order came to attack Zervas. Zack felt very uncomfortable with this mission. Attacking other Greeks was a distasteful task no matter how it was framed. The command justified it as a necessary move because of the alleged collaboration of some EDES members. They said that Zervas had become an obstacle in the fight against Germans and had to be neutralized.

The whole regiment was mobilized; fortunately, the Zervas forces did not offer much resistance, which kept the casualties to a minimum. They opted to retreat to the sea town of Preveza to be evacuated by naval vessels provided by the British, to the Island of Kerkira on the Ionian Sea. A Greek destroyer attached to the British Middle East command kept the advancing ELAS troops at bay by a relentless bombardment from the sea inflicting severe casualties.

The ELAS requested artillery reinforcements. The next day 16 mules arrived carrying 3 small cannons. Foolishly, the ELAS fighters attempted to sink the destroyer by firing these cannons.

The Captain of the destroyer simply pulled back the ship a few hundred yards until he was entirely out of range and commenced firing with his big guns leveling everything in site.

The shelling continued relentlessly day and night keeping the ELAS troops pinned down. This devastating sea bombardment gave Zervas forces the cover they needed to escape from Ipiros to Kerkira. When the Zervas soldiers and the ships were gone, the ELAS regiment marched into the town of Preveza where they were given a hero's welcome.

By that time, the German Army was in full retreat running for their lives. Athens was already liberated, first by the surrender of the Italians and now by the flight of the Germans. The retreating German Army bore no resemblance to the mighty armada that invaded Greece. It was a pitiful assembly of soldiers trying to get out before the arrival of the Allies discarding along the way their weapons and parts of their uniforms. Most of them were young children or old men inducted by the Nazis in desperation when the end of the war was nearing.

A spirit of euphoria was seen all over the country. After several long years of suffering, starvation and fear, the dawn of victory was finally here and Greece was once more going to be free.

CHAPTER 22 .

The Beginning of the End – Italy Surrenders

A major turning point in the resistance effort came when on September 8, 1943 Italy capitulated. Even before the official declaration of surrender, the Italian occupation troops were losing power and showing signs of collapse. The Italian army's disastrous performance in Albania had greatly affected their morale.

Most of the soldiers had no stomach for fighting, hated the war and Mussolini and showed open defiance to authority. The Italian-German "Alliance", that was artificial to begin with, was showing progressive signs of discord. The Italians always regarded the Germans as barbarians and refused to follow the German example of committing atrocities against the civilian population.

They openly criticized their Nazi friends for taking and executing innocent hostages.

As a result the Italians in Greece were a lot more moderate in their treatment of the Greek population than their German counterparts. They opposed the killing of civilians and the burning of Greek villages.

The position of the Italian command was that reprisals "must not be allowed to degenerate into blind brutality ". The Italians were also completely opposed to the German policy towards the Jews. The Italians had no illusions about the fate awaiting the deported Jews and refused to cooperate. In many instances they helped the Jews escape.

Aware of the Italian opposition to the deportations, many Jewish families, with the help of certain courageous Military and Diplomatic figures, fled to the Italian zone. So long as Italy remained in control of the southern zone the Jews living there were safe. Consequently the German demands for the immediate implementation of sterner measures and of the "Jewish problem" fell on deaf ears. The Italians dragged their feet and did not make a serious attempt to collect the Jewish population of Athens. The same was true of the Islands that, for the most part, were under Italian occupation.

Frustrated by the lack of response from the Italians, Adolph Eichman decided to sweep up the Jews from Salonica and the other territories that were exclusively under German control. He then issued an ultimatum to the Italians that he wanted all the rest of the Jews from Athens and the other parts of Greece to be rounded up and sent to Auschwitz. Following that, the Grand Rabbi was spirited out of Athens by the resistance and the planned deportation was not implemented.

These events convinced the Germans that the Italians were weak and unreliable. Hitler issued orders for the total German takeover of the Balkans. Following the Allied landings in Sicily he was convinced that Greece would be the next point of attack. He sent Rommel to Salonica with orders to take defensive positions along the coast and be prepared to move against the Italians whom he regarded as defeatists.

When the Axis forces in North Africa finally surrendered, the possibility of a separate peace proposal by Italy became quite likely. Towards the end of 1943, one would frequently observe drunken Italian soldiers openly cursing out the war and denouncing Mossolini. German and Italian soldiers could often be seen brawling in the streets. The signs of Italian defeatism were progressively and increasingly evident, and all indications were that a separate surrender by Italy was nearing.

When Badoglio suddenly toppled Mussolini in a palace coup, the German tanks took positions in front of the Italian headquarters in Athens and all the German units were ordered to be ready to disarm the Italians.

In a bold proactive move, Pylioritis decided to have a talk with the Italian commander stationed in the town of Volos, which is located adjacent to the foot of mount Pylion. He rode into town in full uniform in a motorcycle accompanied by a British commando officer. He went straight into the Italian headquarters and asked to see the commandant. During the meeting he gave the Italian a full and accurate assessment of the situation pointing out that the war was going badly for Germany in all fronts and that the end was near.

He gave the Italian his personal assurance, as the regional resistance leader, that if he would agree to the transfer of all the military equipment and supplies to the underground before the Germans arrived, he and his men would be accorded asylum in the mountain villages and would be treated fairly and with respect.

Any Italians soldiers that chose to surrender would not be required to fight, would be protected and enjoy the same treatment as the resistance fighters. The Italian commandant agreed and issued the order to turn all the supplies, guns, ammunition, and uniforms to Pylioritis. They left together in a car and headed for the mountain.

The next day there was a frenzy of men and vehicles loading all the supplies from the Italian warehouses and transferring them to the resistance. Within two or three days all the supplies were moved. In addition to the military equipment, a veritable treasure of other types of goods was obtained. They included: wheat, beans, flower and other staples as well as clothing, shoes, blankets, soap and other personal effects.

The captured Italian soldiers were initially assigned duties as cooks and clerks in the various guerilla units. Later orders came from headquarters that they were to be treated as prisoners of war and not to be used in any form associated with the fighting. Since there were no facilities for guarding prisoners in the mountains they were allocated to any peasant family who wanted them and offered to give them food and lodging.

Since many of the captured Italians were skilled craftsmen, they began to rebuild the burned houses and barns and to perform many other useful functions. The British made air drops of gold coins and the orders were to pay each Italian prisoner of war a gold sovereign per month for his services.

On September 8, the Italian surrender was officially announced culminating a series of secret negotiations that had been going on for several weeks between Badoglio and the Allies. In every part of Greece, where there was no German presence, Italian soldiers and Greek civilians held riotous celebrations, dancing and singing in the streets, destroying fascist emblems and waving Greek, American and British flags. Soldiers and officers alike were selling or giving their equipment, arms and ammunition to the resistance as well as food and clothing items to the population at large.

The Germans took immediate measures issuing ultimatums to the Italian command that all Italians must unconditionally surrender to the Germans along with all their weapons. The Italians requested that they be allowed to return to Italy in exchange for a pledge not to take arms against their former allies. Despite that the German ultimatum had no basis in international law, many Italian soldiers, in the face of vastly superior German forces, did surrender to them.

Upon surrendering several thousand Italian men and many Italian officers were summarily executed by firing squads in some of the Greek Islands. This is a most unbelievable example of war crimes in military history, which remained unpunished.

Despite these atrocities, the real significance of the Italian surrender was that it contributed significant amounts of arms and supplies to the fighting units and served as a psychological catalyst for resisting the German rule. Across the country many Greeks that had not yet been actively involved took to the hills believing that the Italian collapse signified the end of the war and the final defeat of the Axis powers.

A few of the Italians that had surrendered to the partisans hated the Germans and actually requested a combat assignment. One of these was a machine gun expert who asked to be baptized Greek orthodox and be allowed to take part in the fighting. Zack obliged and baptized him "Mitsos" (short for Demetrious) and took him along in every operation against the Germans until the very end. Mitsos turned out to be a real expert machine gun operator who knew every machine gun part, how to take them apart, clean them and repair them. He knew more about machine guns than any Greek soldier in the group.

The summer soon came to an end and life in the mountains began to shape up in a similar pattern to the previous winter except that the men had better food and thanks to the Italians most were dressed in new uniforms and had a pair of army shoes. In the past, the only military clothing available for the Greek fighting man came from dead German soldiers.

The military operations also slowed down during the winter months and mimicked the pattern of the previous year namely periodic sabotage missions, and hit and run raids. When the next summer rolled around the Germans were using Greece as the hub for storing and transporting military equipment and supplies to other fronts.

As a result, many more trains loaded with munitions were arriving daily from Germany to Greece. The orders came to blow up and destroy as many of these as possible. Consequently, the fighting intensified and the raids became more frequent with a corresponding increase in the number of casualties. The Germans, out of desperation, took civilian hostages and put them in cars in the beginning and the end of each train, transporting German soldiers of munitions, hoping that this would deter the resistance from blowing up the train. It did not.

CHAPTER 23

Freedom Comes to Skiathos

Dum dum dum dum. Dum dum dum dum. "This is London calling, the European service of the BBC. We are pleased to announce that as a result of a massive joint air and sea operation the Allied forces just landed in Normandy...."

These words had an electrifying effect on all of us that were hovering around the short wave radio listening to the traditional 8 o'clock transmission from England. Before long the whole Island was buzzing with the news. Everyone was in a festive mood realizing that the tide of the war has finally shifted and that it was now just a question of time before Hitler was defeated and our Country was liberated.

In the ensuing days we remained glued to the radio absorbing every piece of news. There were daily broadcasts of the Allied advances and victories on the battlefield. Day by day American and British forces were pushing the enemy back to Germany. In every "Kafenion" in Skiathos self-appointed Generals and strategists gathered to discuss tactics leaning over crude maps of Europe that were drawn on the white napkins or on the tabletops.

"Patton should move ahead with his armor and cut off their panzer divisions while the air force launches an attack on the bridge..."

This kind of dialog could be heard in every spot where idle men gathered.

Frederic Kakis

The news about the relentless bombing of Germany by the RAF and the American Air Force, reducing their cities to rubble, was also music to our ears. After years of killings, torture and starvation the Germans were finally getting a dose of their own medicine. By the summer of 1944 the Red army had the Germans on the run and threatened to cut off their forces still remaining in Greece as they overran Romania and swept across the Balkans. In the meantime Patton and the other allied generals were kicking Hitler's ass all the way to Berlin.

This was certainly a period of hope, optimism and celebration for all the residents of Skiathos but especially for us who had endured so much. The smell of victory was in the air. Mother, Albert and I began to plan our return to our home in Salonica and were praying for the safe return of Zack and Carmen.

Albert, now seventeen years old and with his passion for learning, had befriended a young man who was a teacher in the local high school before the war. With his help he was able to locate several textbooks and began to have regular study sessions on all the basic High School subjects: Math, physics, literature, history, etc.

"Someday the war will end" he would say "and we will have to make up all the years of school we missed".

He insisted that I also participate in these study sessions. I was now fourteen years old and strongly resisted this because I had gotten used to goofing off and planning my own activities but he persisted and got my mother's backing so I was stuck. Thus, at a time when the resistance activities were at a minimum I was kept out of trouble by this independent study supervised and scrutinized by my older brother. As it turned out this became a real blessing at a later date.

Despite the continuing food shortage the last days of the exile were rather peaceful. We were full of hope that Germany would be defeated and that the end of the war was near. Bit by

220

bit we anxiously followed the progress of the Allied march towards Germany.

With each of the BBC's announcements of an Allied military victory our spirits were lifted and our hearts were filled with joy.

This period of optimism and high hopes was marred by the unleashing of a reign of terror characterized by indiscriminate killings, looting and the burning of homes and villages. The worst part was that those responsible for these atrocities were Greeks, not German!

As mentioned earlier the main resistance movement in Greece was organized, dominated, and run by Communists whose ultimate agenda, extending beyond the German occupation, was the takeover of the Government. However those serving in the EAM, ELAS and EPON were not all Communists. The membership of these resistance organizations consisted of an assortment of various types of peoples each having his own special reasons for joining.

Most were fugitives trying to evade capture. Many were idealistic young men and women who wanted to free their country from slavery. Others were fanatics who strongly opposed any form of totalitarianism. The glue that held them together and kept them in line was their common hatred of the Germans and the desire to free Greece from the strangling oppression of the occupying forces.

As the war was coming to an end the concerns about survival and liberation began to fade and were being replaced by fear of being liberated from one tyrant: the Germans, and falling into the hands and the domination of another: communism. The strong support of ELAS and EAM that characterized the early periods of the occupation and reached maximum proportions at the time of the famine was now diminishing as Greek politics once more began to be polarized.

There was an increasing apprehension, especially among the wealthy Greeks about the ultimate goals of the resistance organizations once the occupation no longer existed. Hellenism was by its heritage and traditions, incompatible with the worldview of communism and as the Nazi threat began to diminish, Greek right wing elements began to be increasingly more vocal against the EAM and all the other resistance organizations.

The German propaganda machine saw in this the opportunity to use the disenchanted and fearful anti Communists Greeks to break the back of the Resistance. The anti Communist sentiments reached their maximum when the forces of the ELAS successfully attacked and neutralized the other two right wing resistance groups of EDES headed by Zervas and EKKA headed by Colonel Psarros. A patchwork of Greek anti-Communists of a variety of political persuasions now emerged who were about to write one of the most shameful pages in Greek history.

This movement was stimulated, supported, and financed by the Germans and turned brother against brother. As a result thousands of Greeks died in vain, without reason, being cut down by Greek hands.

The election of Ioannis Rallis as prime minister that took place in April of 1943 signified the beginning of this new "friendship" between the Germans and Greek anti-Communists. The Rallis government passed a law providing for the formation of Greek "Security Batalions" and asked for volunteers. Most of the "Volunteers" were either very poor people who joined as an alternative for going to work in Germany, criminals who were wanted by the police or traitors, informers, and other shady elements who were being hunted by the resistance organizations.

Both the Germans and the Italians were initially very reluctant to arm Greeks but, after the surrender of Italy, the Germans realized that Greek auxiliaries could be useful in the war against the resistance and decided to exploit the anti-Communist movement. The SS and the Gestapo penetrated these organizations and gave them expanded powers.

They also infiltrated the Greek police and used them to their advantage. Starting with several hundred men the "Battalions" by the end of the war numbered 8,000 and had spread a reign of terror through central and southern Greece. Even more shameful than their German association was the complete lack of discipline among these groups.

They were basically a bunch of thugs that under the guise of anti-communism, burned, looted, and terrorized the countryside forcibly recruiting other members.

They also helped the SS to guard Jewish deportees on their way to Auschwitz. Some former members of the defeated right wing resistance organizations joined the Battalions, although towards the end their leaders finally publicly repudiated them.

Piling shame upon shame in addition to the Battalions that were operating in central and southern Greece, the German authorities in the north decided to counteract the ELAS by financing and organizing other "anti-Communist" auxiliary groups who later became known as "Death Squads".

The mission of these squads was to reduce the countryside into a land of terror by random killings. These, the German propaganda said, were "pure Greek patriots that were to make sure that the red flag is never planted on the ruins left by the war."

One such organization of "patriots" backed by the German security police was the EASAD headed by a man called Takis Makedon. In may of 1944 EASAD gangs of thugs attacked the port of Volos and went into a murderous rampage, roaming the streets with clubs and guns, looting stores, attacking passers-by and killing in cold blood unarmed young men.

Others who were unfortunate enough to be there were forced to shoot each other or were taken into a local warehouse and tortured to death. There was no due process, just bands of uncontrolled anarchists that were conducting arrests, interrogations, and executions and confiscating property without any qualifications or semblance of fairness and impartiality. These actions were inhuman and an affront to the inhabitants of Volos who were terrified and were fleeing in numbers. The saddest part of all is that those perpetrators were Greeks!

The end of the war came to Skiathos by the sudden appearance in the harbor of a British destroyer and several other smaller naval vessels.

I woke up to the furious ringing of church bells that told me instantly that a major event was occurring since it was neither a Sunday nor a holiday.

Mother greeted the news of the liberation with great relief but she was subdued and less exuberant than us. When I ask her why she did not appear to be happier, she replied,

"I will celebrate when all my children have returned home safe and sound".

It was obvious that the lack of news about my brother and sister was weighing heavily on her mind.

We all dressed quickly and went out. The whole village was in the streets, carrying Greek, English and American Flags. People were dancing, hugging and kissing each other, friends and strangers alike. Others were shouting anti- nazi slogans and yelling, "Long Live Greece". Several boats in the Harbor began to fill up with people heading towards the destroyer and bringing bouquets of flowers and jugs of local wine.

When we reached the ships we were allowed to go aboard giving the officers and the crew a hero's welcome. They reciprocated by distributing food, chocolates, cookies and biscuits. The crews were given liberty and disembarked to receive the applause of an adoring crowd.

The celebrations lasted nearly three days of continuous eating, drinking and singing. Many of the sailors got plastered on ouzo and had to be transported back to the ship like sacks of potatoes. The shore patrolmen would grab the hands and feet of a drunken sailor and by a swaying motion toss his body from the pier to the bottom of the boat located along side. It was a hilarious sight.

Within a few days the ships left and the people of Skiathos started to pick-up the pieces and began the long process of healing and rebuilding. Everyone had lost something: A home, a relative, a boat or a friend. We all felt numb and for a while were paralyzed into inactivity.

The resistance echelon was trying desperately to maintain control. The indoctrination sessions continued but less and less people attended them. Since there was no longer any threat or any recognizable common enemy the cohesive nature of the resistance movement could no longer be sustained and the organization in Skiathos fell apart.

My young comrades and I began to shift our attention to other concerns. Primary among these was the procurement of food. The departure of the Germans had no immediate effect on the availability of food; however, because the blockade was lifted there was no longer the danger of running into a German patrol boat. We could now expand the search for food by importing supplies from the mainland that had been cut off during the occupation.

For example it now became possible to exchange olive oil that was in abundance on the Islands, for wheat, corn, potatoes and other staples more easily found in other parts. Apostolis, the "Black marketer" began doing a thriving business of importing much needed supplies to the Island and exporting oil.

Albert and I started to work for him while waiting for my mother to decide to return to our home in Salonica.

She was reluctant to leave the Island immediately for fear that Zack and/or Carmen might come back to Skiathos and not find us there. After a few weeks we finally convinced her that we needed to go home and that this offered the best chance of reuniting the family.

Nagging thoughts, concerns and fears that we managed to suppress during our exile now began to surface. There were many questions that were begging for answers: Who of our relatives survived? What happened to our home in Drama? What was left, if anything of our father's business? Were the movie houses still there? What about our home in Salonica? Is it still there? What were we going to do about the years of school we missed during the occupation?

I also was too young and I have never understood why the Jews in general and our family in particular were so hated by the Germans. I never felt that I was any different from any other boy my age. I did not know what being a Jew really was. I did not have the opportunity to receive any kind of religious training regarding Judaism but I could recite by heart major portions of the Greek Orthodox Mass because as part of our disguise and deception we had to attend church regularly even to the extent of receiving communion and going to confession.

Furthermore I was sure that neither I nor anyone else in my family had done anything to make us the primary targets. Why were the Germans hunting us down and trying to destroy us? Before the war I had not even seen a German, why then was I being hunted? The whole thing did not make any sense to me.

Survival is such a strong instinct that overshadows all other concerns and while the occupation was going on it was taking all the energy I had and I suppressed the search for answers to these questions. Now that we were liberated it became important to me to understand.

It was very frustrating and disappointing when, pressing my mother for answers, I discovered that she also did not have a satisfactory explanation. No one at that time could find a rational explanation for the persecution of the Jews. Eventually it became clear that no rational explanation existed. The Nazi anti-Jewish campaign was in fact an insane and barbaric act for which there was no precedent in the entire history of mankind.

Never before were millions of innocent non-belligerent people gathered and systematically been exterminated for no reason at all. This is what made the whole thing impossible to comprehend, especially by a young person.

After a few weeks of waiting to no avail for our siblings to return, it was clear that we had to leave Skiathos and return to Salonica and if possible to resume our "normal" prewar life. Since there was no mail or telephones yet it was impossible to receive any news about the fate of our relatives or the whereabouts of Zack and Carmen.

Mother was visibly concerned but remained optimistic. Leaving the Island that had been our home away from home, for such a long time, was difficult. We had made a number of strong friendships of the type that only sharing common dangers and fighting side by side can forge. This made parting a real sad occasion.

After saying our tearful good-bys we packed our meager personal effects and went down to the dock to board a fishing trawler that was to take us back to Salonica. The sum total of all our belongings consisted of a valise and two small trunks. This was all that remained from the abandonment of three homes!

The trunks contained some family memorabilia that my mother stubbornly clung to throughout the war. Among them was a pair of silver candlesticks, two hand embroidered silk blankets and some other fine items of clothing that were the remnants of the good old days. Mother jealously held on to those few possessions that were the only links to the past and reminders of the happy times when she was the Great Lady in Drama. We had carted these trunks all over during our entire Odyssey.

CHAPTER 24

The End of the Exile – Going Home

We finally boarded the small boat and started our trip to Salonica. As the boat got further and further away I stood motionless on the deck looking, with tears in my eyes at the disappearing outline of the Island. The full realization that an important and exciting part of my life was over suddenly hit me. I was leaving behind a piece of myself.

I was only fifteen years old yet I felt like a hundred. All the years of suffering and my misspent youth were at that moment converging upon my shoulders. For the first time I was feeling sorry for myself. I became overwhelmed by a feeling of profound sadness and broke down crying uncontrollably.

Albert and mother put their arms around me and tried to console me by telling me over and over again that the nightmare was over and things will get better from now on.

The return journey was miserable. We hit bad weather and choppy seas. The tiny boat was bouncing up and down the whole night. Since there was no room below we had to sleep on deck. I had never been so cold in my life. We were huddled together under a blanket but we were still freezing. To make matters worse we all became violently sea sick and were throwing up bent over the railing while holding on for dear life for fear of being tossed overboard.

After this horrible night, exhausted and pale, we arrived in Salonica by 9:00 o'clock the next morning. When we finally reached the pier and disembarked we ran smack into a massive demonstration. Thousands of people had taken to the streets carrying huge banners and red flags with the hammer and sickle.

There was a sea of red as far as the eye could see. The crowd was shouting Communist slogans. Others were chanting the famous Communist song that was written in honor of the Bulgarian Communist leader GEORGI DIMITROV. "Black vultures with long curved claws are attacking the working class. They are crowing wildly and are seeking blood. They want to see Dimitrov hanged...."

Judging from the size of the crowd one would have concluded that the entire city was Communist. An old man standing on the sidewalk leaned over to me and said:

"You see those people? In a little while, when the British troops will come and start distributing food, these same people will shout Long Live the King". It was a very prophetic statement because that is exactly what happened later!

It took us nearly four hours to push through the crowd and travel the distance from the pier to our home on Queen Olga Street, a trip that is normally about three quarters of an hour. What we found was shocking and devastating. Both homes were badly damaged and rundown from lack of maintenance.

Shutters were missing and windows were broken and repaired with pieces of cardboard. Many roof shingles were missing or broken which meant the interiors were certainly damaged by water leaks. Nothing had been painted in four years. The existing paint was peeling and chipping and the stucco was crumbling in several places.

Some of the trees in the yard had been cut and right in the middle, where the beautiful flower garden existed in the past, the Germans had erected a monstrous 20 by 50 feet long air raid shelter that consisted of an underground tunnel made out of telephone poles covered-up by a mountain of dirt on top of which were huge marble slabs. These were actually tombstones taken from the graves of the Jewish Cemetery prior to its destruction by the Nazis.

Both houses were fully occupied and cohabited by several families of squatters that had moved in with the blessing of the army of occupation. The Germans encouraged the local residents to take over any vacant home belonging to Jews. When we identified ourselves as the owners, we were greeted with hostility and we were told that this was now their home and they were going to stay there.

"We were here first. You go away and find another place to stay. We are not leaving and you can't make us".

We were unprepared for this development and did not know what to do. We were obliged to leave for the moment and seek refuge in the home of an old friend and neighbor who offered to take us in until we had things straightened out. During the first night that we spent in the friend's home our two trunks that we carted all over during the war were stolen to my mother's great chagrin. I think this was the signal from God that we had to lose everything before we were allowed to restart our life.

We spent the next few days trying to identify the proper authorities for reclaiming our home. The situation was truly chaotic. All the major administrative posts were taken over by young Communists who had neither the knowledge nor the education or experience to run the offices assigned to them.

The same type of inexperienced persons took control of the official law enforcement agencies, tainted as they were with having collaborated with the Germans. The District Attorney for our area was the son of the neighborhood baker! To make matters worse, the whole society was polarized with the extreme camps on both sides of the spectrum poised for indulging into the favorite Greek game of killing each other.

The most fanatic members of ELAS, under the leadership of a man called Aris Velouchiotis, remained in the mountains and were preparing for the armed take over of the government of Greece. The country, already devastated from years of occupation, was ready to plunge into a bloody civil war. Armed conflict was about to break out between the Communist forces of the resistance on one side, and the right wing Greek soldiers backed by the British forces on the other.

In the days preceding the open hostilities a chaotic situation existed characterized by the total lack of due process, arbitrary rules and regulations without basis of law or reason and rampant executions and killings of people by both sides. A mere accusation was enough to have you arrested and even executed without the benefit of proof or justice. These arbitrary actions by fanatics, on both the right and the left, had served to further fuel the fires of hatred and to perpetuate the conflict.

To our frustration and dismay the Communist rulers that had taken over at the time were openly hostile to us and unsympathetic to our pleas to regain our family home.

"This is not the old bourgeois society" we were told, "The people own everything now, not you, the aristocrats. You make an application and then wait your turn and in due time we may let you occupy one room in your former home".

To come back, after spending years fighting to liberate the country, and be mistreated like this by people who sat on their back sides and did nothing was a very hard pill to swallow. Having no other choice for the moment we did apply and were eventually granted permission to occupy one room in our own family home. We had to share the space with two other families of peasants and a prostitute that was still conducting business from our home.

Each party occupied one room and shared the bathroom and kitchen. It was an unbearable situation, worse than the days of our exile. In Skiathos our home may have been a wreck but at least it was private.

Time was going by with no sign of life from either Carmen or Zack until one day a woman suddenly appeared at our doorstep. She was pale and emaciated. Her clothes were old and dirty, her unkempt hair was a mess and her eyes were sunken in and had black circles. She looked old and ill. It took me a few seconds to recognize that it was my sister.

The years of suffering had taken a heavy toll and the beautiful and vibrant young girl that left Skiathos had returned looking like an old woman. After an emotional reunion with the family she had a bath and slept for two days.

Albert was now eighteen years old and had grown into a young man. He was deceptively strong. Because of his quiet non-flamboyant nature you could easily underestimate him, however, as it is true with most quiet people, if provoked enough to explode you had better stay out of his way.

He could knock me down with one punch so I always made sure not to rile him. Both of us had missed a lot of school. I was now fifteen and found it difficult to revert to a normal routine after the exiting and adventurous previous years in exile. Albert's insistence during the last few months in Skiathos that we keep up with our studies paid off because we were now able to challenge by examination and regain two out of the three years of high school we missed because of the war.

The UNRRA started to distribute food and we plunged into it with voracious appetites. Starved for so long, especially for protein, we started devouring can after can of sea rations. I clearly remember that Albert and I would eat half a dozen cans of corned beef or Spam each! We soon started dealing again, back to our old habits.

We bought, sold, and traded food items in the black market. All of the clandestine activities in Salonica took place in a neighborhood known as "Vardari". This was also the red light district attracting large numbers of male visitors from the surrounding villages. Vardari was a regular hangout of the under- culture of the City.

It was a dangerous place since petty crimes such as muggings and pick pocketing were commonplace. The "Out of Towner's" were greeted by scores of confidence men, each with his own scheme for relieving them of their money. One of the favorite methods was a Greek modification of the American "Shell Game".

The "operator" known as "Papatzis" would shuffle three cards on a small, portable folding table. One of these was a King (Papas in Greek). The object of the game was to identify where the King fell. The "Mark" was first allowed to win a couple of times until the betting got heavy and then taken to the cleaners. If one accidentally happened to guess the right location of the King, one of the shills yelled "Police", where upon they quickly folded their tiny table and took off like lightning leaving the Mark behind empty-handed.

For some strange reason many of the confidence men operating in Vardari came originally from Drama. One day, when I finished peddling my "Merchandise" I was attracted to one of the games that were going on. I watched the "Papatzis" throw his cards on the folding table and I was sure that I knew where the King had fallen. I meekly approached the table and placed a bet on top of the card I thought was the King. The operator raised his eyes and looked at me intently.

"You are Emil's son from Drama, aren't you?" he asked.

I said, "Yes". He immediately got up, asked his associate to take over, grabbed me by the arm and pulled me into a nearby alley.

He then said, "What are you, nuts, betting like a sucker? Don't you know that no one ever wins on this game? I want you to listen carefully. I know your family and I am doing this out of respect for your mother and because we come from the same town. This is no place for you. Here is your money back. Now go home. If I ever see you here again I will rearrange your face". He then walked away. I was amazed that even among crooks there was a code of ethics that did not allow stealing from your friends or co-patriots.

Albert's modicum of knowledge of the English language served us well. He was able to read the labels and identify the contents of the American K-rations. Of particular importance was to know which contained meat or meat products because they were more valuable than those cans that contained only beans or spaghetti. Eventually we had acquired quite an inventory of these American army food supplies, which kept us from starving.

There were also some funny episodes associated with our brief career as food brokers. At one time we came across a couple of packages tightly wrapped in waterproofed paper that contained bars of a dark brown solid that looked and smelled like chocolate. Albert and I decided to try them. It had a peculiar taste, not exactly the same as chocolate, and not as sweet.

We later discovered that they were specially formulated bars of concentrated protein designed to keep alive, for a long time, those who were shipwrecked and stranded on a raft. Each bar was supposed to provide a month's nourishment. We ate them all in one sitting and we were constipated for two weeks.

One day, Albert and I were walking on "Leophoros Nikis", (translated "Victory Boulevard"), that runs along the water for several miles from the Customs house all the way to the south end of the city. This was and still is the traditional place where couples promenaded in the late afternoon hours and where young people searched for companions of the opposite sex.

Suddenly we heard loud laughter and voices coming from behind us. Albert stopped. I took a look at his face and saw it turn pale and then harden, filled with hatred.

"I know that voice and that laugh," he said "its Fokas" the man who arrested us in Skiathos." We turned around and sure enough saw our old tormentor coming towards us with a woman in each arm.

Albert stood in front of him blocking his way. I have never seen Albert, who was normally calm and composed, so angry.

"Dr. Fokas, the Nazi lover, I presume", he said while he spat on Fokas face. "You are pretty good in beating up and torturing children. Let us see what you can do now with a grown man". Albert slapped him twice in the face with the back of his hand and yelled to me "Hit him. You will feel much better". Fokas raised his hands to protect his face while I delivered two hard blows to his stomach. He doubled-up with pain and started to whimper,

"Please don't hurt me any more. I did not harm you, did I? I could have turned you over to the Germans but I didn't. I am not a bad person".

We took a look at him crying on his knees and our anger turned to revulsion. It was a pathetic sight, a broken down old man begging for mercy.

Albert said, "Find a hole and crawl into it. Get out of town because if I ever see your ugly face again I'll kill you" and with that we turned around and left still trembling with rage.

In addition to resuming our studies and fulfilling the role of food merchants, Albert and I also undertook the mission of eliminating that monstrous souvenir of the war, the air raid shelter left in the middle of our garden. Equipped with only a pickaxe, a shovel and a wheelbarrow we began to demolish the shelter, gnawing at it a bit at a time during our spare time. It was a slow and backbreaking process that lasted several months.

Eventually a few holocaust survivors began to drift back to Salonica. They had their concentration numbers tattooed on their wrists and told us the horrible tales of their captivity. Their descriptions of the starvation, the tortures, the mass exterminations in the gas chambers, and the burning of the dead bodies in the crematoriums filled us with revulsion and sadness. Many of them were young girls who had been raped and forced to become prostitutes for the German guards.

Others were victims of the sadistic "medical experiments". Some of the male survivors were former "sonderkommandos" which was a euphemism used by their captors to describe Jews that were forced to work at disposing the bodies of their own people who had been put to death.

Most of those that returned were ill and needed a place to recover. Fortunately a few of the Jews that had survived by being in hiding in Greece had regained their properties and began to take- in any Jew from Salonica that made it back alive from the camps and cared for them until they were back on their feet.

From the several thousand Jews that were deported only about two percent survived. Not a single person from our relatives on my father's side was spared. The Bulgarians took my mother's relatives from Kavala. There were no survivors from the Jewish population taken by the Bulgarians. Consequently their fate remains unknown to this day.

There were rumors that they were placed in barges, which they sank drowning everyone in the Danube River; however, this was never documented. The real paradox is that the Jews that lived in Bulgaria were actually saved by King Boris who stood up to his ally Adolph Hitler and refused to implement measures against Jews that were Bulgarian citizens. Yet the same regime collected and deported the Greek Jews to an unknown destination from which no one returned!

We shortly learned that our home in Drama was severely damaged first by the Bulgarians and then by the local people who cannibalized it after the Bulgarians left. All its contents were stolen and most of the furnishings were loaded on trains and shipped to Bulgaria. Everything that was not permanently fixed was removed.

That included doors, windows, shutters and plumbing fixtures. What was left was just the shell that made the house uninhabitable without drastic repairs. Similarly all the contents of the two movie houses my father operated were ransacked. It was thus impossible to resume operations without a major investment.

The biggest obstacle was the cost of replacing the stolen projection equipment. Another big problem was the procurement of films. There were no film studios in Greece at the time and most of the films shown in Greek theaters came from America and were shown with Greek sub-titles.

However, right after the liberation there were no American film reps in Greece yet to arrange for film rentals.

Basically after all these years of running and hiding we returned to find out that all our relatives had been killed, both our homes had been badly damaged and all our belongings were lost. In addition that there was no place for us to stay, no means of earning a living and my brother Zack was still missing.

Three months had gone by since our return from Skiathos and with each passing day our hopes of ever seeing Zack alive got dimmer. Until one day, late at night, when everyone was asleep, there was this loud knocking on the front door. When mother got up, put on her robe and went to answer the door she saw a man with a long black beard wearing an army uniform standing there. It was Zack. She put her arms around him and said,

"Everybody told me that you were dead but I did not believe it" and then she broke into tears. This was the first time I have ever seen my mother cry!

Zack was outraged with our situation and with the treatment we had received by the so-called local authorities.

The very next day still unshaven and in full uniform bearing Captain's insignia he went to the City Hall and asked to see the man in charge of housing. He pushed his way into the man's office despite the protests of his clerk and saw a skinny youth with glasses sitting behind an enormous desk sipping coffee. Zack said, "So you are the man that had been giving my family a hard time. I came after years of fighting in the mountains to find my home full of squatters and prostitutes and you have not done anything about it'."

The man started to recite the standard party line about equality etc. Zack did not let him finish. He reached across the desk, grabbed him by his lapels and lifted him off the ground. "Shut up, you little shit. Don't tell me about the proletariat and all that junk. What do you think I am, a millionaire? Where to hell were you when we were fighting the enemy? If in a week you don't kick those people out of my house I'll come back, tear you to pieces, and feed your remains to the fish".

He then put him down, pulled out his luger, which he had taken from the body of a dead German officer, and put it against the man's throat. "I have a good notion to kill you right now for all the pain you caused my mother. Here is the address. Remember, one week or I'll come back." He then stormed out of the office leaving the panic stricken weasel behind.

Within three days all the riffraff was kicked out of our house and we were all dancing with joy.

The war had visibly changed Zack. He was no longer the happy-go lucky, almost irresponsible youth who used to think that war was a big adventure. He knew now from personal experience that war was not a game. War was hell, destroying families and killing innocent people.

He was tougher both physically and emotionally. His years in the mountains taught him to take charge. He knew how to handle people and get results. The old mischievous spark was still there but it was now subdued. He was still fearless and daring and maintained his good sense of humor.

With father gone he emerged as the head of the family determined to lessen the burden on my mother who had suffered enough. He knew that in this arbitrary regime imposed by the Communists it was easy to intimidate people by being more forceful than they were. Since there was no legal basis for their position in the first place, all the petty local officials were insecure and if someone threatened them, they panicked.

Consequently Zack was able in a few days to accomplish what the rest of us could not. Not only did he clear our houses from all the illegal residents but also he was able to regain titles for all my Father's real property and secure it from any further attempts to confiscate it.

One day we received a notice that a warehouse containing furniture stolen by the Bulgarians was seized and that in it were several pianos. We were asked to provide a detailed description of our household effects left in our house in Drama. My mother completed the list, which included the piano stolen from our home and the piano stolen from father's theater.

To our amazement and delight several weeks later one of these pianos was returned to us in Salonica. It was the only item from our personal effects ever regained.

The social and economic hardships caused by the German occupation did not cease with the liberation. Life in the first few months after the German withdrawal was only slightly better than the German occupation. The only noticeable improvement was the greater availability of food.

Everything else was in total disarray. Government services were by and large in the hands of incompetent people. Old political hatreds and animosities were flaring up as well as the hunt for the arrest and punishment of German collaborators and traitors. There were many arrests and executions, sometimes with very little proof of culpability.

Greece was in a state of political unrest and conflict at a time when it should have been concentrating on recovering from the occupation. The full extent of the physical destruction was apparent everywhere. Inflation was still rampant, most people were unemployed and in poor health.

In my high school many young people had tuberculosis and most were suffering from malnutrition. Dental care was non-existent. The postal service was in total disarray and the schools lacked books and sometimes even benches. The German occupation was being replaced with a bloody Civil War.

In December of 1944, a period, which came to be known as "Ta Decemvriana", which can be loosely translated as "The December affairs", British troops, clashed openly in Athens with the ELAS forces for control of the capital. This was a bizarre and unique episode in history where British soldiers actually fought the army of the resistance who up to that point had been their ally!

Who is to blame for this still remains as one of the most bitterly contested issues in Modern Greek history. The left has charged that the British had flagrantly violated Greek autonomy by trying to interfere with the internal affairs of the country and reimpose the King upon the Greek people. The right contends that British military action was necessary to prevent the forceful overtaking of the Greek government by Communist forces. There is no doubt that the British Foreign Office and Churchill himself were fearful about Greece falling into Soviet domination, as a result the British found themselves supporting some anti-Communist Greek organizations with doubtful pasts.

Since mother had already sold all the valuables she possessed to keep us alive during the German occupation our family was in deep financial ruin. No one was working and there were no prospects for employment since everyone else in the city was in the same boat. Thus we began to sell whatever real property was left from my father's estate one piece at a time.

This enabled Zack to complete his studies at the University and graduate with a degree in Agricultural Engineering. Albert and I were able to finish High School. Albert successfully completed the entrance exams and was admitted to the Military Medical School.

I returned to Drama and tried to restart my father's Cinema, which proved to be a futile effort. Besides the lack of resources previously described I ran smack into the organized opposition of competitors who had since started another movie house. These people had powerful connections and they used them to harass me and put obstacles in my way.

Hiding behind official rules and regulations they were constantly sabotaging my efforts to run the business. There were constant inspections from the Fire Department to the Tax Collectors office fabricating violations of local ordinances and levying fines. My youth and inexperience made me especially vulnerable because I did not know how to fight dirty.

Eventually I was forced to give up and return to Salonica. Mother, with her boundless reserves of energy, had taken over the management of our affairs. She refurnished the house in Salonica and continued to work hard in keeping the family healthy and strong.

Carmen resumed some of her prewar activities which included her voice and piano lessons and beautiful musical sounds were once more reverberating from 79 Queen Olga's' Street. Zack got married and moved with his new young bride to a small village near Salonica working for an American company that was building roads in post war Greece. The same company was experimenting with the conversion of swamps into agricultural land for the cultivation of rice.

At the same time the British brought in their "Anti-vector" units and sprayed the swamps with DDT. That summer for the first time in my life I did not get malaria.

The effect of the spraying was truly remarkable. For the first time in Greek history there was NO flying insect of any kind in the air. Eventually adaptation to the insecticide took place and the bugs returned.

Carmen met another holocaust survivor who was also a former member of the Greek resistance; they fell in love and they too got married.

Unexpectedly one day a big package arrived from the United States. It was from Uncle Leon and contained a variety of clothes including some enormous ties with pictures of Palm trees and naked women. Inside there was a long and touching letter from him that made us laugh and cry at the same time.

Uncle Leon was my mother's youngest brother who after my maternal grandparents death came to live with us in Drama. He was always eccentric and did crazy things that got him into trouble, such as trying to raise wolf cubs. My father, who was temperamentally at the other side of the spectrum, had a hard time coping with Leon's capers, Finally he got rid of him by sending him to America for the 1939 New York's World's Fair. Little did he know that this act resulted in saving his life!

Apparently Uncle Leon's idiosyncrasies continued on the other side of the Atlantic. We could not stop laughing reading the description of how he locked himself in the bathroom on his wedding day and would not come out unless his in-laws got rid of the Rabbi they had chosen and replaced him with another. Apparently the original Rabbi and Uncle Leon had a heated argument about theology before the ceremony and Uncle Leon refused to be married by him.

The letter also contained many informative and amusing tidbits about life in the U.S, and Uncle Leon's colorful descriptions of some of the local customs.

Eventually all of the Jewish survivors had returned and tried to pick up the pieces. Most of the Jewish businesses were either closed or taken over illegally by Greeks with the encouragement and blessing of the Germans. Most Jewish homes were similarly occupied by squatters or were destroyed.

The lack of the Jewish presence had a visible and pronounced effect of not only the business life but also the cultural and artistic life of the city. Eventually it became clear to us and many of the other survivors that we would never be able to get rid of all of our demons and resume a normal life in Salonica.

There were too many sad reminders of the beautiful prewar life and too many bitter memories of our ordeal during the occupation. Most of us could not cope with the reality of the death of our relatives in the concentration camps and subconsciously had guilty feelings about being spared.

Then there was the anger about the continuing discrimination and unjust treatment we were getting and with the apparent lack of any swift actions to bring the war criminals that murdered our relatives and friends to justice.

The collective impact of all of the above was that a decision began to emerge that we really needed to get away from the country of our birth and get a new start in a country where it would be somewhat easier to distance ourselves from the bitter past and build a better life. Most of the things that would have kept us in Greece were no longer there.

Mother was the first again to suggest that we needed to restart our life. "The world as we knew it" she said "no longer exists. There is no future here for us and what happened this time could happen again. You need to be in a place where if you work hard and build something it would endure- a place where you would not be discriminated upon for being Jews and no one would bother you unless you commit a crime".

America, with its tradition and reputation for personal freedom and opportunity for all, seemed to be the most appropriate place for us. For the next several months we concentrated on formulating a plan that would allow eventually our whole family to leave for the United States.

It was decided that I would be the first to go. I focused my efforts towards obtaining the necessary clearances from all the pertinent Greek agencies, getting a passport and applying to the American Consulate for a visa. At the same time I asked uncle Leon to enroll me in an accredited American School. Eventually all the formalities were completed and we came to the difficult time of disengagement.

There were many emotional goodbyes with friends and loved ones. Finally the day of departure arrived. With a small suitcase in my hand and only $20 in my pocket I boarded the third class compartment of the Orient Express. The train originated in Istanbul and went through Salonica, Yugoslavia, Italy, and Switzerland terminating in Paris. From there I was to go to "Le Havre" and board the ship for the transatlantic Voyage to New York.

This was the first time I had ever been anywhere outside of Greece. As the train began to pull out of the platform I was glued to the window watching the landscape of Salonica, the town of my youth, slowly disappear from view. My entire being was flooded with a variety of emotions that overwhelmed me to the point were it was hard for me to breath.

There was a profound feeling of sadness that stemmed from the realization that I was closing behind me the door to my life as it had up till that moment existed and that I would probably never again see any of my friends with whom we shared so much. Also it was very difficult for me to say goodbye and for the first time in my life be separated from my mother. I was also apprehensive and fearful of the unknown.

I was not at all sure that I was equipped to face the uncertainty of living in another culture, learn another language and adapt to an entirely new set of customs. On the other hand I was excited by the challenge that lay ahead and the prospect of experiencing the adventure of exploring first hand new places and things that up to that time I only knew from the movies and from reading books.

As I closed my eyes, that were full of tears, a number of images flashed through my mind. I saw the face of my father, the house in Drama, and the outline of beautiful Skiathos. The finality of my decision to leave Greece suddenly hit me. This was the end of my bizarre and tormented youth and the dawn of a new life.

EPILOGUE

Eventually everyone migrated to the United States. Learning a new language and adapting to a new culture was challenging. However, after going through the initial shake down period that all new immigrants have to go through, every member of our family excelled and prospered in our adopted country.

Zack pursued graduate studies at the University of Connecticut and eventually became a nationally known expert in agriculture. He was nicknamed the "Garlic King" because of his specialized knowledge of growing and selling garlic. He is presently retired and lives with his wife of over fifty years in Pebble Beach, California. He has three daughters and two grandchildren.

Carmen and her husband, also a holocaust survivor and a resistance fighter, ran for many years a successful business in South San Francisco but she never abandoned her dream of becoming a scientist. Working during the day and attending the University at night she earned both a Bachelors and a Masters Degree in Biological Sciences from San Francisco State University. After the death of her husband, at the age when most people are looking to retire, she managed to obtain a position as a research biologist thereby finally achieving her lifetime ambition. She is now retired living in Pacific Grove, California. Carmen has a son and a daughter, both happily married, and three granddaughters.

Albert finished Medical school in Greece, got married and served in the Greek Army as a medical officer. He later resigned his commission and immigrated to the U.S. After going through the usual hoops facing foreign physicians he was granted a license to practice medicine. Eventually he became a prominent Neurologist in Southern California where he died at a

Frederic Kakis

very young age of a heart attack .He was survived by his wife, four children, two sons, two daughters and three grandchildren. Three of his four children are physicians.

Mother adapted very quickly to her new environment. With her usual energy and superior intellect she learned the language and became an active participant in the life and culture of San Francisco where she resided in her own apartment by herself for many years. She continued her love of music in general and of the opera in particular. For every year until her death she had a season ticket for the San Francisco Opera. Mother died at the age of 87 in Mountain View, California. She had thirteen grandchildren and five great grandchildren at the time of her death.

At the age of twenty-one, I landed in New York and attended a technical electronics school graduating as a radio and TV repairman. I then got married and enrolled at the City University of New York. Working during the day and going to school at night I eventually completed my studies and received a B.S. degree in Chemistry, with special honors, Magna Cum Laude, and Phi Beta Kappa. After receiving a Ph.D. in Chemistry from Stanford University I became a University professor and administrator. I reside in California with my wife of over fifty years. We have two daughters, two sons and four grandsons.

About the Author

The author is a native of Greece where during WW II, at a very early age, was forced to abandon his home and flee to avoid capture by the Germans and deportation to the death camps. The family managed to survive and narrowly escape capture by defying the German orders and ultimately joining the resistance movement. This book is a detailed account of the trials and tribulations the family went through in order to survive

At the end of the war the author migrated to the United States and enrolled at City College of New York graduating "" Magna Cum Laude" and Phi Beta Kappa.

He pursued graduate studies at Stanford University and earned a Ph.D. degree.

He then joined the faculty and administration of Chapman University where he served as a professor of Chemistry, Chairman of the chemistry department, Chairman of the Division of Natural Sciences and associate Vice President of Academic Affairs.

Dr. Kakis received numerous grants and conduced a variety of research programs involving students. He carried out postdoctoral research under the auspices of The Oak Ridge National Laboratory, the National Science Foundation, NASA, and the Department of Defense.

In 1970-71 he was on sabbatical as a visiting Professor at the Ecole Polytechnique in Paris, France.

Dr.Kakis is a popular speaker and a prolific writer He has written many scientific papers and contributed numerous articles to National and International Journals and publications. He has published a well-known book entitled "Drugs-Facts and Fictions." and was one of the co-authors of a book on Steroids. For a number of years he had his own Forensic Column in a magazine entitled " Claims People."

Dr. Kakis received numerous honors and awards. Among them a senior Fulbright Fellowship and Citations from NASA and the American Institute of Chemists.

His biography is listed in American Men of Science and most of the major "Who is who" Directories.

Printed in the United States
17779LVS00001B/363